Angel's Den

a novel

JAMIE CARIE

PUBLISHING GROUP

Nashville, Tennessee

978-0-8054-4814-6

Published by B&H Publishing Group,
Nashville, Tennessee

Dewey Decimal Classification: F
Subject Heading: ROMANCES \ WIFE ABUSE—
FICTION \ OVERLAND JOURNEYS
TO THE PACIFIC—FICTION

Scripture quoted from the King James Version.

Publisher's Note: This novel is a work of fiction. Although
it is based on actual historical events, some of the names, char-
acters, places, and incidents are the products of the author's
imagination. In some cases, fictitious words or actions have been
attributed to real individuals; these, too, are imagined.

The lyrics to *Amazing Grace* used on page 273
are considered public domain.

1 2 3 4 5 6 7 8 • 14 13 12 11 10

To women round the world,
Across all of time . . .
Who have endured and survived
Who have endured and died
For another's creed.
For a grown man's need.
Your sorrow will be heard in heaven.

And to Karen Ball
Who saw it through
This one is for you . . .

Prologue

St. Louis, Missouri Territory—1808

*R*obert Frazer woke to the sound of a click in his ear.

"Get up, nice and slow."

Whaat?

The voice triggered a faint memory—a hazy image of a roll of money being thrust at him. Robert's eyes shot open, but he lay perfectly still not wanting to nudge the barrel of the gun at his temple. His heart pounded as he looked up at the man's face. Hardesty, wasn't it? The man who had tried to buy his journal, his Lewis and Clark journal.

Robert pulled back the covers and swung his legs over the side of the bed. The chilly air slapped his body awake as he stood. His gaze swung from the man with the gun to roam the room. A chair had been dragged into the middle of his bedchamber floor. An ordinary wooden chair—*his* ordinary chair—but now the curved wooden slats glared at him in a menacing smile. He gritted his teeth and felt his heartbeat roar in his ears.

"Have a seat." Hardesty's voice growled and coaxed at the same time. This man seemed to really enjoy his job.

Robert's face swung up toward the stocky man. The arm that held the gun on him bulged with muscle. Hardesty motioned toward the chair, the gun cocked and ready to wreak its havoc on his chest.

Maybe pleading would help. "Look. You can have the journal. I'll give it to you. No cost." He held his hands up in surrender.

"You got that right." Hardesty's big head cocked to one side as an insidious smile slid across his lips. "Now sit down, and we'll get started with the business of it, eh?"

Robert's feet shuffled against the rough wood floor as he made his way to the chair. Ever since the Lewis and Clark days, he had stiffness in his legs and feet every morning upon waking. But he didn't regret it. Best days of his life. Others called the journey the Corps of Discovery, but to him it was always just two names, two men—Meriwether Lewis and William Clark. What they discovered was a vast land of heretofore unknown terrain graced with animal and man and water and lush vegetation. He hadn't been able to write it all down. He'd wanted to, but he hadn't been schooled in that way, and he knew that the small, stilted entries in his journal had been just that. Small. How could anyone want his paltry efforts? Robert had already refused to sell it twice now. He should have known better. He should have recognized that look of grim determination in Hardesty's eyes the last time the man came by and offered a small fortune for the book. Robert should have lied, told the man and his rich boss that he hadn't kept a journal.

He could lie now. They would never find it if he didn't tell them where to look.

"Out with it then." Hardesty moved in front of him and pointed the gun, it bobbing around toward his chest and shoulders, his neck and face.

Robert swallowed hard. *Don't look at the gun.* He'd never been good at lying. It always came out weak, his eyes darting about, his fingers curling into his palms. As a kid, he'd never been able to fool his parents. But this man didn't know him. "I buried it. Beneath the biggest oak tree on Fort Belle Fontaine's grounds, on the west side of the fort."

Hardesty's face grew red, a vein popping out on his forehead. "You buried it on the fort's grounds?"

Robert looked up and met those wrathful eyes. "It seemed the safest place." It would be difficult for Hardesty or anyone to dig around the grounds without causing all sorts of questions. But Hardesty might think he needed Robert to help find it, and that might be enough to save his life—for a little while anyway.

Apparently Hardesty thought differently. He circled around to the back of the chair, and Robert heard a rustling sound above the pounding of his heart. He dared not turn around.

With a suddenness that sent new tremors through Robert's body, a cord wrapped his throat. His eyes bulged as his hands reached up to claw at the rope. Hardesty leaned down, his putrid breath hissing into Robert's ear. "If you are lying . . . I will cut you up, piece by piece. Fingers then hands"—he squeezed Robert's shoulder so hard that Robert gasped around the cord—"your arms . . . then snap your neck." He let the pressure of the cord ease enough for Robert to drag in a wheezing breath. "Are you lying, Frazer?"

Robert's heart drummed louder and louder, faster and faster until it seemed nothing could stop it from bursting through his chest. He gasped out the truth. "The Ace Saloon . . . in Margarite's room. Don't hurt her! Please—"

"That's more like it. Always good to tell the truth, that's what I say." The man chuckled into Robert's ear, but instead of lessening its cruel pressure, the cord grew taut.

Robert heard rasping, choking gasps echo across his bedroom. The sounds were coming from his throat—he knew that. But he couldn't really connect the scene with reality. It couldn't be real, could it? Someone was really murdering him in his own bedroom? And yet his body reacted—fighting, twisting in the chair—his legs kicked out as he struggled.

As the cord did its work, he felt himself fade from terror to a twilight sense between life and death. It was a bit more comfortable here, the panic fading, a heaviness over him that he could no longer fight. He allowed his thoughts to wander, float, linger over past images. He saw Clark's face. Robert had wanted to be like the strong, sure William Clark, but he never even came close. And then he saw Lewis. A little touched in the head but not in a slow-of-thought way. Robert never figured out if he liked him or despised him. But together Lewis and Clark had been the perfect team. Together they had accomplished the impossible.

The cord jerked against his throat, and he grew very still. The words he had always wanted to write finally poured through him.

He saw Lewis standing in front of a log cabin. He was crying out to Clark:

> *Where art thou?*
> *I await you in the twilight of my distress*
> *Come and save me*
> *My friend*

I watch for your shadowed form
Against the red of sun
I have set out the robe you love
My friend

Your face is all I long to see
It sets me free
That clear-eyed smile
Make the ghosts vanish
For awhile—stay
Bring back my peace
My friend

The sun—it fades so fast
Your voice grows ever dim
If you do not appear
I cannot bear
The rising of the same
Appear to me
My friend
Or I will be no more

Robert saw Lewis's face flash bright and then fade away into nothing . . . and knew Lewis would be joining him in eternity soon.

Chapter One

St. Louis, Missouri Territory—1808

*D*o stand still, Emma." Her mother raised a thin hand to her bosom looking for a moment close to tears.

Mrs. Daring—the elegant, staid, proper Mrs. Daring—did not cry. Emma had never seen her mother even tear up, and the thought that she ever would hadn't entered Emma's mind. Her mother was always . . . well, perfectly perfect. But there it was, emotion spilling over in quivering lips and watery eyes. Emma's own eyes widened, and she bit back a choked laugh as her mother glared at her. Of course it would be *her* fault if her mother finally broke down!

Emma looked down at the glorious skirt of the gown she wore, *her wedding gown,* and stilled her fluttering hands, trying to imitate her mother's usual decorum.

One must not let one become overset with emotion. Or so her mother had said on many occasions. But this? This moment was more than she'd ever thought to have in her life—her special moment in time. She couldn't have any more squelched her delighted squeal than made the sun cease to rise. "Please! Can I turn around now?"

1

"Patience, Emma." But a crack of a smile hovered around her mother's lips. "Margery is almost finished."

Margery, the maid hired to help with the wedding, was a young woman with a calm demeanor and a knack for elaborate hair dressing. Emma tapped her toe, her fingertips brushing across the sides of the silken skirt as the maid fussed with the folds at the back of the gown. "There, Miss!" Margery's face was wreathed in a pleased smile as she took a step back.

Emma locked excited gazes with her mother, both looking quite terrified with glee. "Now?"

Her mother swallowed hard, the sound loud in the room, then nodded once.

Emma held her arms out a little, her fingers pointing up and out in a graceful arc. She took a deep breath, held it in, and turned in a tottering circle toward the long mirror.

Oh.

Tears rose up sudden and strong. Her hands came up to her cheeks.

Oh my.

She stared at the woman looking back at her and forgot to breathe. She took it all in . . .

Her blonde hair set in a mass of elaborate curls atop her head. A small glittering tiara peeking back at her from the center of the curls. Her pink cheeks and glowing eyes. And the dress! She could hardly believe she was wearing a replica of none other than Empress Josephine's wedding dress. Was it really true? Was it really her? Would she really marry the man of her dreams this day?

Emma's mother's came up from behind her, catching Emma's attention. There was no denying the tears in both their eyes.

Her mother sniffed. "I do wish Aunt Violet could see you."

Aunt Violet's name was rarely spoken in their house. Emma had impressions of the woman from the few stories she'd heard—adventurous, the younger and prettier of the two sisters, and a hint of scandal. Aunt Violet had done well enough in the end though; she was happily settled with a wealthy husband on a plantation outside of Williamsburg.

"Would she be pleased? She went to such effort to find the pattern for this dress." Emma swung toward her mother and then back to the reflection.

"You will write a long letter of thanks and describe the dress in detail."

"Of course!" Letter writing was not one of Emma's favorite pastimes, but she would have no trouble describing the high-waisted, white satin gown with its delicate puffed sleeves; green-threaded scrolling embroidery that ran in a long, elegant strip down the front of the dress; and the matching green ribbon. Emma turned to admire the short train that spanned out like a fluttering fan on the floor behind her. Yes, she would be quite happy to write this letter.

Turning back toward her mother, she leaned over and kissed her wrinkled cheek. "Thank you. I feel almost as beautiful as he is."

"Of course you are, Emma." Her mother said it, but they both knew it wasn't true. No one matched her husband-to-be for pure physical perfection.

"Are you ready, dear?"

Emma nodded, and a rush of excited happiness burst through her. She hadn't realized until this moment that happiness could be almost painful.

She walked from her bedchamber, the room she'd slept in and played in, the room she had grown up in, and turned to take one last glance, expecting to feel some sadness. It surprised her that the emotion didn't come. She could only see ahead and feel the happy bubble of her future surrounding her. Turning toward her mother she followed her down the long staircase to the stately entrance with its elegant chandelier that twinkled with pinpoints of dancing candlelight.

They rushed toward the front door, but Emma turned to a long window where she could see her parents' lawn.

"Oh, look!" She gasped as she clasped her hands together and stared at the wedding scene before her.

Her mother waved a hand at her. "Wait here for your father. I must take my seat, my dear. We've tarried too long." She opened the door, and Emma heard the shouts of the children and the voices of their friends adding to the happy scene. She dashed to the door and peeked around it, careful to stay hidden from sight.

So many people had come to witness her wedding! She bit her lip to hold back the tears. The sun bathed the scene in a soft yellow light; the sky was an aquamarine shade of blue, like robin eggs. Not a single insect buzzed, nor an ill wind blew against the piled-up hair, the decorated bonnets and staid hats, the opulent gowns and crisp coats. Why, the whole of St. Louis had gathered for her wedding day!

Her perfect day.

Music began to play, and as if on cue from some long-forgotten lesson, Emma watched the crowd quiet and find their seats among the long rows of white-painted benches that had been arranged to afford each guest the best view. She leaned further around the door so that she could see around a large tree blocking her view and tried to catch a glimpse of the altar, trying to see *him*.

She leaned a little further, and the door began to swing open with her weight pushing on it. Oh no! The thought no sooner surfaced than she fell with a shriek onto her side, half in and half outside the front door.

"Emma!" Her father rushed from the back of the house toward her. "Are you all right?" He grasped her arm and helped her up. Emma shot a mortified gaze at him and then back at the crowd. Relief, instant and profound, poured through her as she noted that the music must have been loud enough to cover her cry—no one seemed to be looking their way. But her next thought struck terror in her heart.

The gown! Had she ruined the gown? Emma turned this way and that to study it from all sides, frantic that she would find a dirt smear or a tear in it. Seeing nothing wrong, she took a deep breath and collapsed into her father's waiting arms. "Praise be to God! It's still perfect."

Her father chuckled and patted her on the back. "Yes, your mother would cheerfully strangle you if anything happened to that dress. Now we must hurry. I believe we've missed our cue, and they are starting up the song again." Her father always forgave her clumsiness and covered for her as best he could.

She would miss that!

They walked forward arm in arm, and then stood at the end of the grassy aisle. Everyone turned and stared up at them, making Emma's stomach feel kneaded like bread dough. Her gaze scanned the scene that looked as perfect as a painting: the people like colorful birds in their best summer finery, giant flowerpots flanking the altar, overflowing with white lilies—the flower of purity and virginity, a flower that held a meaning as sweet as its fragrance: "heaven with you." Or so her mother said, anyway. The altar was of rosewood, with its matching arch of delicately carved birds of paradise and lilies. Her perfect day indeed!

Her grasp tightened on her father's frail arm, a shaft of compassion filling her as she felt the bones beneath the thin fabric of his suit. She'd been a late addition to her parents' marriage, the only addition, and lately they seemed to be aging before her eyes. She looked eye level into his washed-out blue eyes and saw his tears.

"I'm sorry we kept you with us for so long," her father whispered as they waited for the march down the aisle to begin. "It's just that we love you so much."

"I didn't want to ever leave you, Papa. It took a very special man to steal me away." It was true. She had turned down a few suitors, and anyway, twenty-five wasn't so very ancient, was it?

"Just so," her father said with a sniff as he looked toward the man who had captured her heart.

Emma realized she hadn't yet mustered the courage to look at *him*! The man who had swept into her life and changed everything.

The next song began. A harpist strummed something her mother had chosen. Emma's glance swung to the seat where her mother sat, so prim and stately in her lavender gown with its matching bonnet of deeper purple. Emma smiled at her straight back and high-held chin. Her mother would be sure not to cry in front of all these people.

Their footsteps started down the grassy, petal-strewn aisle. Emma looked down and saw her pretty, satin clad shoes. They were her only insistence against her mother's wishes. Pink. A soft pink with ribbons and lace and satin bows. She loved those shoes more than the dress, though she would never reveal that secret to anyone. She smiled thinking of how she'd tried the shoes on and watched the satin gleam back at her in her bedchamber mirror. She had stood there several moments admiring the turn of her ankle, watching the sheen of the fabric glisten as she turned her foot this way and that, running her fingertip along the height of the satin-covered heel. Now, she almost giggled, happiness rising like a giant bubble in her throat as she walked arm in arm with her father, remembering when she'd lifted the hem of her dress high enough to see the tops of her stockings where the garter met and how she'd stared in the mirror at her legs in these shoes and wondered what *he* might think of such a sight.

Suppressing her anticipation, she looked up at him. Her husband-to-be . . .

Eric Montclaire. The prized catch west of the Appalachian Mountains. "Ungodly handsome," they called him. Every woman who uttered his name said it in a breathless way, no matter their age. He was wealthy and he'd promised Emma a house—a plantation, if she wanted it. A mansion on a hill. A comfortable life filled with children and *him*.

She looked toward him for the first time this day, and their gazes locked like two puzzle pieces fitting together. The sight of him with his blondish-brown hair, piercing blue eyes, and broad-shouldered stance sent an immediate shiver down her spine. For a moment she forgot everything, everyone, even her prized pink, high-heeled shoes. She stumbled, just a little, at the passion glowing across the yellow-bathed expanse from his eyes to hers. No one knew she almost ended up on the ground, save her father, who grasped harder to her arm and made it seem like he'd been the one to stumble. And then there they were. At the altar.

At the beginnings of their future together.

Her father stopped, took a firm hold on her arm, his fingers tight for a moment; and then, little by little, he let go. He nodded toward Eric, who came down the one step of the raised platform and grasped her arm just where her father had left it. It was as if she were being passed between these two men, as a prize, as a possession. She looked up and into the eyes of her new keeper.

Silly thought, that. A keeper? She breathed a deep gulp of air as her lips lifted into the veriest smile, the smile of a happy bride, and then took the final steps to the altar where they stood under the elegant arch.

The preacher began the ceremony that would forever make Eric hers and Emma his. She listened intently to the words as Preacher Hollis read one of her favorite passages from the Bible:

And the LORD God formed man of the dust of the ground, and breathed into his nostrils the breath of life; and man became a living soul. But for Adam there was not found an help meet for him. And the LORD God caused a deep sleep to fall upon Adam, and he slept: and he took one of his ribs, and closed up the flesh instead thereof; and the rib which the LORD God had taken from man, made he a woman, and brought her unto the man.

And Adam said, "This is now bone of my bones, and flesh of my flesh: she shall be called Woman, because she was taken out of Man."

Eric squeezed her hand, and then together they walked to the table and each picked up a slim, flickering candle. At the same time they tilted each flame, representing their individual lives, toward the larger candle in the middle, which represented their new life together. Emma's hand shook with suppressed gladness as she held her flame to Eric's. The wick of the large candle caught, and a larger, brighter flame burst to life. Then they turned to each other, and, as her mother had instructed them, Eric leaned over to blow out Emma's candle while Emma leaned to blow out Eric's. A rush of joy constricted her throat.

They were no longer two; they were truly one.

They set down the slim candles, turned, and stepped back to their place where the ceremony continued. Now they would receive the blessing.

Emma turned toward the man who would soon be her husband and followed his white shirt front, up to his neck where the dark stubble began. Did he know? She flushed thinking of it and then squashed the desire to reach up and draw her fingertips along the line of his throat, up to his jaw. How she longed to run her fingers through his curling hair.

Pressing her lips together, she stilled her body, made herself look up into the depths of his eyes. They were gray-blue and like a glowing, silent moon. They bespoke the truth that everyone said about him—Eric was a man who knew what he wanted and got it. A force to be reckoned with.

And he wanted *her.* She still couldn't fathom it.

Preacher Hollis came forward to bless their union. He placed his hands on the tops of their heads, causing them to close their eyes and bow their heads. Emma heard his ringing prayer as a mere echo against the grandness of the man she was fortunate enough to marry. Eric Montclaire. How lucky was she? How fortunate among women? How blessed.

Lord, thank You. I don't deserve such a man. I am not beautiful. I am not grand. I cannot imagine why he chose me. He could have had anyone.

At the collective "Amen," she opened her eyes and looked at her new husband like a desert wanderer would look at a cup of water. His cheeks were high and imposing, his hair fell back from his forehead in waves of gold-streaked brown. She looked back into his eyes. She had first fallen in love with his eyes. They were large and wide and purpose filled. No matter what he spoke of, from the weather to the running of his trading company or the flower he had most recently plucked for her. A gray-blue that at times looked silver—determined, sure, passionate eyes. When he looked at her, into her ordinary, cornflower-blue eyes, she ignited and flamed—engulfed in him.

Emma took a long, deep breath of the fresh air as she gazed into those dark, silver-blue depths. The words of the preacher rolled over her like gentle waves. Wave after wave of deep voiced convictions that said she would be forever tied to this man. That she would bear his children, God willing, that she would bathe his fevered brow when he was sick, and he would sit at her table when he was well. That she would be everything anybody human could be for another living soul. And that he would be that for her.

Thank You, God. The thought whispered through her as he slipped a massive sapphire on her finger to claim her.

She was, now and forever, his wife.

Emma's mother leaned down to whisper in her ear at the lavish, sit-down dinner reception after the wedding ceremony. Emma smiled. What motherly words would she share on this, Emma's wedding day?

"Don't drink the red punch while wearing that dress, my dear."

Heat filled Emma's cheeks as she placed the glass back on the table and nodded. She always did have a penchant for spilling or tripping or bumping into things. And the odds for an accident always increased in pace with the importance of the occasion, especially when wearing her best dress. It wouldn't do at all to be sporting a giant red stain on the silken material of her Josephine wedding dress.

Thinking of a red stain brought to mind her looming wedding night. She ducked her head over her plate and took a small bite of roast goose oozing in cream sauce, all the while fighting the blush still heating her cheeks.

Her new husband leaned toward her bent head with a voice of concern. "Are you quite all right?"

The sound of his deep voice made her jump and clamp her lips against the squeak that almost came out. Had he read her mind? Were her thoughts plain on her face for everyone to see? She blushed deeper and reared back, her gaze guilty as it swung toward him. She frowned at the pull on her wrist and looked down to note that the delicate bracelet on her wrist had caught a loose thread in the tablecloth. Oh bother! She stared down at it and then jerked her wrist hoping to free it. Her mistake registered at the same time that she heard Eric gasp. Horror filled her as her dinner plate slid toward her and then slipped over the edge of the table. In slow motion, but too fast to stop it, the plate flipped and then fell, food first, into her lap. She shrieked and pulled her arms back, dragging the tablecloth further toward her. The bright red punch tottered as everyone in the room gasped and watched as the glass followed the plate. She lunged toward the glass, which only made matters worse as she dragged the plates of her dinner companions toward her. The punch tilted over the edge in a slow-motion agony that had her reaching and missing. She could only watch the liquid splash down the side of her lap. She pulled her feet under her chair so that the punch couldn't drip onto her prized pink shoes.

"Oh, heavens!" She looked up into the appalled faces of the guests, who were grasping tight hold of their own plates and glasses. She heard an indignant gasp of breath.

Eric.

"Look what you've done!" His voice no longer held the soft purr of new love. It had become snarling and sharp as he wiped food off the side of his trousers with his cloth napkin.

Her brows came together. She opened her mouth to speak, paused, and then rushed the words out. "Oh, my goodness. I am so sorry."

His scowl reached down into the tender place of her heart and twisted like a knife. Was he really so angry with her?

"Please, Eric. It was an accident." How many times had she said that to her mother when she'd tripped over a stone on the walkway and turned her ankle, or insisted on helping the cook wash the dishes only to drop an entire stack of rare china to the floor where each and every one of them shattered into a hundred pieces, or the time—

No. Stop it, Emma. Now, with everyone staring at her in jaw-dropping silence, was *not* the time to remember all her transgressions.

"Of course it was an accident." Eric's voice interrupted her self-loathing. "Only a clown would do it on purpose."

All eyes were on them, and though Eric's voice had lowered to a staccato hiss meant for her ears alone, she saw her father's face grow dark with protective disapproval. "No great harm done," her father cheerfully barked out. "Just go and change, sweetheart." He turned toward the crowd with a bright smile. "The good Lord knows she has dresses enough to fill a ship to China."

The assembled cream of St. Louis society smiled at the joke and began talking again, breaking the tense moment.

Emma pushed the food back onto the plate in her lap and attempted to scoot the tablecloth into place with shaking hands. She'd forgotten her bracelet—still attached and giving the cloth little room to move unless she moved her wrist with it.

Eric leaned toward her. "Hold still or you'll only make things worse," With deft movements he removed the thread from the tiny chain link. "There. Now hurry."

Emma shoved the plate back onto the table and fled the room as fast as was decorous. She held back the sobs that threatened to explode from her chest until she had stripped off the heavy gown and threw herself down on her bed. With a great sob she covered her face with her hands and asked the silent room what she'd wondered all her life:

"What is *wrong* with me?"

Chapter Two

A knock sounded. The door creaked open.

Emma rose from the curled position on her bed and wiped the tears from her cheeks. She sighed her relief as she recognized the swish of her mother's skirts.

Her mother cast a glance—a familiar mix of love and frustration—over her daughter. "You can't hide up here forever, dear." Determination threaded her voice. "You must come down. The guests are beginning to notice this . . . this"—she waved an elegant hand in the air around her—"tension."

"Oh! I've ruined everything, haven't I?" Emma ran into her mother's stiff arms. "I've ruined the dress! And Eric! He was so angry. He's never spoken to me in such a way before."

Her mother sighed against her, then pulled back. "It was ill-timed to be sure, but you are only making matters worse by hiding. We will soak the dress and hope for the best. But for heaven's sake, Emma, it's your wedding party, and the bride cannot go missing." She braced Emma's shoulders in a firm grip and made her stand up straight as she inspected the replacement gown Emma had chosen to wear. Her lips pursed. It was obvious she didn't approve of the simple blue-green frock that Emma knew brought out the blue in her eyes and made her pale hair seem brighter, but it was also obvious that her mother was in a hurry. "Oh, well," she murmured. "Let's have a look at your coif and that tear-stained face."

She grasped Emma's shoulder and led her toward the low, ornate, cherry-wood dressing table where Emma had lit a single candle. Her mother held her chin and stared at the damage. "Here, now. Just a bit of powder on those cheeks. Powder covers a multitude of sins, you know."

Emma had heard the phrase countless times and stilled herself while her mother brushed on the powder and fussed over the crooked tiara that held up her massive curls. "There is nothing to be done about it," her mother muttered. "We would have to redo your entire coif if we take it out, and there's no time." She tucked in a stray curl and straightened the band, pinning it tight to Emma's head. "There now. Let us go. And, please, Emma. For the rest of the night . . . be careful."

Emma nodded. After all, nothing worse could happen. With renewed hope and a spirit of determination, she took steps toward the door. Looking down at her pink shoes, she looked up at her mother with raised brows. "Well at least the punch didn't ruin my shoes."

Her mother glanced down at the offending footwear and grimaced. "Indeed."

Emma smothered a smile, feeling her spirits rise a notch.

Emma walked side by side with her new husband down the dusty street toward her new home. Eric had been kind, apologetic—

whispering admiration for her new gown and squiring her about the room on his arm to chat with this group and that group in a way that put everyone at ease. He was a master in every situation, and she marveled again that he would pick her. What quality did she possess that he saw for his future? For his wife? Taking courage in hand, she ventured the question as the sun set, spilling a rosy glow across their feet and ground beneath them.

"Why did you marry me, Eric?"

He hesitated, as if a question of such ilk had never entered his mind. "You have to ask?"

"Well, yes. I mean, you've shown your devotion, your love in so many wonderful ways." She thought of all the gifts, the jewelry—brooches and earrings, necklaces and bracelets, the bouquets of flowers on every occasion and even when there was no occasion, the times he held her hands tight against his chest and gazed into her eyes like he wanted to kiss her, their one brief kiss, a touch of his lips to hers that sent chills all the way down her spine and into her toes when he asked her to marry him. "But you've never really said. What was it about me?"

She knew it must be foolish to ask. Shouldn't his actions be enough? His stony-faced look didn't encourage the prying, but the puzzle gnawed at her and . . . well, he'd never said it.

"You are everything I have ever wanted in a wife."

"But what does that mean?" She might be frightened of pushing him toward anger, but she couldn't let that be the answer.

Eric stopped as they came to his house, her house now. He turned to her and grasped up her hands. "You are from the right family. In my business that is important."

She nodded, noting that his grip tightened. Was he nervous to declare his love out loud?

"You're beautiful."

"I am not."

"All the more so because you don't believe it. And, you are the one woman who captured my heart. We will be happy together, Emma. I promise."

Emma smiled up at him. "You have captured my heart as well." She turned toward the front door a little disappointed. He hadn't said the three words she most wanted to hear, but it had been close.

In a sudden move Eric leaned toward her, swept an arm under her legs and lifted her into his arms. "My bride must be carried over the threshold."

"For luck." Emma laughed, loving the feel of his skin against her cheek. His neck smelled of the soap he used to shave, and a feeling of giddy lovesickness for him rushed through her like an unstopped fountain.

Eric opened the door and stepped across the threshold. They were both smiling as he set her down in the small foyer and then drew her into his arms. He leaned back to close the door with a slight slam and then wrapped his arms tight around her. She held her breath as his head lowered, knowing what was to come. He would kiss her now, finally kiss her.

His lips touched hers and then pressed harder. They moved across her lips in a way that was as different from their only other kiss—a mere brush of contact across her mouth—as night is to day. The unexpected nature of it made her stiffen.

The pressure of his mouth grew harder, causing her neck to strain to stay aright. His breathing became more labored. "Relax, Emma," he rasped out.

"Oh."

His lips found hers again, a crushing force that left her gasping for air. Astonishment—and fright—reverberated throughout her body. Before she had time to accustom herself to the onslaught, one of his hands came around toward the front of her gown. She didn't like it—him or her reaction to him—not knowing whether to be afraid or excited.

Emma pressed her hands against his chest and pushed away with a gasp. "Eric, wait."

Her husband stood before her, breathing heavy and looking as if he'd entered another world. Slowly her words sank through his haze.

"Wait?"

She started. He was angry again. Why was he so angry?

"I've *been* waiting for months. *This* is why I married you."

Emma took a step back, her hand pressed against her galloping heart. "Only this?"

Eric huffed out a deep breath, ran a hand through his golden-brown waves, and looked off to the side. After a few moments he looked back at her, and she saw the man she knew, the man she had agreed to marry.

"Of course not." He offered a slight, self-deprecating smile. "Dear Emma, a man . . . a man has needs. I don't know how to explain it to you, but you can trust me. You trust me, don't you, sweetheart?"

Emma nodded, though no longer sure she did.

"Why don't you go into the bedchamber, put on that pretty nightdress I saw you unpacking. I will be there in a few minutes."

She must have looked as wide-eyed and shaky as she felt because he continued.

"I am just a little overeager. It will be better now, I promise."

He gave her that slow, sensuous smile that never failed to turn her knees to mush. What was wrong with her? Of course he would be eager. He was a man and her husband. She would just have to get used to his . . . male vigor. "I'm sorry, Eric. It was just something of a shock." She smiled feeling shy and unbalanced. "I will go and get ready."

She could feel his gaze boring into her back as she retreated to the bedchamber, and she suppressed a shiver despite the lecture to herself to be brave.

Going over to the bureau that she now shared with her husband, she pulled open the top drawer and drew out a nightdress of white silk that she and her mother had commissioned to be made when fitting out her trousseau. Laying the soft garment on the bed, she worked the buttons of her dress free, slipped it from her shoulders, and let it fall in an aquamarine pool around her ankles. She stepped over the pile, untied the corset, and slid it down her body to lie on the floor next to the dress. A chemise soon followed suit.

Walking by a long mirror, she turned toward it and saw a pale woman staring back at her. Would Eric be happy with her? She pushed back the anxiety that threatened to clog her throat and hurried into the nightdress and then sat on the bed to take off her shoes. They landed with a loud thud-thud on the wood floor, causing her to look up at the door. Swallowing hard she berated herself for a fool. Of course she would be nervous on her wedding night.

Just calm down!

Repeating the phrase over and over in her mind, she walked back to the mirror to take down her hair. What she saw made her gasp. Her nightdress was nearly transparent! What had her mother been thinking to *suggest* such a thing? Forgetting about her hair, she ran for her side of the bed and slipped beneath the covers, pulling them to her chin. Her eyes widened as Eric's tall form filled the doorway.

"I heard such a racket in here that I thought you might need some assistance." He walked further in, looked down at her as the corners of his mouth kicked up a notch. "You're not hiding, are you? You know you can trust me, Emma. I am the only one you can trust."

She nodded her head and made herself lower the covers from her chin but couldn't speak. What would he do next?

He looked at the floor and frowned. "You shouldn't leave your clothes scattered about on the floor, you know. We don't have a maid yet, but I see we will need one despite my hope for some privacy during our first weeks."

"We don't need a maid. I-I was in hurry is all. It won't happen again, I promise."

Eric pointed to the offense. "Come now. Let us start out as we will continue. Come hang them up, and then we will go to bed." Was he really serious? She studied the smug satisfaction in his eyes and had her answer. Emma ground her teeth together, took a long breath, and then swung her legs from the bed. She darted over to the dress and corset and scooped them into her arms to cover herself. Turning, she walked to the armoire, opened the door and hung the dress up, then folded and put away her corset.

"You forgot the shoes."

Emma turned her head and blinked at him, true anger simmering inside her now. She wanted to tell him to stop ordering her about as if she were a child, but she didn't want to have their first argument on their wedding night so instead she bit her tongue and nodded. "Of course." Without turning toward him she backed up and snatched the dangling pair from his hands, gritting her teeth and resisting the urge to throw them into the bottom of the armoire.

"Excellent. Now turn around." His voice was as smooth as silk but held a dangerous purr that reminded her of his kiss.

She turned, her arms crossed in front of her chest.

Eric took the steps necessary to gain her side. "Come now, don't be shy." He reached for her arms and pried them away then took a step back. "You *are* beautiful."

His words drew a rush of air from her reddening chest. Was it relief? She could hardly fathom what she felt anymore. She looked down at her bare feet, her hair still up in rows of fat curls, tiara still in place.

If only it were dark! But no, it was too early. The soft evening sun filtered through the two windows of the room undeterred by her wishes. She heard Eric move and peeked up at him through her lashes. He was unbuttoning his waistcoat and shirt with quick economy as his gaze traveled up and down her form. She watched in some awe as he slid the garment from his back, seeing her first glimpse of a man's chest. He startled her as he turned toward her, but he walked over to the armoire where he hung up his clothes. Turning back toward her, he smiled. "Help me with my boots?"

Emma nodded.

Eric sat on the bed and held out his hand as Emma stood rooted to the floor. She took a long breath and walked over, standing just outside his legs. His gaze roamed over her body, his eyes grew darker.

"Come here."

Emma took another step toward him, commanding herself not to be afraid. Eric reached up and grasped her around the waist, pulling her toward him.

"Wait, your boots." She scrambled out of his arms and leaned down to grasp one of the tall black boots. She grabbed hold of the heel and pulled with all her might. Eric reached down to help, wiggling his foot a bit, which did help, but then the boot came off all of the sudden sending Emma rearing back to land flat on her backside.

Eric made a disgusted sound from his throat, his eyebrows drawn together. "I've never seen such a clumsy woman on her wedding day."

Emma smothered a pained chuckle. "Yes, let us hope my luck improves." Emma agreed, deciding to make it funny instead of sad. "I think you should take off your own boots from now on, don't you?"

She forced mischief into her voice, but Eric didn't seem to care for it. "An excellent plan," he recounted, as dry as dust. He took the other boot off, set it on the floor, and then stood. Before Emma had any notion of what he might do, he stripped off his trousers.

She turned away.

"Come and get into bed, Emma."

Half-terrified but resolute, she walked over and slid beneath the covers next to him.

Chapter Three

Sweat dripped into his eyes, stinging and warm. It ran a wide path down his neck and bare back and then into the thin skin of linen trousers. Luke Bowen paused, one hand hanging onto the slow-moving wooden handle of the plow, the other hand shielding his eyes against the mid-afternoon glare as he lifted his gaze to row upon row of the yet furrowed field. His jaw clenched then worked in an agitated manner. Looking up toward the westward sun, that round glow of promise unknown, he drew a deep breath, pulled his grimy handkerchief from his pocket, and wiped the sweat from his brow.

"Good girl." Ginger always seemed to know moments before he did that he would need a rest and stopped, puffing air through her large nostrils, looking back at him as if to say, "It's all right. We both need a minute."

Luke trained his expression into stillness and then his heart to determination. He looked back at the acres of rows of plowed, dark earth—black lines of heaven. Or so they claimed. Kentucky land was rich. Not in folks, though the country was filling up; not in culture or East-Coast fashions or goods. No, its wealth came in what mattered most out here—rich dirt that meant rich crops. He knew he should be giving thanks. This land held the sweetness of gentle rising hills, soft soil that could grow a stick into an oak, cane thickets and wooded coppices of every kind of wood a body could need: sycamore, ash, beech, and hickory. Folks here thrived on bluegrass and abounding streams, scantily placed log cabins and one another . . . Kentucky had an infant country's dreams for greatness.

Luke repeated all of that to himself many times a day. This was his father's dream. A dream as distant to Luke as his father's face had become. Patrick Bowen died four years ago, but somehow it seemed longer. All he could remember about him was the sweat-plastered shirt he always wore and the words, "Time to farm, son. Time to farm."

A sound broke out from behind him, and he turned. "Luke!" His little sister Callie propelled her short legs toward him as she tore across the field at a quick gate for a ten-year-old. Something white waved in her hand above her head as she ran. Luke checked the horse and stood waiting, hoping nothing was wrong. But no, Callie's face glowed with excitement, her lips curving up, her eyes bright. He couldn't help but grin at the vision of her happy face and bouncing brown curls.

She paused in front of him, leaned over for a moment to catch her breath, the paper clutched in her hand at her knee. "Reverend Thomas brought it from Clarksville. It's a letter for you." She stood and held it out like a queen knighting a servant. Her chin jutted out as she solemnly announced. "It's from St. Louis."

Luke walked the few steps toward her and took the letter from her hand. He flipped it over and saw the red wax of an elegant seal that he didn't recognize. His heart did a little jump as he pressed his thumb against the wax to pry it up. What could it be? He hadn't been to St. Louis since his Corps of Discovery days.

Dear Mr. Bowen,

I have heard from a reliable source that you are an expert car-
tographer and adept at drawing wildlife and landscapes.
I am about to embark on a journey to the Pacific Ocean in the
footsteps of our great explorers Meriwether Lewis and William
Clark in the effort to set up trading posts along the route they
have paved for us. As partner in the ownership of The Ohio
Company, I must explore trading opportunities in the West;
and, as such, I would like you to consider joining my expedi-
tion as guide and to record, both in journals and in drawings
and maps, our westward prospects. If you would be interested
in such an endeavor, please present yourself in St. Louis by
mid-August. Ask for Eric Montclaire. I am looking forward to
meeting the man who traveled with this country's great explor-
ers. I would be honored to have you among our company.

Sincerely,

Eric Montclaire
The Ohio Company

Luke's heart pounded in his chest. He reread the letter,
clutching it tight between his thumb and fingers. Another
expedition? What he wouldn't give to be back on the Missouri
River, sketchbook in hand, his gaze sweeping land that few
men had ever seen. And to draw maps again? His throat locked
with excitement as he remembered how easy that talent came
for him. He seemed to have an instinctive ability to know the
turns and twists of the rivers and their tributaries, the size of the
land masses, where it would sink and swell—a bird's-eye view.
He saw the world as if from above instead of the usual linear
way most people saw it. But he hadn't made it far enough to see

the land swell into the majestic Rocky Mountains that he heard Lewis and Clark had found. What he wouldn't give to see those mountains . . . and the Pacific. He still woke in the middle of the night, excitement pulsing through him from a dream about the Pacific Ocean.

Luke looked up from the letter into the curious eyes of his little sister. She wore a faded calico dress that showed her ankles and recent growth spurt. Her feet were bare, but she didn't seem to mind or even feel the tough clods of dirt. His gaze roamed over her young, eager face. She looked like their mother—"a spitting image," everyone said. And she had her same big smile, the kind of smile that never failed to jerk at his heart.

Luke let out a long exhale of held breath as he stared into her eyes. A moment of decision passed within his chest and then he crumpled the paper in his fist.

Confusion lit Callie's eyes. "What is it? Bad news?"

Luke shook his head and reached out to tousle her brown curls. She had a smattering of freckles across her nose that reminded him of his own face so many years ago. "No, honey. It was nothing of any importance." He leaned down and stroked her cheek with his dirty thumb. She shook her head, her smile drooping to half its usual exuberance. "Momma will be disappointed. She thought it was important."

Luke ruffled her hair again, causing giggles to rise up as she twisted away. "Nothing important." He stood and turned toward the plow, then reared back his arm and threw the crumpled ball of paper up and into the clear blue sky. They watched together as it arched and then fell into the rich, dark earth where the plow would bury it. Luke turned back to her, a genuine smile on his face even though his heart sat like a lode of metal in his chest. "Have you worked on your figures today?"

Callie shook her head and looked down at the tips of her toes, dusty with dirt. "Not yet. Momma's kept us busy doing the washing."

"Catherine Bowen, you'd best get at it." She flinched slightly at his use of her proper name, but she had to learn. "I'll be in from these dirt clods in less than two hours, and I want to see neat rows of figures." He made the command as stern as he could, but she gazed up at him with the big, round eyes of hero worship.

He forced a smile. "Go on, now. I'll be in before you know it."

Thank You, God, for my sisters. But I'm not their father. How can I be their protector . . . caretaker?

Once again he faced the plow—his enemy. He hated to admit that, wouldn't most days. Usually he held fast to doing what God wanted him to do in the face of his father's death. But today . . . he couldn't deny the truth.

There just wasn't any love in it.

His father had loved this land, loved plowing rows, loved planting seeds, loved seeing them sprout up and show their curling green heads. Luke closed his eyes and saw his father's face clearly for the first time in a long time. Luke heard his laugh and remembered when they had walked the fields together among knee-high crops, marveling aloud how each plant had come from a tiny seed pushed into dirt.

But every year was the same. Every year they watched the crop grow only to have it half eaten by locust, deer, rabbits, and other predators. Every year they prayed for rain, then had to run with water buckets up and down the young plants in the middle of the hot sun when moisture seemed sucked from the earth. Every year they hoped so hard to make a living—

Luke shook his head and slapped the reins on the horse's back to start the cycle again. It didn't make sense, all this hope in things beyond their power. But his father had loved this life, and now . . . he had no choice but to love it too.

"You have to go." His mother bent over the flames of a wide kitchen fireplace, her pride and joy. She'd had his father build it to her specifications, and an admirable job he'd done. With a sigh, she straightened and turned to face him.

Luke dropped his empty canteen onto the scarred wooden table in the main room of their four-room cabin and looked askance at his mother. She picked up the letter that he'd crumpled and thrown away. It had been smoothed out and quivered now in her hand as she held it toward him. How had she gotten a hold of that? His gaze swung toward Callie, who turned and scurried off.

"You must go."

"No." Luke stalked over toward the hooks on the wall and hung his hat. He couldn't look at her. "You know I can't do that."

"I don't know anything of the sort." Her tone turned mulish as Luke stood staring at his hat. He heard the ringing of her shoes against the puncheon floor as she approached. "It's your second chance. I won't let you give that up for us again."

He turned and looked at her, then wished he hadn't. Her lips were trembling and her chin quivering. Her hands clutched the letter like she sometimes held the sketch he once made of his father.

The sight of her thus brought searing pain into Luke's stomach. He pushed it down as he had so many times in the past

28

four years. His voice held more heat in it than he meant as he demanded answers to all the questions that lay between him and his dreams. "Who will plow the fields? Who will plant them?" His voice shook. "Who will look after you and the girls? Who will hunt for meat?" He paused, feeling the tension on his face, sweat breaking out across his shoulder blades. "Tell me, Mother, who will provide for you all?"

"I suppose God will." Her voice was soft and quiet but held a thread of conviction.

Luke looked around the room and saw his sisters crowding around the table so that they could hear. There was Callie, who apparently felt safe from his anger now, with her sisters flanking her. Sweet Josephine . . . Sophie, they called her . . . the middle daughter at twelve. Torrie, the eldest and so quiet since their father's death, a young woman at sixteen. It took all of Luke's charm and wrangling to convince her to write her stories, which were always so light and funny and brought a moment's joy to their Saturday evenings.

His lips firmed. If he left, who would pull that gift from her? Who would still the shadows in her eyes? "My place is here."

His mother punched the letter into his chest. She looked up at him, her face white—almost as white as he was sure his face must be. Their mother had *never* shown anger in front of the children. She turned her face away from him, lips pressed together as she studied the wide eyes of the girls. Luke grasped the paper from her hand, and when she looked back at him, her words rang with conviction.

"You can't replace him."

He stared hard at her. "God knows I've tried."

"Yes, God does know that you've tried. God knows, and so do we. And we have loved you for it. But, Luke, my son"—she reached out toward him, touched him on the shoulder as tears reached her eyes—"you have a chance here. Another chance." She looked at each girl in turn. "We won't let you miss this again. To see the West? The Pacific? To see lands none of us have imagined." She tightened her grip on his shoulder until it hurt. "It's your future. *Your* purpose. I won't let your father's death rob you of that."

Luke's breathing quickened, and he felt as though he'd been running long and hard. Until this moment he hadn't allowed himself to consider going to St. Louis for such a job. There had been rumors of others following Lewis and Clark's trail westward, but none he'd taken seriously. But this. This time they'd heard of him. They'd asked for him.

They needed *him*.

"I can't do it." He said it like a plea. "How would you manage without me?"

"We can hire someone to plow. The girls and I can plant. Heaven knows many others have made do with less." His mother reached out and grasped hold of his cheek. "You have done your duty well. Better than most. Now it is your turn to live your life as God designed you to live it."

"I don't know . . ."

His mother smiled up at him. "Yes, you do. You know."

"I know I want it, but I'll feel guilty the whole time if I leave."

His mother's lips pressed into a small smile. "And I will feel guilty the whole time if you stay." She laughed. "Do it for us if not for you."

Luke turned and gave his sisters a long tortured look. "I guess I have a letter to write."

His mother shooed him from the room with a broad smile. "Dinner will be ready soon. Just say . . . you are on your way."

Chapter Four

"You have acquired the journal? I told you, whatever it takes."

"As I've said, he wasn't going to part with it," the man with her husband insisted. Emma frowned. The man sounded so . . . smug.

"So it came to that."

A long pause. "Yes sir, it did."

"Well?" Eric sounded impatient. "Where is it then?"

Emma stood on the threshold of the parlor, balancing the silver tea tray in her hands and looking between the two men in the room. The visitor must be one of the men going on the coming expedition. He had visited on several occasions, but she had never spoken to him. He had a harsh face, in a mean sort of way, with a jutting chin and beady eyes that gave Emma a shiver every time she saw him. If his white-knuckled grip on his hat was any indication, the man was quite frustrated.

The two men realized she was there at the same time and turned to look at her.

She had tried to rattle the tray as she approached the room. Not that she'd known about Eric's meeting—he never felt the need to tell her what he was doing—but she did know far better than to disturb him unnecessarily, regardless what he was doing. She had already made that mistake twice this week.

They'd been married a month now. She should have learned her lessons better. She stood, feeling her knees shake beneath the folds of her silken dress as she looked up into her husband's frowning face. "I'm sorry, Eric. I didn't know you were meeting with someone." She gestured toward the tea tray. "I thought, perhaps, you would like some tea and-and"—curse her stuttering tongue! Why couldn't she speak clearly any more?—"S-Sara made some genoise sponge cakes." She smiled up at Eric, a small movement of her lips, not daring to glance again at the other man in the room.

Eric nodded once. "Set it on the table." He gestured to the low table in front of the sofa. Emma gripped the tray much as the visitor had gripped his hat and walked into the room. *Graceful, Emma. Unobtrusive . . .* She deposited the tray, wincing at the clatter it made. She couldn't help glancing up at Eric, her lips curving, her face feeling hard and brittle.

"Well"—her gaze slid to the other man staring at her—"if you need anything else . . ."

Where should she say she would be? In her room? With the door bolted? No, she'd already tried that once. There was nowhere to go, nothing to do. She tilted her chin toward her husband in a tiny nod and turned.

"Emma."

Her back stiffened, but she didn't turn around. "Yes?"

"Mr. Hardesty was just leaving. Stay, won't you?"

She turned in slow-motion dread. "Of course." She walked back into the room, her gaze locked to the floor.

"I, um, could write down the address of the object, if you would like. I thought you might like to pick it up yourself." Mr. Hardesty's tone said he wanted to flee as badly as Emma did.

"Of course." Her husband gestured toward the desk, upon which were fresh paper, quill, and ink.

They all stood silent as the man wrote something in slashing black ink and then rose, tipping the hat he placed on his head toward Emma. "Ma'am."

"Good day." Emma directed her gaze at the rug under her feet. As Eric saw the man to the door, her mind worked swift calculations as to her most advantageous position. She could stand, but that might imply she didn't want to be here. She could sit on the striped sofa, her head down, but that might anger him. He didn't like it when she showed fear. She eyed the afternoon repast of tea and cakes, how pretty it appeared, and made her decision.

She was here to serve him.

She was happy to see him.

Emma sat on the sofa and slipped into the role of devoted wife. This was only the beginning of an act that would last a lifetime.

Despair slammed over her in drowning waves.

Eric's footsteps sounded across the wood floor. As he walked toward her, she lifted the heavy, silver teapot. She turned her face a little to the side and placed a contented, happy-to-be-married smile on her face. She lifted the pot and locked her eyes on the steam and brown liquid pouring from the delicate spout. She must not spill a drop.

He stopped in front of her.

She added a spoonful of sugar, noted the glittering ring on her third finger as she lifted the small, elegant cream pitcher and poured in a tiny dollop of milk. She could feel his gaze hot upon her face as she stirred it in. She must not falter. She must remain calm.

Above all, she must not show fear.

Emma held the delicate cup and saucer out to her husband. She forced the smile curving her lips into a curving smile, but she knew it had to reach her eyes too. That was the hard part. "Won't you sit down?"

He stared hard at her. He looked deep into her eyes for long seconds, the cup suspended between them. She blinked, wanting to turn away. And then she knew her mistake. She could paste falsity on her face, but they were married, they were *one*. He had rights to her—body and soul—and he knew it. He could see down into her very being . . . and he knew her black void of terror.

"I've told you not to come down here when I am meeting with my men. This mission is more important than anything I will ever do. I can't risk a woman ruining it."

Emma put the cup back on the table and folded her hands into her lap in an effort to stop their trembling. "I'm sorry. I didn't know anyone was with you, and I-I missed you." She didn't look at him this time.

"If you missed me so much, come here."

The heated timbre of his voice brought back the night before. Her wrists throbbed anew at the memory and her stomach rolled so that she wondered if she would be able to obey him or have to run for a pot in which to heave the contents of her stomach.

Dear God in heaven . . .

Was there a heaven anymore? Or a God for that matter? She rose, smoothed any invisible wrinkles from her skirt, and then closed the distance that separated them. He reached out and grasped a firm hold on her chin, lifting her face, her eyes, to lock with his.

"Don't ever come down here again unless I call you."

"I'm to remain upstairs? Always?" Shock gave her the courage to ask it.

"Of course not, Emma. What kind of a monster do you think I am?" He barked the answer out, now the wounded and loving husband. "I meant when I am meeting with my men, of course. Don't come downstairs then."

Emma shook her head as the pressure of his fingers grew on her chin. Pain throbbed like a pulse. Tears filled her eyes. "I won't. I didn't know. I promise not to do it again."

He glared at her, moving closer so that she bent back, away from him. "How long were you standing there, listening, before I saw you? What did you hear, Emma?"

She shook her head again, even as she knew she'd never convince him. "Nothing. I promise."

"You're lying. Tell me."

The pressure on her chin increased. Pain radiated into her jaws and cheeks. A tear slipped down one side of her cheek and then clung along her jawline, running its path along the curve until it gave up, gave way, and dripped to her collarbone. "A journal. Something about a journal, that's all."

She knew what was coming next, but the slow motion of his hand rearing back still came as a shock to her system. Her breath whooshed out as his hand made contact; her head jerked as the rest of her body followed to her knees.

"*Tell* me!" He leaned down and yelled into her face, his own features masked in hate and rage. His quick, heated breath blew across her hair. He was so close she could see the dark pinpoints of stubble beneath his immaculate shave. "What do you know? What do you think you know about the journal? Tell me everything your mind has thought about it."

Emma could hear the ragged quality of her voice as she spilled out all her thoughts. She swayed on her knees, trying to stay upright, one hand held to her burning cheek. "You said to get the journal at any cost."

Eric knelt in front of her. He took her face between his hands and gripped hard. Shards of pain throbbed into her temples. "And what might that mean, Emma? What do you think I meant by that?" His voice lowered and she trembled anew. Softness promised suffering.

"I don't know," she wailed as his fingers intertwined in her hair, closed into fists, and jerked hard.

"You're a smart girl. Come on, Emma. What did I mean?"

Emma closed her eyes as he jerked her face up to look at him. The left side of her face stung so that she couldn't feel the tears she knew were rolling down her check. Without looking at him, she gave in, told him what he wanted to hear. "You told Mr. Hardesty to kill the man if he had to. T-to get the journal at any cost. *Whatever it took.*"

Eric chuckled.

How she used to love that sound. How attractive it was to her, so mysterious . . .

Now the mystery was gone. She knew what that laugh meant.

He pulled her close, locking her in his arms. "You know me." His voice whispered into her ear, even as his hold on her hair turned into a tangled caress. "Only you know me. And you'll never tell. You'll never tell anyone, will you?"

"No." She shook her head as he took her down to the floor, to the fancy rug that he'd insisted she buy weeks ago with its garish colors that she hated. She concentrated on the feel of the rug beneath her grasping hands and a light in the distance. A light that sometimes visited her in her dreams. A light that might—if she was lucky enough or good enough or dead enough—someday come.

A saving light.

The bruise wasn't too noticeable this time.

Emma leaned in to apply the loose talc. No one would know. She brushed on more of the powder and then sat back to study the effect against the purple hue of her cheek. Who was she kidding? She was to have a luncheon with her mother today, and she was sure to notice. Eric, perhaps, had not thought ahead last night when he'd given in to his rage.

Her chin rose. She stared back at herself in the mirror, saw the stern set to her lips, the thin hollows of her cheeks, the deadened ache in her eyes, and the purple-hued smudges beneath them.

This was not life as it was supposed to be.

No bright happiness of a new bride here. She looked haggard, tight, constrained, . . . broken. Shell. What would she look like in a year? Five? Ten?

Father in heaven, if You can hear me, please help.

She stood up and studied the rest of her form in the wavy mirror. The dull ache in her back made her wince. She was too thin. Thinner even than on her wedding day when nervous anticipation had distracted her from eating. Now her dress draped loose around her shoulders; the waist of her gown hung in forlorn folds around her narrow hips.

If only she'd known.

Oh God, I want to die.

She swallowed against the sob in her throat and reached for her pearl drop earrings. A knock at the door made her start and turn. "Yes? Come in."

Eric opened the door a crack. He peered from around it. "You're to luncheon with your mother today?"

Emma looked away from him, back at the mirror to put on one of the earrings. "Yes."

She watched in the mirror as Eric entered the room and closed the door. Her stomach flipped over. He came up behind her and stood, silent and still. Her gaze met his in the glass.

He pulled something from his pocket, a porcelain box. "A present."

Emma turned toward him and stared at the prettiness of it. It was square with a pink rose enameled on the top and smaller roses circling the gilded edge. She schooled her features into a smile. "For me?"

"Open it."

Emma took the little box and lifted the hinged lid. She peaked inside and gasped. Luminous pearls gleamed at her from the box.

"Turn around." Eric reached for the necklace.

She turned toward the mirror but didn't look at him, focused instead on the quick up and down of her chest.

He laid the strand of pearls around her neck like a tether line. It moved and rolled on its cord with each breath against her collarbone. His hands, like spiders, crawled across the nape of her neck to fix the clasp.

Her hand went to the pendant hanging from the pearls, a large amethyst that glittered from the center of a gold, filigreed top. "Oh . . . my."

"Do you like it?"

"Of course." She lifted her chin and mimicked a smile. "Thank you."

"It suits you, you know."

"How do you mean?"

His hand slid down the curve of the piece, stroking the tops of her breasts in a feather-light caress. "You were meant for such things."

Emma looked up in the mirror and locked eyes with her husband. Her hand rose to the purple smudge on her cheek. Her fingertips followed its blue-hued outline much as his had the necklace. "Am I?"

Her lips curved up without warmth.

His eyes turned dark.

He stepped away, the necklace still within one hand, tightening the hold on her neck. Then he stepped forward, a sudden movement, leaned toward her and placed his mouth next to her ear. "You are my wife." His voice was as chilling and dark as any nightmare, only this was spoken in the full light of day. This was real.

Emma shivered and shrank from his hold. "I am your wife."

"Don't ever forget it, Emma."

Emma reached for the glittering pendant against her throat and pulled it a little forward so that she could breathe. Her eyes met his in the mirror. "No. I won't forget."

He released the piece, walked from the room, and slammed the door behind him.

Her eyes in the mirror glittered back at her like the amethyst around her throat.

She reached up, frantic to undo the clasp around the back of her neck. She tugged the elegant piece into her hands, where it lay illuminated in the soft light. Her fingers curled around the strand, making a fist. She wanted to throw it into the mirror where it might shatter into the sharp shards of the broken dreams around her. But she didn't. He might hear and come back. Instead, she uncurled her hand and, as if handling something very precious, set the necklace in a careful pile on her dressing table.

She picked up the powder. Leaning forward toward the mirror, Emma swept more powder against the purple of her cheek. "Powder covers a multitude of sins," she whispered to herself as she pushed back from the dressing table.

She gathered her parasol and gloves and left the room, knowing she wouldn't die. She wasn't so fortunate.

Her nightmare had only just begun.

Chapter Five

*E*mma's mother opened the door to her knock. How odd to be knocking on her childhood door, but it didn't seem right to just walk in anymore.

Her parent's three-story brick house lay on the side of St. Louis that boasted some elegance. St. Louis was a Spanish city mostly with some French citizens and their carefree culture from the other side of the Mississippi River thrown in for good measure. Emma and her parents were neither French nor Spanish. Her father was of good English stock and a speculator. Her mother was a mix of Scottish and Irish heritage. But no one would have guessed that from a meeting with her. No, the venerable Mrs. Anna Daring had labored to squelch any hint of such a heritage, taking on the staid, sure mannerisms of her husband. Everyone agreed that Mr. Daring wouldn't be the man he'd become without Mrs. Daring.

Her mother answered the door, a mixture of annoyance and relief on her well-schooled features.

"I'm not late, am I?" Emma kept her head down, her bonnet brim covering her face.

"No, of course not. Why are you knocking? You know you are welcome here anytime."

Her mother backed away to allow her to enter the entrance hall. The home might have been a simple brick structure on the outside, but its interior boasted ornate touches in the hand-carved woodwork, the ornamental plaster ceilings, and the gleaming wood floors. All testimony that a well-heeled family resided herein.

Her mother reached for Emma's parasol, handed it to the maid, and then held out her hand for the bonnet.

"It's such a beautiful day," Emma prevaricated. "I thought we might take our meal outdoors on the terrace?"

Her mother frowned. "We never eat out of doors, Emma. What's gotten into you?"

Emma sighed and pulled on one of the satin ribbons under her chin. She ducked her head and pulled the hat free, handing it to her mother without lifting her eyes or chin.

Her mother didn't seem to notice as she tossed the headpiece into the maid's waiting hands, turned away, and strode toward the back of the house.

"I have a surprise. Come along."

Oh no, what could her mother have planned? Emma kept her head down and to one side as she followed her mother's clicking heels toward the dining room.

Her mother smiled at Emma over her shoulder, turned the knobs on the double doors, and flung them open. She turned, took Emma's elbow in a tight grip, and propelled her through the doorway and into the room. Emma heard it before she saw it. A twittering, suppressed laughter and movement. She glanced up and sank inside. All her friends—all her *mother's* friends, she corrected—all the women they'd known in the last few years were here. To see her.

She gasped, panic rising, and turned her bruised cheek away from the women.

She couldn't do it.

She couldn't let them see her face.

Emma pulled away from her mother's grasping arm and fled the room.

"Emma!" Her mother shouted after her. "Emma, come back!"

Emma reached the door, pulled it open, and stumbled out into the bright sunshine. She hitched up her skirts and ran, as she used to run as a child, down the half-stone, half-dirt walkway toward the middle of town.

Her eyes watched the ground but were blurry with tears as thoughts rushed through her mind at a speed that made her dizzy. She couldn't see—didn't want to see. *Don't fall!*

Her hair fell loose from the pins and cascaded down her shoulders, to her waist. It was unseemly to be in public without her bonnet much less with her hair down, but at least it hid her face. She slowed to catch her breath and saw that many of the townsfolk were out on such a beautiful day. What if she saw someone she knew? She had to get out of the busy streets, but where to go? She couldn't go back home yet. Eric would know something had gone wrong and force the story from her. He would be furious when he heard what had happened. Worrying her bottom lip, she rushed ahead to where she knew not, just plunging toward First Street.

A sudden thought struck her. What if she just kept running? Would anyone stop her? *Escape.* The word echoed . . . so sweet, so seductive. Head down, she pushed on. Her breath whooshed in and out of her chest. Her heartbeat thudded loud against her ribs, and her throat tightened even as she savored the forbidden word.

A sudden slamming into her shoulder spun her, then dropped her to the hard ground. Her shoulder hit first and then her face smacked down hard. Sharp pain registered as pebbles embedded into her cheek. She heard a grunt and then firm hands grasped around her waist—lifting her, realigning her, standing her upright before she had time to absorb that she had fallen.

She lifted her head into the bright light, dizzy and shaken. "Miss. Are you all right?"

Her gaze stopped on a face, but the sun was too bright to see him clearly. She blinked and wavered, started to slide and fall. She was dimly aware of strong hands on her shoulders and then, as she tilted, her waist. Suddenly her feet were no longer on the ground; he had lifted her into his arms. She gasped, panic streaking through her like a lightning bolt. "Put me down at once!"

"You're hurt. You looked ready to faint."

The words came from far away; the edges of her vision grew dark and wavy. "No." She tried to argue that she would not faint, had never fainted in her life. But even as the words formed on her lips, an odd darkness overcame her.

Luke stared down at the woman in his arms. Her body had gone slack, and a cascade of luxurious, blonde curls framed the face that lay open to his gaze in the full, mid-afternoon sun. Her skin had gone white except for the spots of red where blood oozed from the rocks in her cheek. And what was that?

His artist's eye gave him the unique ability to see details that others missed and to see them with an immediate clarity that sometimes astounded him. This time it brought a frown as he took in the purple hue on her cheek . . . powder applied to hide it, the indentations of fingers, a palm.

She'd been smacked with an open hand.

The realization rocked through his thoughts. When? Why? Who would have done such a thing? The only women he could imagine being abused in such a way were prostitutes. But this woman was no such thing. Her dress was a costly, demure gown of crystal blue; her skin like a fine painting, ivory and pure, supple enough to see the creaminess without touching it. Her blonde hair, the color of honey and the wheat of his father's field, hung across his arm, falling in waves to his knee. He looked down the length of her and saw delicate, expensive, bright green shoes.

No, this was no coquette. She was a lady of some consequence.

She'd been in a hurry, that was for sure. Ran right into him without seeing him. Was she running from something? Someone?

A quick look around the vicinity told him that he would have to search for help. He studied the storefronts wondering where to take her. She needed a doctor.

She weighed little more than the traveling pack on his back, the bag that held all his belongings—clothes, cartography tools and drawing implements, a compass given to him by Clark, the letter he'd thrown into the sky of his father's farm, and his Bible. But he didn't want to carry her far, so he turned and carried her toward the nearest shop doorway. When he entered the room, it took a moment for his eyes to adjust. He'd entered a woodworking shop.

A man came from a back room.

"Can I help—"the man faltered as he saw the woman in Luke's arms.

"Some water, please. And a place to lay her down. Do you have a doctor in this town?"

The man motioned him to another small room where a bed stood next to the wall. "Put her there. I'll get the water and then fetch the apothecary. He serves as doctor most times."

Luke looked up into the man's concerned eyes and nodded. "Thank you, sir."

Luke gently laid the woman on the bed and placed his fingers against the side of her throat. Her pulse was rapid but seemed strong. The carpenter came back with a cup of water and a clean cloth.

Luke reached for the supplies. "Thank you, sir. Maybe I can wake her before you return with the doctor."

The man nodded, grabbed his hat, and hurried away.

Luke turned back to the woman and pressed the cloth against her cheek. It bled pretty badly in one place, but he was more worried about getting the rock out. When he picked out the largest pebble, she began to move and moan. Then, before Luke could do or say anything, she sat bolt upright, fear lighting her features and filling her voice.

"I have to go home."

"Miss, you were hurt. We've sent for the doctor."

She turned toward him, shaking her head. "No. No doctor." She swung her feet to the floor and then stood, steadying herself by placing a hand on his arm and then, as though realizing what she'd done, jerked it back. She reached toward her cheek and winced. "I fell, didn't I? Silly of me. I'm so clumsy."

He watched, at a loss for words as she marched toward the door. She turned back toward him for a brief moment. "Thank you, sir."

"You can't go. You need looking after."

She turned away. He could have sworn she said something, but it was too low to be sure. He thought she said, *I am always looked after . . .*

She couldn't just leave! What if she fainted again?

Luke followed her out of the store, then down the street, careful that she didn't hear or see him. A feeling of disquiet assailed him, but it made no sense. It seemed this woman had been dropped in his arms, and so it had become his duty—his mission—to see that she came to no further harm.

He shook the feeling off. He was probably just used to playing the father figure, the protector to helpless females. Not that his family was helpless now. His mother had already hired a man to do his job. He sighed at the thought and concentrated on the task at hand—make sure this unbalanced, half-conscious woman, mysterious and lovely woman, knew where she was going.

He watched from the shadows of one of the town's houses as she let herself through a door to what must be one of the wealthier homes of the city. He'd only arrived in town this morning and had meant to ask around, find out where to find Eric Montclaire, but it was as if his whole world, his mission, had been turned upside down—or maybe righted.

That was a brainless thought. Stop it. Luke swallowed hard and tried to turn away, . . . but he allowed one brief cursory glance. He saw her hurry in and close the door behind her. An unaccountable, overwhelming sadness struck him.

She was gone.

He would never see her again.

He leaned against the rough-hewn wooden planks of the house and let out a breath. A psalm came to mind: *LORD, thou hast heard the desire of the humble: thou wilt prepare their heart, thou wilt cause thine ear to hear: To judge the fatherless and the oppressed, that the man of the earth may no more oppress.*

He looked up at the bright afternoon sky filled with blue as far as the eye could see. He noted the fluffy clouds that dotted the blue, but felt like a storm was coming. "What is it, Lord?"

Not knowing what else to do, he turned back toward town. He should go back to the carpenter's shop and explain their disappearance, talk to the doctor.

The shop's door stood open so he stepped in, smelling sawdust and seeing pieces of furniture in various states of completion. "Hello. Anyone here?"

Two men came out of the back room.

The apothecary came up and shook his hand. "I am Ross Rolland. Where is this woman who collapsed?"

"She was here, but while you were gone"—he looked toward the carpenter—"she came to. Said she had to go home and busted out of here as if her skirts were on fire."

"Do you know who she was? Where she lives?"

He knew one of those answers, but something inside held him silent. "She walked out just fine. I think she made it home." Time to end the conversation. Luke turned as if to go. "Sorry for your trouble, sir."

The man stopped him with a hand on his shoulder. "She just up and walked out, eh? Did you know her?"

Luke shook his head. "Not at all. I'm here to meet with a man about a job—Eric Montclaire. I was walking up the street, deciding who to ask about the whereabouts of Mr. Montclaire when she ran smack into me." He shrugged, placing a slight grin on his face. "I picked her up and carried her in here."

"What did she look like? I know most of the citizens here."

Luke shrugged, taking on a more nonchalant mien as his irritation grew. "Can't rightly say. She'd fallen on the ground and had some gravel in her cheek. Blonde hair. That's about all I can remember."

"Well."

The carpenter motioned toward Luke. "Mr. Bowen was just helping, Ross. Could have been anyone."

The apothecary nodded. "I suppose. I suppose." He nodded to Luke and then to the carpenter. "I guess I will be going then. Let me know if you need anything else."

Both men watched in silence as he walked from the shop, the door clanging shut behind him.

The carpenter turned toward Luke, pondered him for a moment, then held out his hand. "John Sumner."

"Luke Bowen, of Kentucky. A pleasure." Luke paused, measuring the man's gaze. "You knew her?"

"Not sure." John shook his head. "But I know the man you're looking for." Disquiet colored his eyes.

"Mr. Montclaire?"

"Yes."

"Could you direct me?"

"Oh, he's not far." John led him to the door and pointed down the street. "Just about three streets that way, a straight shot. It's one of the big houses. Red brick and pretty. The second one—"

"On the left."

John eyed him but asked no questions. "Yes, that's the one."

Luke met the man's gaze, held it. Then nodded. "I guess I'll be on my way then."

John stilled him with a hand on his shoulder. "Mr. Montclaire ordered a piece for his wife. Would you mind delivering it?"

Luke raised his brows. "I guess not."

The man disappeared and then came back with an elegantly carved box. "It's for his wife's jewelry."

Luke took the heavy box in his hands. He lifted the lid and saw row upon row of silk compartments. There were slim drawers and a tinkling music that stopped when he shut the lid. "A beautiful piece of work."

"Thank you." John gazed at the box for a long moment. "He had very exacting instructions as to how to fashion it. I hope he is pleased with it."

"Do you mean, you hope *she* likes it?"

"No. I don't think she will care as much as he."

"You don't want to deliver it yourself to see?"

John chuckled. "You're approaching a lion's den. I'm happy to escape it this time."

Luke placed his hat low on his brow. He looked up at the man, a stranger and yet, oddly enough, not. He shrugged and grinned, trying to lighten the mood. "I guess it's my turn then."

John walked him to the door and then paused.

Luke noticed it and stopped. "Something else?"

The man pressed his lips together and then glanced up and down the street. When he saw that they were alone, he gestured the other direction. "Mr. Montclaire might not be at home at this hour." John's eyes went from shuttered to shattered. His voice cracked as he pointed toward a tavern, painted a garish green. "I have it on good account that he frequents The Ace on many afternoons."

Luke looked down the street and then back to the man. "Should I go there instead?"

The man shrugged, his suddenly slumped shoulders making him seem years older. "If you do, don't ask for him. Ask for Maggie." He paused and shook his head. "Ask for Margarite."

Luke looked down at the jewelry box and then back at the man. He clapped him on the shoulder and nodded toward the gift. "You made it for her, this Maggie, didn't you?"

His thin chin lifted and his eyes hardened. "I make everything for her."

"Then she should have it."

The carpenter started to shake his head, then changed his mind and smiled a sad smile instead. "Yes. She should. I will make another one for Mrs. Montclaire."

"And risk Mr. Montclaire's displeasure at the delay?"

John looked off into the distance in thought. "I believe God would have me do this. Tell her . . . tell her it's from her father."

The words gave Luke a start; he'd thought she must be a lover of some sort. But a daughter? In a place like that?

What was he getting himself into?

Chapter Six

*E*mma picked her way through the empty hall, her shoes clicking too loudly as she came to the kitchen. She opened the door a crack and saw Sara, their cook and maid of all work, bent over a pot, stirring something that made Emma feel queasy. Without opening the door further and with a forced brightness to her voice, she called out, "Sara, please have some hot water sent up to my room." The woman turned toward her, but Emma didn't open the door further. "And if my husband asks, . . . is he at home?"

"No miss, he left about an hour ago."

He rarely stayed at home in the afternoons—her favorite part of the day, the only time when relief from the constant pressure to be perfect lifted from her.

"Yes, well, tell him I am taking my afternoon rest." Eric favored her afternoon naps as it gave her energy for the social events and plans he had for her in the evenings.

"Of course, miss. Oh, mistress?"

"Yes?"

"Your mother came by. She left a note."

Emma's head dropped, but she let the silence hang.

"I've left it on your bureau."

"Thank you, Sara. I'll be in my room."

She made her way to her bedchamber on trembling legs. She didn't want to read a letter from her mother but knew she must.

She thrust open the door, going to the pitcher and bowl on a low table by the window. She poured some water into the bowl and then carried the heavy porcelain to her dressing table and mirror. Sitting down, she took a deep breath, lifted her head and studied her reflection.

Her cheek and one side of her chin were spotted with blood. Taking up a cloth, she dipped it into the water and bathed the redness away, feeling the dirt and tiny rocks embedded in her skin. She winced as she picked the stones from her flesh, fresh blood flowing onto the cloth. The stinging increased when she rubbed at it, leaning into the mirror to make certain she removed all the dirt and debris. The pebbles dropped into the bowl, making a clanking noise that reminded her that she would have to dump and hide this evidence of her escape from the luncheon.

After cleaning her cheek the best she could, she patted the rest of her face dry and brushed out her hair, pinning it into some semblance of order, and then pushed back the chair. Her gaze flashed toward the gleaming white note on her bureau. She hesitated and then walked toward it, picked it up, and flipped it open.

My dearest,

I don't know what became of you this afternoon, but I was humiliated beyond measure. I blamed it on a new bride's nerves. You have no idea the trouble I went to. Why, all of the food, the invitations, the perfect timing for such an event. And all for you! You can't have known, or you never would have run out as you did.

I will come to call tomorrow afternoon. I shall expect an explanation.

Your mother,
Mrs. Daring

The letter shook in her hands as she stared at it. An explanation? What could she possibly say that would sound convincing? She would apologize and blame the state of her face on her fall. She would grovel and give the *Emma was stupid again* apology. Her mother would never want the truth, never believe such a thing of the prized catch of Eric Montclaire.

Her fingers crushed the note into a ball. No one could know what her life had become. Anyway, he'd been sorry, hadn't he? He had given her that necklace. Maybe it wouldn't happen again. Maybe she would finally learn to please him. She walked toward the low burning fire and threw the note into the flames. Everything in her wanted to scream as she threw it, but she didn't. Instead, she allowed a tight noise to escape her throat as she watched the letter fly through the air, land, catch fire, and, for a few seconds, turn into a blaze that embodied her silent pain.

Luke swung open the door to the saloon and stepped inside. He didn't like establishments like this; they were dark and desperate—people looking for peace in a place where it didn't exist. But the weight of his mission took him toward the long, wooden bar.

He sat down and turned on his stool to study the room. A group of four men played cards at a table, a piano sat in one corner, empty of a player this early in the afternoon, a couple of scantily dressed women eyed him from the other side of the long counter. Luke turned away from their full-bosomed display.

"Whatcha got there?" The bartender wandered over and eyed the jewelry box.

Luke lifted his chin. "A delivery. From a friend of mine."

"Oh yeah?"

Luke nodded. "Does a Margarite work here?"

The man looked at Luke long and hard before answering. "She might. Who's asking?"

Luke stretched out his hand in an effort to be friendly. "The name's Luke Bowen, but I'm just the messenger. She down here?"

The man took his hand, lifted a glass from under the bar, and poured a shot of whiskey. He passed it over the polished wood planks of the top and waited.

Luke didn't particularly like whiskey. The few times he'd tried it, it had given him a headache in the morning. He ignored the glass and asked. "Like I said, is she down here?"

The bartender leaned in, scanning the room, his small eyes roving the place. "I don't see her."

"Well, do you know where I could find her?"

"She ain't cheap, you know."

"I'm not looking for that. Just a delivery. It's a gift."

"I know that girl, and she don't have no patrons with the wherewithal to give that kind of gift." He paused. "Except maybe the one she's up there with now, but he ain't gonna give her any presents, I can tell you that for sure."

Luke let his gaze rove the room in a moment of silence. "Maybe you don't know all her friends. Maybe she has more like Mr. Montclaire."

The man laughed. "Mr. Montclaire is the best thing that girl will ever see. Don't know how she got him." He leaned further in and said in a low voice. "Have you seen his wife? Why, if I had a wife like that"—he shook his head back and forth, lust lighting his gaze—"hmmm-mmmm. All them curves and blonde hair. I hear it's so long it reaches her knees. I can just imagine her without all those fancy clothes on." Luke gripped the box in his hands to keep from knocking the leering grin from the man's face. "She must be a dead fish where it counts if he's still visitin' Margarite."

Luke took a deep breath and jerked his chin in the direction of the stairs. "They up there now?"

"Likely so. Not been the full hour yet."

"He comes in every day?"

"Naw, not every day. But several times a week." The man shrugged. "I'm not complainin' you know. Business is business."

"Sure."

"You ain't gonna tell me, are you?"

"Well . . ." Luke drug out the word. "It's supposed to be a surprise. I guess I'll just wait here a bit for them to come down and deliver it to her personally."

The man took the news surprisingly well. "She deserves something like that." He motioned toward the mahogany wood that gleamed with elegance in stark contrast to the rough wood bar top. "She is somethin' special."

Luke inclined his head in agreement and turned away. "I think I'll just watch this card game while I wait. Thank you."

Luke deposited money for the whiskey he hadn't touched on the bar and walked toward the foursome playing cards. He pulled out a chair nearby and propped his feet on the table, crossing them at the ankles. Leaning back into his chair, he pulled his hat low over his eyes as if he wanted to take a rest.

No one bothered him as he waited, but his mind spun with everything he'd learned since he walked into this town. And since he was walked into by a woman running away from something. Or—his gaze drifted up the stairs—someone.

A few moments later the sounds of feminine laughter caught his attention. A stunning young woman appeared at the top of the stairs. Her dark brown hair was neat and pinned up. Her ample bosom was half falling out of her low neckline, and her skirt clung to her hips and legs. She held on to the man beside her as they walked side by side, down the steps. The woman looked up at the man, adoring.

Luke took a quick look at the man and then looked down at his chest as if asleep. It had to be him.

After receiving the letter from Eric Montclaire, he'd done a little asking around, a little investigative work about the man who might be his future employer and more, the leader of a dangerous expedition. They were going to need someone strong, wise, and levelheaded to lead them, a man like Lewis or Clark.

In all Luke's questioning he'd only learned one thing, and it had perplexed him. Eric Montclaire, according to everyone he spoke with, was the best-looking man west of the Appalachian Mountains. And wealthy. He was reputed to gain wealth with every business speculation he made. But people kept going back to his looks, as foolish as that seemed to Luke. Who spoke, men and women alike, about a man's good looks?

Well, now that he'd seen him, Luke understood. The man resembled a painting of an angel, like that drawing of Michelangelo's *David* that he'd seen once. All Montclaire was missing was the wings.

He was, plain and simple, like physical perfection come to life.

"I guess you're going back to her now."

Margarite's voice was low and sulky but clear enough to Luke as the two of them walked past him. Luke shifted as if uncomfortable so that he could see them. Montclaire reached out a hand and brushed the woman's cheek with a caress.

"You know I don't want you to speak of her." His voice lowered, silky but deadly.

She laughed, a tittering sound of nervous energy. "Sorry. I just think about it sometimes."

"Don't."

"I won't." Margarite grasped his arm and then, seeing his look, let go. She rallied though and dimpled at him, her head cocked to one side. "Until next time then."

Montclaire dipped his head in her direction—and then glanced around the room.

Luke closed his eyes, schooling his breathing to feign a man asleep. He could feel his future boss's gaze upon him, studying him, but Luke's hat sat low enough that Montclaire wouldn't get a very good look at him. At least Luke hoped that was the case.

He heard the door open and close. Montclaire was gone. Luke knew it before he opened his eyes. He could *feel* that the man was gone. For as good-looking as Eric Montclaire was, Luke had a gut-deep certainty that the man's heart was as black as sin, and everything and anyone who touched him would be tainted by that same darkness.

Chapter Seven

*E*mma woke to the distant sound of a knock on the front door. She rose up, an abrupt movement of sitting and then standing, of throwing back the covers and landing on her feet before she was fully awake.

Had her mother arrived?

She looked about the room . . . no, wait. Her mother was coming tomorrow. She was just muddled because she'd been napping. "Thank goodness." She breathed out a sigh of relief as she smoothed down her skirts and made her way to the mirror. Some of her hair had fallen from the knot at her nape. She jabbed the pins back in place, wondering if Eric had come home. He hadn't mentioned any plans for them tonight, but she could never be sure. She had to look her best at all times. Not that that would be possible now.

She hurried to dust powder onto both injuries. Eric was sure to notice, and she was dreading telling him about her fall. He was always so disappointed in her when she was clumsy. With a resigned sigh she walked to the door, took a deep breath, and then opened it and stepped out. As she made her way down the long, grand staircase, she heard male voices coming from the sitting room.

"Mr. Bowen. A pleasure. I'm so glad you were able to make it. I've been looking forward to meeting you."

Should she go back upstairs? Eric had been clear that she was not to come down when he met with his men. She started to back away, to slink back up the stairs, but something in the stranger's voice made her hesitate.

"As have I."

That voice. She knew that voice . . .

"You received my letter?"

"Yes. I am humbled that you thought of me for your expedition."

The man talking to Eric sounded more hesitant than his words expressed.

"I need a cartographer, Mr. Bowen. I've heard from many sources that you are the best."

"Thank you, sir. It's an odd talent, but I seem to have a knack for it. I've mapped much of Kentucky for the American government."

"And you were on the expedition with Lewis and Clark for a time, I'm told. Some family tragedy forced you to leave them?"

"Yes. My father passed away. I had to return home to take care of my mother and my three younger sisters."

"I'm sorry to hear that. It would seem this might be your second chance."

The man paused and Emma strained to hear. "I was hoping so." But he didn't sound at all sure of that.

"I have acquired a journal from one of the members of Lewis and Clark's expedition. With that and your abilities to read the land," Eric paused, "I have full faith that we will accomplish our mission."

Emma pressed back into the wall. Eric really did have the journal. That meant the author was dead, his blood on Eric's hands even though he'd ordered someone else to carry out the deed. She was married to a murderer! A sick feeling rose to her throat. She had to get upstairs but she couldn't seem to move.

"What exactly is the purpose of your mission, sir?" It was as though the stranger read her mind. She'd wanted that question answered for months. What was Eric doing? He told her nothing. Would he leave with the expedition? Would he leave her here in St. Louis alone? It was her greatest hope.

Emma held her breath at the direct challenge. This could be the end of the mapmaker, and he didn't even know it. But her husband surprised her.

"Why, to set up trading posts along the route." A short, arrogant laugh followed the remark. "It won't be long before the Americans follow Lewis and Clark's trail to find land in the West. We'll be there to help them, supply them."

"A worthy plan."

"Yes. I think so."

Emma backed away, needing air. Her skirt rustled against the wall as she took a step.

"Emma, is that you?"

Her hand rose to her throat. What would he do to her this time? But he sounded like he wanted her to approach. She stepped back and then, making her movements more brisk, walked to the doorway and locked gazes with her husband, judging his mood. "I was just coming down to check on din—"

"Emma." Eric interrupted with a wave of his hand. "Come here and meet my new cartographer."

She walked forward with her eyes on her husband, every-thing in her trying to judge her husband's motives. "Certainly."

She came up to Eric, smiled at him, and then turned to face the man who would join him on the expedition that would take her husband away for over a year—her breathing-room time.

The man's face registered with a double beat of her heart before her mind made the connection. She stifled the gasp in her throat. He stood, held out a tanned hand toward hers as if they'd never met before, as if he'd never carried her in his arms.

"How do you do, Mrs. Montclaire."

She saw the flash of recognition in his eyes, then the backing away, and recognized what he offered her: protection.

Above his disinterested smile, his eyes were shuttered but aware. "Luke Bowen, at your service."

She reached for the hand knowing Eric's eyes were upon her. She looked down at their clasped hands, feeling the warmth within the stranger's strong grip. She hadn't let herself think of him since their encounter. Rallying, she lifted her head, stared into his eyes with the appropriate blank stare, and smiled. "So nice to make your acquaintance, Mr. Bowen. I'm sure my husband will see to it that you are successful in your mission."

Luke's gaze communicated his doubt in her words, but he agreed. "Yes, ma'am. I am sure he will."

"Well"—Eric interjected as their hands quickly released—"why don't you have some refreshments brought in, Emma, while we discuss the formalities. There is something I want to tell you. Good news."

Emma forced a smile. "Yes, of course." She nodded at each man and left the room, feeling both their gazes upon her back.

Luke watched Mrs. Montclaire leave the room and was struck again by the stab of sadness, the grief for her that opened like a dark hole within him. She hadn't known. She couldn't have known what she would marry. He couldn't believe that she could have known and still married this monstrous man.

Recovering, his gaze swung back toward Eric to find the man watching him, eyes intent.

"She is lovely, is she not?"

Luke shrugged. "You're a lucky man." He made sure to say it like he didn't care. "What exactly do you have in mind for me to do during this expedition?"

Eric motioned Luke to sit back down across from him. "Like I said, we have a journal, but it doesn't have many drawings in it. We'll need someone who can interpret the reports and help us find the route. We need an expert like you."

"What's the pay?"

"One hundred dollars and any land that you can take as your own. There are Indians to deal with, you know."

"I'm not interested in their land. How about two hundred dollars without the land."

Eric appeared to be thinking it over. "Not a farmer, eh?"

"Not a thief, either."

The men stared at one another for a long moment, then Eric inclined his head. "I am not planning to take land from the Indians, Mr. Bowen. That's between them and the American government. I plan to set up trade in the area, which will benefit both sides."

The man had a glib tongue, that was for sure. But even knowing what Luke did about Mr. Montclaire, he found he still wanted to go.

The clatter of a tray drew Luke's attention. A maid, with Mrs. Montclaire following behind her, came into the room.

"Ah, thank you, my dear," Eric said to his wife. "Just set them there, Sara, next to Mr. Bowen." The maid did as requested and then curtseyed from the room. Mrs. Montclaire came near and bent down with the second tray, her back toward her husband. She glanced at Luke and their eyes locked. The tension in the room roared in Luke's ears. Realizing they were being scrutinized, he stared at the food and forced a bright voice. "Thank you, ma'am. I'm already missing my mother's cooking. That looks mighty fine."

She straightened. "Our Sara is a wonderful cook."

Another stab of sadness. A woman like this should have sweet laughter, a tinkling bell. But it was tight, strained.

Mrs. Montclaire turned toward her husband. "Isn't she, Eric? Much better than I am."

Eric came around and placed a tight, grasping arm around the back of his wife's waist and pulled her close. He looked down at her with adoring eyes as he stated with pride, "You're a wonderful cook, my dear. Just much too busy with your social duties to take on such a task."

Mrs. Montclaire's wan smile pierced Luke's heart. "Much too busy. Thank you, Eric." She had stiffened in her husband's grasp and appeared eager to move away. "I'll just go upstairs and leave you to your business."

Eric nodded at her, but the narrowing of his eyes showed his displeasure. "I will call you down soon. The surprise, remember?"

She nodded at her husband, then glanced at Luke, fear stirring in her eyes. "Good day, Mr. Bowen."

"Ma'am." Luke inclined his head toward her, clasping his hands tight together. There was nothing more he'd like than to land a punch in her husband's face! He never could abide a bully. But there was nothing he could do, and it wasn't any of his business anyway, so he reached out for a fancy little cake and shoved it into his mouth. Smiling around the mouthful, he nodded to Eric. "Good cook, indeed."

"Pour the tea, will you, while I get out the documents for you to sign." Eric frowned at the room in general. "Emma should have known to pour before leaving the room. Did she seem in a hurry to escape to you?"

Walking on cracking ice wouldn't be any more dangerous than this conversation. "Probably just wants to leave us to our business. Must seem tedious to women folk."

"Yes, of course you're right." Eric pulled out some papers from a drawer and passed them across the desk.

"Cream?" Luke questioned, feeling his eyebrows rise and trying to make light of it all.

"A little, yes."

Luke poured a great dollop in, stirred up the tea, sloshing a little over the cup's rim onto the silver tray. "Oops. Sorry about that," he chuckled as he passed the brimming cup over to Montclaire.

Eric came around his desk and grasped the cup, reaching for a cloth. "You have to wipe it off first." His face grew redder by the second.

"Sorry, sir. I'm a little out of practice." He couldn't help the sarcasm that laced his words but then regretted it. If anyone would pay for his mistake, he knew it would be Emma.

Eric placed the cup back on the tray. "Never mind the tea. Let's go over the papers. I want you to sign that you will continue with me to the Pacific, no matter what. I understand the circumstances of your last expedition, but, Mr. Bowen, you are my only cartographer. I can't risk you leaving mid-trip for any reason."

"There is nothing short of death that would cause me to abandon this mission, Mr. Montclaire. You have my word."

"Very good." Eric inclined his head, then reached for a leather-clad book. He stared at it for a long moment and then looked up at Luke. "I am giving you this journal. It came to me at a heavy cost so take care of it. You need to study it, be thorough and quick. We leave in four days."

Luke reached across the table for the worn book. He looked down at it, wondering who had written it. He remembered the men of the Corps of Discovery who had kept the records. He knew they wouldn't sell it cheap. "That's soon. I will do my best."

A few minutes later Luke walked from the room toward the front door. He paused, then turned around for a brief look toward the stairs.

Lord, what am I doing here? Is she all right? And if not, what am I supposed to do about it?

Chapter Eight

*E*mma! Emma, come down, sweetheart."

She heard Eric call her from the bottom of the stairs. She had been sitting at her dressing table, looking at herself in the mirror and telling herself not to be lost . . . not to be terrified. She could manage him. She just needed to learn how. It wasn't Eric's fault she was so slow to learn her lessons. And he was leaving, would be gone for a year or more, giving her a much needed reprieve. She might even be able to escape. Leave this place and him and simply . . . disappear.

She rose at the sound of his voice, demanding her beating heart to slow, her shaking hands to still. She pasted a contented smile on her face, the one she'd practiced in the mirror, and descended the stairs.

"You've finished your meeting?"

He clasped her hand in his and led her back into the sitting room. "Yes. What did you think of Mr. Bowen?"

"I hardly had enough time to make his acquaintance. I am sure you know what you are about, Eric. I am sure you know best who you should hire for your expedition." She played the naïve woman card with silken care, looking up at him a little doe-eyed, hoping to extinguish any anger, any frustration, and dispel any thoughts that the man might mean more to her than a stranger.

"Sit down, Emma. I have news."

She sat, her knees wobbling a bit. He never spoke in such grand terms. A great foreboding came upon her as she tilted her chin up toward him. "What is it?"

Eric smiled that special smile that before their wedding had always made her melt inside. "I have decided that I can't abide the thought of being gone from you for so long. That you should come with us." He paused as if to let the information sink in. But a sudden stupor seemed to fall over her, filling her mind with sodden, heavy wool.

"I . . . go with you? To the Pacific, do you mean?"

"Yes. That is exactly what I mean."

Emma looked to the side toward the mahogany armchair and then down at her lap. Her mind was spinning; she couldn't seem to get a foothold on the shifting sand. "Eric . . . I—"

"Don't say you can't do it, Emma. If an Indian woman could accompany Lewis and Clark on their journey, then you can come with us. We'll be better provisioned and have more knowledge of what is necessary." Eric came over, sat down next to her, and lifted her chin with his thumb. Their gazes locked. "You will have your own cabin on the barge. I won't let anything happen to you. You will be safe."

"I am safe here, Eric."

He leaned toward her and gripped the sides of her face in his hands. "I don't want to live without you. I *can't* live without you for that long." It was a whispered plea, but the tone of it sent a shiver racing down Emma's back.

There would be no reprieve . . . ever. He would hunt her down, he would suck her dry, he would take everything—until there was nothing left of her.

No light.

No life.

Nothing.

Emma watched as the hired man loaded her trunks onto the large boat, complete with a water-tight cabin at the stern. She stared at the cabin, and realization struck her. Eric had planned this all along. He would have never built such a structure if it were only for the men. And he'd allowed her no time to adjust to the news that she would come with them. He'd purposefully waited until the last moment to tell her.

She looked down at the dark, murky water of the swift-moving river. Something inside her shifted from despair to genuine, numbing hopelessness. She stared, unseeing and unbelieving, at the flow of the river, the way it moved south. Their expedition would be moving north and west, against the current, every mile gained at great cost. This river and she had more in common than anyone knew.

"Emma!"

She turned at the sound of the familiar voice. Her mother. Her father followed a few steps behind her, huffing with the effort to keep up with his wife. Emma pasted a smile on her face, but a little sob escaped her throat.

Her mother wrapped her arms around Emma's thin frame. She smoothed back tendrils of loose hair in the wind and demanded. "What is he thinking? You cannot possibly go!"

Her father came up to her side and took her into his arms. "I'm sorry." It was all he said, but it said it all. There was nothing he could do, and they both knew it.

"Sorry?" her mother squawked. "We cannot allow this!" She launched into near hysterics, directing her stare onto Emma's father. "He cannot know what he is doing, asking her, a lone woman, to join such a business venture. You must talk to him."

Her father glared back at her mother. "As I've told you, I have already spoken to him. I assured him"—he turned toward Emma—"that we would watch over you while he is gone." He paused, looked up at a point over their shoulders and then continued in a tight voice, as if the conversation was difficult to recall. "He would not listen. He wants her with him."

Emma placed a hand on her father's shoulder. "Thank you, Papa." She hadn't called him that in a long time, and it brought a sad smile to both of their faces. "He is my husband. There is nothing anyone can do."

Her mother sucked in her breath, her chest rising, her bosom threatening the square neckline of her elegant, green silk day dress. "I'll not have it. Someone has to talk some sense into that man." Her cheeks puffed out, and her eyes flashed at Emma. "All the way to the Pacific? My daughter? Do you have any idea the hardships?" She gripped Emma's face between her white gloved hands. "You could die. What have we done letting him marry you? What have we done?"

Emma reached up and clasped her mother's hands, bringing them down to hang between them. She had never seen her mother lose such control over her emotions. Especially in public. "Mother." She squeezed her mother's hands knowing that she would have to lie. "I will be fine."

Her mother turned toward Emma's father, her voice a whisper. "I can't bear it."

"I will speak with him again."

Emma shook her head. "It won't do any good. He is determined."

Her father's shoulders slumped. He took a leather bag from his coat pocket. "Don't tell anyone about this. Hide it. In case you need it someday."

Emma opened the drawstring bag and peered at the sparkle of so many coins. She looked up at her parents. "Thank you. I'll be back. I promise."

Her mother pulled a cloth-wrapped bundle from a bag she carried. "It's the family Bible. I thought"—she gave a sudden shake of her head—"I haven't read it myself like I ought, but it may give you strength."

Emma reached for it, clutching the small book to her chest. She stiffened as she heard Eric coming up the river's bank behind her.

"Eric Montclaire," her mother demanded when he was close enough to hear. "You *cannot* be serious. This is not the kind of journey suited for a woman."

Eric inclined his head toward Emma's mother and then father. "Mrs. Daring, Mr. Daring. I had hoped Emma would have said good-bye from the house. It will make it more difficult for you to see her off here."

"Now, look here"—her father's face turned a telling shade of red—"she might be your wife, but she's still our daughter. Of course we came to see her off. We might never see her again!"

"You must both stop worrying," Eric returned in a stern voice. "I have taken every precaution to assure Emma's safety. She will be comfortable, well-provisioned, and have the opportunity to see amazing country."

"What of the Indians?" Her mother's shrill voice attracted the attention of the men loading the barge. "You can't guarantee the Indians won't attack you. Just who do you think you are, God Himself?"

Eric took a sudden step back at the insult. Emma held her breath, looking off into the distance, her mind going blank, her insides shifting, shutting down.

"No," came the razor-edged response, "but I am sure God agrees that a woman's place is with her husband. There will be many men, women, and children following in our footsteps to make a life in the West. We are doing a good thing. A Christian thing to set up trading posts along the route so that they will be well-provisioned on their journey."

It seemed her mother could not be stopped. "Don't pretend you care about the people going west years from now. You are doing this to make money and nothing else."

Eric smiled a tight smile. "If I recall, my fortune was a great part of the reason you accepted my suit."

Her mother gasped. "My daughter's well-being is more important than any amount of wealth. Don't ever accuse us of putting wealth before our love for our daughter."

Eric inclined his head, his eyes hard. "I apologize." He turned, his arm stretched out toward the barge. "Please, go aboard and see for yourself how well provisioned we are, how comfortable your daughter will be. It might give you a measure of peace."

"She'll be able to write letters to us, won't she?" her father asked.

"Of course. For some of the journey, anyway. I plan to send a man back every three to four months with news and to get news if possible. As I said, we are taking every precaution for the safety and the success of this venture." Eric bowed. "If you will excuse me now. I must oversee the loading."

He looked at Emma. "Say your good-byes, my dear. We will push off in a few moments, and I want you safely ensconced in your new home." He turned from them without waiting for a reply and walked back down the bank.

Emma looked back and forth between her parents, her heart in the throat. "I told you nothing could change his mind."

Her mother took her into her arms and squeezed tight. "We will pray for you every day."

Her father gave her one last hug. "Try to get letters to us. Write down what happens."

"I will." Emma swallowed back the tears. "I love you both."

"Good-bye."

Luke watched Mrs. Montclaire as she turned from her parents and made her way down the bank to the river's edge. He watched as she walked the wide wooden boards that had been set up to board the barge, watched her jump down onto the deck and turn for one last, long look at her parents. She waved at them and then turned and made her way to the astonishing dwelling that had been erected at one end of the boat. He saw Montclaire come over to her, put his arm around her waist, and lead her inside, the door closing behind him.

The shock of what he had just heard immobilized him. He'd been a little distance away, checking off supplies from a list that Montclaire had given him, half-hidden by a stack of wooden crates when he looked up and saw her.

She was coming with them.

He still couldn't fathom it. There was no reason to put a woman at the mercy of all this trip might hold. No reason save a man's selfishness. The more he learned about his employer the more he had to pray that he wouldn't put a bullet in him one day. But he knew now, deep in his gut, that he hadn't been sent here just to make maps. His mission in God's kingdom had turned into something far more dangerous and important.

God had sent him here for her.

Chapter Nine

*I*t was nearing midnight on the second day of the third week into the voyage. They were on shore, camping for the night, but Luke had moved far away from the noise of the camp to complete his final task for the night—measuring and recording their location. Luke pulled out the octant, an expensive little piece of equipment, to measure the angle between the North Star and the horizon. Even though he was tired from helping to navigate around the treacherous sandbars that plagued them, and even acting as helmsman at times, this was still one of his favorite parts of the journey. Especially with a sky as clear as it was this night.

Joshua Obermeyer strolled over toward him.

Luke smiled at the tall man. "Guard duty tonight?"

Josh yawned and stretched his arms out wide. "Yep. Better than last time though, I can tell you. Last time it was raining buckets."

Luke chuckled. A young, quick-to-smile man, Josh was one of the friendlier men of their party.

"How does that thing work?" Talkative, too. Luke had forgotten that. He curbed his impatience with the question. The sighting needed to be done at the same time each night to ensure accuracy. Still, maybe he could just explain it to Josh as he went. "Well, this is the sighting telescope; that's what you look through."

"Sure is small for a telescope."

"Yes, not a typical telescope for stargazing. This octant works more with mirrors." Luke peered through the sighting telescope at the image in the horizon glass. "One mirror reflects the North Star"—Luke pointed up at the bright pinprick of light above their heads—"and this other mirror"—Luke made another adjustment to the index arm and there . . . the two images of the star and the horizon came into view—"reflects the horizon."

"How can you see the horizon with all these trees around?"

At Josh's puzzled frown Luke grinned. "Dead reckoning. It's a talent some people have. Of course when we get further down the trail into prairie land, which won't be long, we'll be able to see the horizon."

"I heard you were on that other expedition—the Corps of Discovery. What was that like?"

"Very much like it is this time, so far. Lots of rain, the barge running aground on sandbars and hitting sawyers, the mosquitoes—"

"What's a sawyer?"

"Well, you know how the banks wash away into the river?" Josh nodded.

"Sometimes a tree goes down with it. Its roots are heavy enough or still rooted enough to keep it from floating away, and so it bobs up and down. You can't see them sometimes until you are right up on them, but I've seen them do serious damage to boats."

"You saw the prairie lands then? I heard Mr. Montclaire say he wanted to build his first trading post at the eastern edge of the prairies."

"Yes, he does. There's an abandoned Indian camp, the Little Osage, around those parts. I'm hoping I will remember where it is." Luke flashed him a smile. "So back to the job at hand." He pointed at the arc of brass on the bottom of the octant. "I can use this to tell the angle, and that gives me the latitude. Looks to be about . . . 32°."

Josh nodded, his mouth agape. "You must be awful smart."

"No, just have a knack for this sort of thing. Everybody is good at something, don't you think?"

Josh chewed on the side of his lip in thought, "I don't guess I've figured out what I'm good at yet."

"Well, what do you most like to do?"

Josh's face broke out into a big grin. "Dance with women folk." They both laughed.

A rustling sound came from the trees and their laughter died down to silence as they strained to hear. Luke reached over for his gun, propped against a tree at his side. Josh already had his.

They heard the sound again, louder and closer.

"It can't be Indians," Josh whispered. "They'd never let us hear them coming like that."

Luke backed away toward the camp. He agreed with Josh, but a person never knew for sure what the Indians would do. It would be nice to have the others alerted if trouble came upon them.

The sound died down and then, *crash*! An enormous brown bear broke from the brush and trees.

Luke heard a strangled gasp come from Josh. He took a slow step back and whispered, low and demanding, "Don't run."

Josh looked askance at him. "What do we do?"

"If he starts to charge us, we shoot. Go for the head or chest."

They both watched, aghast at the sheer size of the creature. He rose up on his hind legs to tower above them by several feet. The animal opened his mouth, filled with razor-sharp teeth, and roared.

Josh made odd sounds from his throat, and Luke prayed his young friend would hold still.

The bear looked back and forth between them, as if deciding which one looked the tastiest. He roared so loud that Luke's legs began to shake. Slow and easy, so as not to startle the bear, Luke lifted his rifle and pointed it at the massive animal's head. "If we have to shoot, I'll go first, and then you take your shot. If we take turns, we might have more time to reload."

"Take turns?" Josh's face went white and his eyes widened. "Why would we need to take turns?"

"I've heard it sometimes takes six to ten musket balls to bring down one of these creatures. We won't get much accomplished with two shots."

"That doesn't sound good, doesn't sound good at all."

All this time the bear continued to roar at them, swaying on his hind legs, waving his front arms that had long, sharp claws that slashed the air.

Then, as if he noticed they had a plan and they weren't going to run, the bear stopped roaring and stared at them for a long moment. He dropped to the ground and, to the astonishment of both men, trotted off.

Josh let out a giant breath.

Luke chuckled weakly, still pointing his gun and backing away. "Let's get back to camp. The hunters will want to hear about this."

"Oh, sure." Josh's attempt at bravado was belied by his still shaky voice. "I've heard them bragging about bagging a famed brown or yellow bear. After seeing one up close though, I can't say I want to join them."

Luke silently agreed.

The two men turned to hurry back toward camp when they heard a scream—a woman's scream—coming from the direction of the river. They tore off down the bank, rifles ready in hand. When they got to the water's edge, they saw the bear and Emma Montclaire, and the two were facing each other.

Don't faint. If you faint, he will eat you. Don't faint, Emma. Don't you do it!

She repeated the commands over and over in her mind, all the while staring up into the glittering, black eyes of a nightmare. And it must be a nightmare. Creatures like this didn't really exist, did they? That thought, that she was safe in her bed having a bad dream, kept her from fainting. She even smiled, feeling a little brave. In dreams she would reach out and touch the creature if she wanted to with no real harm done. She might wake up sweat soaked from fear, but she'd been through worse.

A niggling in the back of her mind told her to be careful, told her that she was in some state of shock and making things up as she went, but she ignored it and reached out her arm.

The bear looked as surprised to see her as she had been to see him . . . or her . . . who could tell in the dark with a monstrous beast? Not that she would try! Oh, now she *had* lost all grasp on reality for certain. A bubble of laughter escaped her.

The sound startled the bear, and it rose up on its hind legs, leaned into her face, and roared.

Emma fainted dead away.

Luke yelled and waved his arms in the air to draw the bear's attention. The beast swung toward him, then dropped to run at him.

"Now, Josh. Shoot it!"

The men took turns loading then shooting, loading then shooting. The racket brought some other men from the camp, and before long the gigantic animal lay still on the ground. Luke felt a little bad, the magnificence of the animal was undeniable. But if they hadn't come, Emma would be dead.

Emma . . .

That he thought of her thus—no longer *Mrs. Montclaire,* but simply *Emma*—had just dawned on him when he realized Eric must have been awakened by the shots. He saw the man standing on the barge, watching the scene. The Montclaires never slept in camp with the rest of them. Eric kept his wife in the cabin. Luke hadn't even seen her much on this trip. He'd forgotten how she looked, the impact of her on his senses, until he saw her facing down that bear, and it all rushed back to slam into him.

When she reached toward the bear, he'd almost gone mad with fear.

Now, though, he fought to bring his breathing and heartbeat back under control as he watched Eric Montclaire bound over the boat rail and run up the bank to his wife. He wished he was the one who was running to take her into his arms. While

Josh held the men captive with the story of what had gone on this night, Luke walked over to Montclaire, who patted his wife's cheek—rather hard, Luke thought.

"She all right?"

Montclaire looked up, annoyance darkening his eyes. "She will be fine. Thank you."

Luke pulled on the back of his neck with his hand, deliberated what to say, and then just shook his head. "That's good, I guess." He turned to walk away.

"I'll hear a full accounting of this event in the morning, Mr. Bowen."

Anger rose up like a searing fire from Luke's belly, but he bit back a nasty reply. Instead he looked a little to the side and, without turning to face his boss, said only, "Yes, sir."

They were the hardest two words he had ever spoken.

Chapter Ten

She was a princess.

And this was her castle.

A log castle that just happened to be on a boat but a castle nonetheless. Emma closed her eyes and imagined herself being transported to a magical kingdom. The way was filled with dangers and dragons; and her guard, her fair husband, protected her by locking her inside the castle. If she concentrated hard enough, she almost believed it.

And if she didn't . . . she feared the panic of being a prisoner would overwhelm her.

She lay back on the bed and flung her arm over her eyes. Something inside warned her that she shouldn't play such a game, that it might be a step toward madness. But she had only occasionally been out of the cabin since St. Charles, months ago. Eric allowed her to go ashore when they stopped at the little community of Indians and French villagers where they traded for more supplies. He'd nodded his approval of her dress as she stepped upon the muddy shore wearing her most serviceable gown of tiny-flowered cambric. Some of the women invited her to have tea with them, which Eric had sanctioned, saying she wouldn't find many women whose language she could understand after this village. It had been a welcome change from the stuffy sameness of these four walls.

She closed her eyes, drifting . . . drifting . . . forever drifting.

She must have fallen asleep as she woke to pitch darkness and the sudden swing of the barge as it rolled her across the bed. Another monstrous heave of the craft sent her crashing to the floor, a whooshed "humph" forced from her chest. She held still for a moment, looking up at the flickering lightning through the window and hearing the shards of beating rain on the little cabin's roof. She could feel the rumbles of thunder vibrate the wood beneath her hands.

Before she had the chance to sit up, the boat rocketed her toward the door, a quick slide that propelled her shoulder into the wood of her prison. She cried out, a small sound against the shouts of the men outside. She grasped at the uneven boards of the wall, braced her feet beneath her swinging skirt, and then stood to take hold of the door's metal latch. She pulled herself up against another dip of the boat, her shoulder throbbing almost as much as her heart.

Pushing down on the latch that was never locked but always seemed so, she shoved the door open against the wind. She took a step and then another, standing in sheets of cold, pouring rain. She lifted her face toward the opened darkness of the sky, the moon still somehow bright and round. A shout sounded. She turned toward it, took a tottering step forward as men ran about, shouting, scurrying like ants whose hill had been disturbed.

The rain and waves of river water splashed over their wooden vessel to slap against her quivering legs and up into her face. Her gaze darted around, but she didn't see Eric. Emboldened, she took stilted steps forward, her arms outward for balance.

A sudden swing of the stern had her turning round, sinking down, and covering her head. Her feet slid out from under her, a move that caused her chest to land with a breath-robbing thud against the deck. Rain washed down on her, covering her, soaking her, but something inside her welcomed it.

She felt alive. For the first time in so long.

She smiled in horrified delight as she clawed her way up the deck toward the wooden rail.

Another jolt and she slid down, down—blinked up into the rain, her face lifted into the wind. Like a dandelion puff in the wind, she came up against the side, fought to stand, then grasped hold of the edge with white-knuckled hands.

Emma looked down at the heaving crests of dark, foaming water. She looked up at the bright moon and opened her mouth so that the rain could wash in. As she drank from God's own fountain, a little laugh bubbled out of her chest. Head thrown back, eyes closed, she considered it.

Let go and fly . . . fly far, far away.

She looked down at her hands and saw the wedding ring Eric gave her sparkle back at her in the meager light. It mocked her, taunting, promising so much . . . giving so little. Emma tugged the ring free, pulled back, and threw it into the storm. She laughed, a great shaking laugh, as she looked down at the roaring river and saw her salvation.

Emma took a deep breath and looked back at the sky. The rain pelted against her face like little needles, the wind ravished her hair—hair that had blown out of all its pins and whipped long and free, wet and slick around her face and body. Her throat ached with the answer to her misbegotten life.

Of course. It was the only way. She looked up toward God and uttered the words she never thought she would say: "Forgive me this"—she looked down again at the heaving darkness of the water, the grave—"but I have no other choice." She studied her hands. As if outside herself, she watched as they loosened their grip on the wood rail. She stood for a second, suspended, then smiled as the boat dipped, spun, cooperated with her plan. She laughed as her body propelled up and out. A long, last inhale and she stretched out her arms into the wind as if to help lift her up and over her pain.

A sudden, mighty pull stopped her mid-flight.

Something grasped tight hold of her hips. Like an anchor it pulled her back onto the deck with a solid, hard impact that knocked the held breath from her chest.

Tight hold, impossible savior.

She fought and kicked, turned toward the man, clawing at him, not knowing who it was but hoping it was Eric. She wouldn't stand still this time! She would not submit!

She heard a grunt as her elbow struck his chin. The arms around her tightened as she and her savior rolled toward the cabin that had held her prisoner.

"*No!* I won't go back. I won't." She sobbed with the moaning of the wind. "Let me go. Please, just let me go."

The man pulled her up against his chest as he leaned against the cabin. "Mrs. Montclaire. It's me . . . Luke Bowen."

His voice rose with the wind, up and out like a song that was never supposed to be sung, but she knew, somehow she knew. She pulled away from him, away from the hard solidity of his chest. She turned to face him. "You should have let me fall. You should have left me alone!"

The rain washed her tears away faster than they could run down her cheeks. The wind whipped, hard and stinging, into her face. She saw the compassion in this man's eyes, and her insides recoiled in shame. He knew. How did he know?

As if to validate her suspicion, he leaned toward her and yelled against the voices around them, the running feet and the rushing wind. "I won't let him hurt you again."

"Stop it. You don't know what you are saying."

"Why are you protecting him?" The mapmaker's eyes penetrated her sorrow and astounded her at the same time. Emma didn't know the answer to his question.

Luke stood and held out his hand to help her up. Emma stared at his hand. She didn't want help from a man who knew so much, who knew she had tried to end her life this night, but she needed assistance to get back to the cabin before Eric discovered her. So she swallowed her pride and grasped Luke's hand.

The storm began to subside; the boat seemed a little more under the men's control. "Let's get you back to the cabin," Luke shouted as he took hold of her waist and led her, step by staggering step, to the door of her cabin. As they approached it, the wind blew her hair around his body, wrapping them together in its rebellious, silken threads.

"Emma!" Eric came around the corner of the cabin, soaked to the skin, his clothes clinging to him, his hair plastered against his handsome face, a face that went from worry to jealousy to rage in seconds. His voice shook. "Emma, what are you doing out here?"

She felt Luke Bowen drop his arm from her lower back. The strands of her hair clung to him, caught under his arm, around his waist, and snagged against his belt. She pulled back, her hair tugging against her scalp, and stared in mounting terror into her husband's eyes. Luke worked to untangle her while she rushed to explain.

"I fell. I opened the door to see what was happening and rolled into the wall." She pointed to the place she'd almost allowed herself to be swept over, remembering her white-knuckled grip on the railing and then letting go. "I was nearly swept overboard. Mr. Bowen saved me."

Eric's glare swung from Emma to Luke. He didn't look like he believed her, but she didn't really expect him too.

"Did the mast break?" Luke had to shout against the wail of the wind.

Eric gave him a glare. "The tow rope too. It took all the men's attention to keep her aright. We could have used your help."

"I think I helped where needed." Luke stared back at her husband, and even in the darkness Emma saw the mapmaker's hard eyes, heard the edge of warning in his voice. Both men looked at Emma.

She glanced into Luke's eyes for one brief moment, then turned away and ducked back into the doorway of her wooden prison. She pulled the door shut behind her, a small rebellion, a way to tell Eric in front of Luke that she didn't want him following her. She would pay for that later, but exhaustion filled every limb, and she couldn't make herself care.

Her body shook from her curled toes to her wet head as she stripped out of the sodden clothes. She dried herself and slipped into a night dress, buttoning the pearl buttons one by one. She was truly a prisoner now. If Luke Bowen knew . . . then others must know too. Her body flushed scarlet with the thought.

She lay down on the bed and pulled the blanket up and over her wet head, and then she wished . . . no, *prayed* to die.

Chapter Eleven

*E*mma heard the sound of Eric's solid, slow steps enter the cabin. She lay as still as she could in the dark, feeling him move as he walked around to the narrow space between the bed and bureau, where he hung his dripping garments on hooks to dry. She lay still, pretending sleep, her hair still damp against her quivering shoulders.

"Emma?" The stern tone to his voice twisted her stomach.

She didn't want to answer him, but it was no use pretending; he would just shake her awake. She allowed some small movement, as if awakening to his voice.

"Yes? How is the barge?"

He didn't answer. Just seemed content that she was awake. He turned and took off his hat, unwound the cravat and then reached for his soaked shirt. With deft movements of hand and wrist, he flicked his clothes over the back of a chair to dry. She watched in the dim light as he shrugged out of his pants.

He eased into the bed beside her. His hand grasped around her middle and pulled her into his stomach. Nausea assailed her as he leaned his head into her neck. She gritted her teeth and waited . . .

His hand ran along the length of her side, her thigh. She didn't move, barely breathed, still pretending, pretending something, she didn't know what anymore.

"Your hair is still wet." He lowered his voice, silky but accusatory.

She didn't speak. Didn't move within his arms.

"Emma." Commanding now.

She didn't know how to answer. Before, she would try to answer something, but now there was nothing. There was a great black nothing that didn't seem to care what he would do if she didn't answer the way he wanted.

"Emma. Look at me."

She didn't have the strength. She knew if she looked into his eyes this time . . . "No."

It was a whisper but he heard it. He shook her shoulder. "Emma. Look at me!"

Eyes clenched shut, she pulled away. "Leave me alone."

He jerked her shoulder, pressing it back against the bed. She allowed it, allowed her body to be pliant as he pressed her onto her back. But she kept her eyes closed.

"Don't think you can play games, Emma. Look at me."

She kept her eyes squeezed tight.

"Emma! Emma! Stop this foolishness!" His voice sounded panicked.

His hands pressed down on each shoulder. His breath grew stifling in her face, but Emma kept her eyes closed. Behind her lids she saw colors. She saw a flickering light that flared and then faded and then flared to life again. She saw the roaring of the wind and waters and darkness but . . . light. She saw light. Her lips curved into a smile.

Something must have frightened him about that smile because he pushed away from her and rolled over. The last thing she heard was his low voice.

"Don't think this is the end of it, Emma."

She took a shaky breath, lay very still, and little by little relaxed into sleep.

Luke lifted his journal up into the morning sunlight to study the bird he'd captured on paper. An unknown specimen to him, something perhaps no hand had ever captured in a drawing before, a jolt of joy at the discovery made him smile. He wondered what the natives might call it, but they'd only seen a few natives thus far, paddling by on their canoes with trade goods. Peaceable Indians and the occasional French trader. The expedition didn't hail them yet as they weren't to the part of the journey where they needed knowledge of unknown terrain. In another month or two they would be hoping to meet up with friendly Indians.

He brought the journal back into his lap and stared at the passing shoreline. There was little sign of the storm of the night before except for the damage on the barge and some soaked supplies. The men had laid the trade goods and some wet food in the sun to dry out. He'd heard that some of the food was ruined though. That couldn't be making Montclaire happy.

He pressed his lips together and wondered about Emma Montclaire. Who could have known her husband would keep her penned up in that cabin all of the time? Everyone thought it strange, but no one had the nerve to question Montclaire over the matter. She was his wife, most of them agreed, but when the men spoke of her, their eyes darted away, and their feet shuffled. Someone always rushed in to turn the topic.

But after last night Luke couldn't get the memory of her from his mind. She had just about thrown herself overboard. He knew it as sure as he knew the sky had turned gray, and he knew her husband was the cause of it. Montclaire had been mighty displeased to see them together. And her hair! The memory of it wrapped around him, caught on him—

He took a deep breath. "Dear Lord." He stopped, unsure how to go on.

He had prayed often during his life. Prayers of youthful thanksgiving when his father's fields had yielded much-needed crops. Prayers of supplication when he entered a young man's time, afraid of what he wanted, praying God would help him when he told his father that farming wasn't his path. How to tell a man who valued sweat on the brow and arms stretching against plow lines that his son loved to sit on a hill, looking out over the rise, and draw birds, bushy-tailed squirrels, shy foxes, and the grandness of a sunset?

Lewis and Clark's expedition had given him the opportunity he'd been looking for. He still remembered when old Thomas Ernie from Louisville had winked at him and handed him an advertisement from his penny paper. They were looking for men who were interested in joining an expedition to the elusive Pacific Ocean. Thomas had pointed out the words that said they needed an artist and cartographer. He'd winked at Luke, knowing what he could do, even though his father hadn't any idea of his son's small acclaim to such things.

That had been quite a day! Luke drew up a knee and leaned against it huffing with the memory. As his father came in from the fields, Luke walked over and took off his hat.

His father's face lit up upon seeing him.

"Pa."

"You did good today, son. Let's get these horses fed before mother has dinner cooling, eh?"

"Yes, sir. But there's something I need to speak to you about."

Luke paused, slung a hand onto his hip and then dropped it. Courage failed him as he dropped his gaze from his father's direct gaze and stared at his mud-caked boots instead.

"All right, son. What's on your mind?"

Luke gripped the sketch pad while sitting in the bow of the barge . . . remembering the moment. It was the first time his father had ever paused in his work and directed his full attention on him. He'd stopped. Really stopped and looked him square in the eye. Luke realized in that moment they were the same height.

Then he'd tried to explain the magical moments of creating something from a blank page.

Luke looked back down at his drawing of the bird. He'd only caught a glimpse of it, but it stared back at him as if alive. The head, cocked to one side and looking at him, the ruffled feathers of his body as he was caught mid-pruning, the stick legs, ready to leap, to take flight. Luke had been ready to take flight that day.

"I got a letter. It's from some men who are making an expedition out west, over the mountains and all the way to the Pacific. President Jefferson wants it done. They plan to find the river that leads to the Pacific, map out the land."

His father looked at him like he'd just sprouted wings.

Luke plunged on. "Pa . . . they've asked me to come along as their cartographer and, well, artist. They want me to draw maps and sketch some of the wildlife. They want me to keep a record of what we find."

Luke stared into his father's weathered face, saw the tanned skin, the wrinkles around his eyes, brown like his and a little blank at what he'd said.

He hurried to explain. "It's a big opportunity. No one has ever done this before."

His father took off his floppy hat and brushed it against his leg while he wiped Kentucky sweat from his brow with his other arm. "Done what, exactly? What are these men trying to prove?"

Luke pressed his lips together, looked down at the grassy earth of their land, the land they'd both worked hard to produce a crop and a living. He saw the sway of the blue-green blades in the breeze and knew he would not be able to explain such a thing to this man. A man he loved. A man he respected.

A man he was about to disappoint.

Luke took a long breath then looked back into his father's perplexed eyes. "I'm going with them."

A long silence followed as they stared at each other. Luke couldn't remember his father ever looking at him in the eye for that long. He watched as his jaw clenched and then relaxed. His chest thudded as his father nodded. He saw his father reach out and clasp his shoulder in a strong grip.

"I guess you've made up your mind then."

Luke wanted to waver. Some part of him wanted to ask if he was making a mistake, but he didn't. He nodded. "I guess I have."

"All right then. When do you leave?"

"Pa?" He fought the sudden tears, wanting to be strong.

"No, you are a man now, ready to make a man's decisions about his future." His expression was clear—he respected Luke's stand, though he didn't quite comprehend it. "I can't say I understand why you'd want to leave us . . . leave this"—his pa's gaze swept the sunset, the golden-lit fields—"but if this is what you really want, you won't be happy until you have given it a try. We will miss you, son."

Luke controlled the tightness in his throat. His father was giving him his blessing, and he'd never thought it of him. How little did he know this man? The thought struck him as a blow. He'd lived with him. Saw him live out his life for his family. But he chose to let him go.

Fear ate at him those first days away. What if he was making a mistake? What if he was supposed to be a farmer? What if he followed some unfamiliar path instead that led to something so . . . well . . . unknown? Could he do it?

He'd left that week. With tears from his mother and sisters. With a pack full of food. With blank journals and ink and quills. With a young man's excitement of the first day of his life as a man. He'd left his family and their farm and all that he'd ever known, except that still, sure part of his heart that said, *This is right. This is what I was meant to do.*

The next contact he'd had with his family had been a letter. From his mother. While he'd been gone chasing his dream, his father had died. In the middle of a field, they'd later told him. He had gripped his chest and fell in the furrow he'd just plowed, gulping for air.

The fact that Luke hadn't been there haunted him. He hadn't seen them lower him into the earth or heard the last words spoken about him. He'd seen his mother's crumbling face and felt her arms around his neck while she sobbed into his shoulder when he'd returned.

And his sisters . . . they'd been so afraid.

And now here he was, on the way to the Pacific again. He looked down at the new drawing he had mindlessly sketched while his thoughts roamed the pages of his past.

It was Emma.

With her hair wrapped around him like the silken threads of a spiderweb.

The word *unfair* rose up within him, but he squelched it. Life was not fair. He would endure, knowing that his endurance was nothing compared to hers.

Emma woke to the tendrils of a dream. She was riding a white horse through a rushing stream, a sword gripped in her hand. She turned back to face an enemy, but his face was clouded by mist.

She sat up, slow and easy, noting that Eric still slept. The images faded away as a fog lifting, but the feeling of the dream, how strong she'd seemed! The thought that she could overcome filled her chest with a spark of hope.

She eased from the covers and tiptoed over to her clothes. With a wisp of sound she slipped off the night dress, careful to fold it and place it in the drawer, and then slid her arms through the sleeves of a pale yellow, high-waisted dress. She picked up golden-hued slippers and eased open the door.

The fresh morning air revived her as she walked across the deck of the barge. She nodded to the men who were rowing.

Surprise lit their faces but they rallied, one by one, and nodded or smiled or even murmured, "Good mornin', ma'am."

Emma nodded back to them. "Good morning, gentlemen." She ducked her head to hide her smile at their eager faces. Why, they must have thought she lay near death, they were so cheerful to see her. Turning her back to them, she walked over to one side of the boat, taking in the sunrise and enjoying a moment of freeing beauty. The sky was gray but with a hint of blue in the west where they were headed. The trees they passed were bright in their autumn colors of gold and red and fiery orange. The sun rose, almost perceptible on the edge of the horizon, spilling light and warmth across her face and bringing her a jolt of joy, even though there was no reason for her to feel joy.

A sound of scratching made her turn and brush aside a blowing tendril of her hair. Her hand rose to shield her eyes as she searched for the sound.

Luke Bowen.

He sat in the bow of the boat upon a bench, his knee brought up, one of his journals upon it. She turned her head away. Heat flooded her cheeks and her heart fluttered. What must he think of her?

When nothing happened, she peeked through her lashes at him. Maybe he hadn't seen her. He *did* look absorbed in whatever he was working on. As she watched, he flipped a page and began making wide and small slashes with his writing tool. He dipped the quill back into the ink pot several times as she stood transfixed against the rail, her hair blowing against her shoulders. Occasionally, very occasionally, he glanced up at her.

Immobilized. Caught. Like one of the wildlife he drew. Why he would draw her—for she felt certain now that that was what he was doing—she couldn't fathom. Didn't he know how dangerous sketching her could be? What if Eric found the drawing? What would he do to this man who had saved her from drowning? She swallowed hard. Eric would kill him.

She wasn't sure that was true. But it might be. Should she stop him?

She looked down at her hand resting on the railing. Just the night before her hand had released from a tighter grip. Just hours ago . . . she'd been ready to give up the fight. What was she thinking? She couldn't even save herself.

Luke finished the rough sketch in minutes. She didn't know it, but in turning away she showed him the line of her jaw, the curve of her neck, the delicate, little hollow against her collar bone, the tendrils of hair dancing in the wind around her exposed throat.

With a few more deft strokes he had captured her in the morning light. He stopped, put down the quill, and then held out the drawing. What he saw made his breath catch. Closed but open, sorrowful but sweet, afraid but courageous. He hadn't meant to be so . . . so accurate! The word was wrong, but his gift had showed him things about her that he'd not allowed himself a long enough look to see.

A part of him said to ignore her—turn away and pretend he didn't know. Another part said that if he did, no one would hear her pain, her desperation. Could he let her drown unheard? He took a long breath and realized that by pulling her from the river he had already made up his mind.

Chapter Twelve

*L*uke watched Emma's face tense and then heard the closing of a door and the thud of footsteps. He shut the journal and looked away but didn't move from his seat. No sense moving and drawing attention to himself. Sure enough, it was Eric. He walked up to Emma and grabbed her wrist. Luke clenched his teeth together. The Montclaires' muted conversation wafted toward him like an ill wind. Luke listened, reaching for the journal that Eric had given him to study, wanting to appear deep in concentration.

"I was just getting some air." Emma sounded panicked.

"You should have awakened me," Eric ground out, his voice a hiss of displeasure as his gaze turned, swept over the men at their morning work and then swung back to his wife's face.

"You were sleeping so soundly. I didn't want to bother you."

"You know I don't like you out here alone."

Emma laughed, a false tinkling sound that made Luke's heart ache. Some day . . . he would hear her true laughter. "I'm not alone, Eric. I was just getting a little fresh air and sunshine." She pointed away from Luke, directing Eric's attention toward the stern. "You did promise that I would get to see this amazing country. I miss so much cooped up in the cabin all of the time, don't you think?" She looked up at Eric and Luke's heart lurched. Anxious energy filled her actions. "Are you hungry? Let's see about some breakfast."

She took Eric's arm and nudged him toward the men who were grouped around Billy Lang, the young, redheaded cook who passed out the day's rations.

Eric glared at her and then glanced over his shoulder. His squinted eyes locked with Luke's. Luke held up the journal, nodding toward it, and shouted to Eric, "A true treasure, this. It will be a help with the maps."

Eric turned toward him and looked like he was coming over, making Luke regret he had engaged him in conversation. If Eric asked to see his journal, he would have no choice but to hand it over. The thought of the sketches of Emma in Eric's hands was not pleasant.

Shouts from some of the men at the stern stopped Eric cold. He turned back around, took a firm grasp on Emma's arm, and led her toward the commotion.

Luke stood, gathered up the journals, and shoved them inside his coat. He followed the others toward the back of the barge. It looked as if they had company coming.

A canoe approached, the men paddling at a mighty pace up the Missouri toward them. Luke could just make out three men. His gaze darted toward Emma. She'd paused, taking the moment of distraction to pull away from Eric's side, to brush her hand against her hair like a woman with unexpected company. She fell back a step as they faced the men hailing them.

Luke grew closer and heard Emma ask, "Isn't that the new circuit judge? Judge Littleton? My parents had him over for dinner once."

Eric's head snapped toward her, his brows coming together in some kind of warning. Luke had heard of Judge Littleton. He was a newly appointed judge in the land west of the Mississippi and, from all accounts, good at his job.

"Don't say a word to him, do you hear me?" Eric turned and glared at Luke as he had at Emma. Luke returned the stare, spine straight, jaw tense.

A shouted command from the canoe to stop and bank the craft made them both turn back around.

"Mr. Eric Montclaire?" The judge shouted across the expanse of river between them.

"Yes. What is the meaning of this?"

"We'll be needing you to bank, sir. Got a few questions we need to ask you and your men." Two soldiers in American army colors of red, white, and blue held rifles and looked ready to use them if the situation called for it.

Eric, hands on hips, back as stiff as one of the oars, just stared. His men were exchanging glances, looking up at their boss with a mixture of curiosity and caution. The few who were armed fingered their guns.

After a few moments of nerve-wracking stillness, Eric gave a decisive nod and the orders to pull up on the north bank. When he turned around, he sought Luke's gaze and motioned him over. He glanced down at the journal in Luke's hand. "Take Emma in the cabin and stay there with her until these men have left."

Luke could feel the shock spread across his face. "Why?"

Eric looked off to one side, his fair curls waving in the wind. What was he up to? Luke was the last man Eric would want alone with his wife. Why would he do this?

"I don't want her in the middle of this. I know she'll stay put if you are there with her."

The logic made sense, still . . .

Eric looked back, stared hard into Luke's eyes. They were the same height, though Luke's chest was broader, more muscled from all the farmwork.

"You will not touch her, of course." Before Luke could answer that astounding comment, Eric leaned in and continued. "She will tell me. She can't keep secrets from me."

Eric turned and strode away. Luke watched him jump to shore, struggling with a mixture of anger and a sense of being trapped. He turned back toward the cabin and found Emma walking toward him. "Mrs. Montclaire?"

Emma stopped, a slight frown on her smooth brow.

"He wants you to wait in the cabin. And he wants me to wait there with you."

"What?" Emma's chin rose up, her eyes flashed wariness.

"He said to wait with you. He doesn't want you mixed up in whatever is going on down there."

Emma shook her head. "Eric would never want me alone with any man. Especially you, after last night."

"I know. It doesn't make much sense. He did threaten me if I touch you." Luke grinned, trying for lightness. "I guess we'll have to be careful not to bump into each other."

A small crack of a smile skittered across Emma's lips. "I guess so."

While everyone else headed ashore, Emma and Luke walked toward the back of the boat and stepped into the cabin. Emma went over to the small window and pushed back the curtains, causing the morning sunshine to spill into the room. Next she walked over to a small table and lifted up a pitcher. "Would you like some water?"

Luke sat down on a high-backed wooden chair and nodded. "Thanks."

As she poured it, she asked, "What do you think Judge Littleton wants? Do you think my husband is in some kind of trouble?"

Luke reached out and took the cup, careful not to let their fingers brush. The last thing he wanted was to have Eric force some story of an innocent touch out of her, make it seem disloyal, and punish her for it. "Wouldn't surprise me. Can you think of anything?"

Emma sank down on the edge of the bed and clasped her hand together in her lap. "Yes. I can think of something." Emma pointed to Luke's chest. "The reason you are here with me now isn't to keep an eye on me. It's so those men won't know Eric has the journal." Emma's laugh rang hollow. "Clever, isn't he? He knew you wouldn't refuse such a request. He knows everything about manipulation, Mr. Bowen. You are being used."

Luke reached for the journal tucked inside his jacket. "What is so important about this journal? Was it stolen?"

Emma lowered her voice to a whisper. "Worse. Eric had the author of it killed because he wouldn't sell it to him."

"How do you know this?"

"I overheard him talking to one of the men. Eric told him that if the author wouldn't sell it . . . he said to do *whatever it takes* to get it."

Luke stood and walked over toward the door. "I have to give it to the judge. We can't let your husband get away with this."

Emma rushed toward him, placing a hand on his arm. "No. Eric will kill you. He will make it look like an accident, but he will kill you."

"I'm not afraid of him."

"Please, don't go out there." Her anxious tone, her face so pleading and open. The impact of her nearness streaked all the way to his toes. "I-I couldn't bear it if anything happened to you."

"I can take care of myself, Mrs. Montclaire. We can't let this happen."

"You are underestimating him. He always gets what he wants."

Emma took hold of the journal and slid it back beneath Luke's buckskin coat. "Keep it hidden for me . . . please."

A sudden knock sounded at the door. Emma backed away while Luke buttoned up the coat, the journal hidden next to the sketches. He pulled the door open to find one of the men who had accompanied Judge Littleton.

A soldier of tall, erect carriage and a serious face. He was probably stationed at Fort Belle Fontaine, just a few miles from St. Louis.

The soldier looked back and forth between them then turned toward Emma as he took off his hat and held it to his chest. "Sorry to bother you, ma'am, but I've been ordered to take a look around this cabin."

"By whom?" Emma asked in apparent concern. "Whatever for?"

"The judge gave the order. Your husband has agreed it would be all right."

"What are you looking for, sir? Maybe I can help you find it."

The man looked over at Luke and motioned him to step outside. "That won't be necessary, ma'am. If you and Mr. Bowen could both step outside."

"Dear me"—Emma pressed a hand against her chest—"well, if Eric said it would be all right."

"Yes, ma'am, he did."

Emma and Luke walked away from the cabin and made their way over to the railing. Eric stood on shore with Judge Littleton and the other soldier that the judge had brought along.

As if he sensed his wife's presence, Eric looked up at the two of them. He gave Luke a warning glare.

Beside Luke, Emma gasped. "He knows I've told you." Her voice was threaded with fear. "He knows I would have begged you not to hand it over." She turned her back on the scene, looking out at the other side of the river. "He planned it, as soon as he saw the judge, he planned all this out."

It was likely she was right, and Luke didn't like it one bit that he was being played for a fool. A grim contemplation settled on him.

The soldier came back out of the cabin and approached them.

"Did you find what you were looking for, sir?" Emma asked him.

"Lieutenant William Arthur, ma'am. And no, I did not." He gave Luke a considering appraisal.

"Maybe if you told us what it is, we could help. Is someone in some kind of trouble?" Luke asked.

"I am not at liberty to say anything at this time." He touched the brim of his hat and nodded to Emma. "Thank you, ma'am." The soldier strode over to the edge of the barge and leapt onto the grassy bank.

"Emma! Come and meet the new judge, my dear." Eric didn't invite Luke, but Luke followed her anyway. They walked together over toward the judge, Eric's eyes assessing Luke.

"This is my wife, Emma Montclaire," Eric's arm reached out and snaked around her low back. He pulled her into his side, then nodded toward Luke. "And this is my cartographer, Luke Bowen."

Luke shook hands with the man. "Glad to meet you, sir. Heard you are doing a fine job in this new territory."

"Why thank you, son. It's a duty and a privilege to keep folks out this far west in some semblance of safety."

"What's brought you our way? Has someone committed a crime all the way out here?"

Eric broke in. "The judge's business is his own, Luke. Now, Emma, why don't you make these men some of your tea. I'm sure they could use a rest before heading back to St. Louis."

"Oh, we won't be going back just yet, Mr. Montclaire. I'd like to question your men. Find out for myself if anyone has seen this mysterious journal."

Eric turned, brisk and ramrod stiff. "You don't trust my word?"

"Well, now I didn't say that." He looked at Luke with interest lighting his brown, intelligent eyes. "Just don't know that you know all the goings on with your men." He chuckled, his belly shaking as he laughed. "You're not God, now are you? Can't know everything."

Eric looked ready to throttle the man but took a long breath, forcing his fists to unclench at his sides. Luke tried not to enjoy seeing him so discomfited.

"That tea sounds mighty good, though." The judge looked around. "This looks like a good spot to camp for a bit." He clapped Eric on the shoulder. "Don't you agree, Mr. Montclaire?"

"I don't believe my feelings on the matter will have any sway on your opinion, judge."

"Well, you're a smart young man, I'll say that for you. Smart indeed."

The four of them made their way to a clearing among the cottonwood trees. Some of the men were huddled around talking, but they broke apart and stared as the four of them neared. Luke knew they were as curious as he to know what was going on, and it looked as if they would find out soon. They would all be questioned about the journal.

God, help me know how to handle this.

As if in answer to his quick prayer, words flowed through his mind: *"Behold, I send you forth as sheep in the midst of wolves: be ye therefore wise as serpents, and harmless as doves."*

Wise without causing harm.

That's going to be a tough one, Lord.

Chapter Thirteen

*E*mma crawled from her tent the next morning and blinked the sandy feeling from her eyes. The judge had taken the cabin on the barge for individual questioning, so Eric allowed Emma to join the men at camp where she and her husband slept in a large tent. Eric told the men they would camp for a couple of days to replenish meat stores, but they all knew better.

They were staying until the judge's questions were answered.

The interrogations began almost immediately upon the judge's arrival. Emma saw Luke go to the cabin for his turn but had not seen him since. She'd tossed and turned all night wondering what had happened. Had he told the judge about Eric? Was her husband going to jail? And if he did, would she finally be free?

A chirping, tiny bark of a sound made her turn around. A squirrel? A raccoon, perhaps? She didn't see the source of the noise but wasn't afraid. Emma loved being out of doors. Their camp sat in such a pretty spot, she reflected as she picked her way around cottonwood trees and an old oak tree with its round, glossy acorns on the ground. She saw the squirrel then, peeking out from the side of a tree, and smiled.

"Hello." She laughed as he ducked back behind the trunk. Turning away, her foot landed on a nut, which promptly rolled and sent her off balance. She let out a little screech, her arms windmilling wildly. The men closest to her turned and watched as she fell flat on her backside.

"Ow." She wished she could take back the whimper, but since she couldn't, she just turned aside. Why didn't those men look away? It wasn't seemly to stare at a woman . . . even when she did something so ungainly. As she pushed to her feet, Luke separated himself from a group of men and walked toward her. He didn't look distressed from yesterday's interrogation. Rather, he looked as though . . . well! The horrid man was trying not to laugh.

"No need to come any further"—she ground out the words, holding her hand out as if to ward him off—"I'm fine."

Luke paused, a grin spreading across his face. "You sure?"

To prove her assertion, she straightened and took a step and cried out as pain shot up her leg. Surprise filled her, but it shouldn't have. She was long overdue for an injury.

Luke came up to her side and put his arm around her waist.

"What are you *doing?*" she hissed. "Eric will be furious if he sees you."

"Eric is on the barge with the judge and"—he grinned—"I think he has plenty to occupy his mind right now."

She let him support her. "What happened yesterday? The judge had you in there for so long, and Eric was steaming mad he wasn't allowed near the boat while you were being questioned."

"Well, it's a story, that's for sure." Luke seemed happy. A fact that, oddly enough, sent a lightness surging through her own heart.

So confused was she by the direction of her thoughts that she forgot about her ankle—until, that is, she put weight on it. She cried out again, a little squeak this time, and grabbed hold of his shoulder.

He caught her and righted her. "Looks like you may have sprained your ankle."

"On an acorn? How mortifying! I can't tell Eric."

"Well, seeing as how you can't walk, you'll have to tell him something." Levity filled his tone, and she ground her teeth. He couldn't even keep a straight face!

"This is horrible! Now I'll be stuck in that cabin for sure."

Luke lifted her into his arms. His face was inches away as he looked down at her. She caught her breath. She'd never seen eyes so deep a brown . . .

"What you need is a project."

As though his words brought her to her senses, she struggled against him. "Put me down this instant!"

"I'm just going to carry you over to that fallen tree so we can have a look at that ankle. Hold still." Luke's grip tightened. "And yes, a project. You know, something to keep you occupied."

What was the man talking about? "What kind of project could a woman have out here in the wilderness?"

"You could sew. You can sew, can't you? Or knit, some . . . womanly thing?"

"Of course I can sew," Emma snapped, hanging on for dear life as they strode into the camp. "I didn't exactly have time to plan and pack anything like that. I might have some needles and some thread, but no cloth to sew together."

Luke deposited her onto a fallen tree that the men had been using for a long bench. "Well, how about drawing or reading?"

Emma watched, wary and nervous as he squatted down in front of her and grasped her leg. He brought the sore ankle onto his thigh and with slow, careful motions removed her slipper. When his hand started to go up her leg, she pulled back with an outraged squeal. *"What* do you think you're doing?"

Luke squinted up at her. "Mrs. Montclaire, that ankle needs looking after, and since I've become the medic, more or less, for this outfit, the job falls to me."

"What skills do you have as a physician? You're a cartographer."

"Which gives me steady hands."

Emma's cheeks flushed—though Luke's placid features told her he hadn't meant anything by the comment. *What* was wrong with her? Her heart raced with so many emotions: embarrassment, fear, excitement . . .

Lord, help me. Why am I reacting this way?

Luke stared at her, waiting for her to make a decision.

Emma thrust her ankle toward him, "A quick look. Don't touch me."

The corners of Luke's mouth turned down as he stared at her foot. "Move your foot up and down and tell me when it hurts."

Emma did as he requested and gasped.

"Is the pain bad?"

"A little." Emma bit her bottom lip and stared down at it. "Is it swelling?"

Luke nodded. "A little." He looked up at her with a half smile. Small lines appeared around his eyes, and dimples showed through the short growth of dark beard on his face. Luke Bowen was as opposite to Eric's bright good looks as one could be. And yet Emma couldn't deny that Luke's dark hair, dark brown eyes, and tanned skin made an attractive combination. Were there

111

really men in the world who were as good and noble as they appeared?

Thankfully Luke seemed oblivious to her inner turmoil. He studied her ankle again and nodded. "I believe it's just a sprain. It should be wrapped with a long strip of cloth to keep it stable while it heals. You'll have to rest it for a few days at least."

"I will wrap it." Emma sighed. "Eric will be so angry."

"Maybe he will leave you alone for awhile."

Emma started at the words, and Luke frowned and clamped his mouth shut, as if he wished he hadn't said it. Emma looked down, unable to meet his eyes. "Maybe this is God's way of protecting me."

Luke allowed a small smile. "I'll keep praying then."

Emma couldn't hide her astonishment. "You're . . . praying? For me?"

"Just about all of the time." He looked up, suddenly serious and quoted, *"Be sober, be vigilant; because your adversary the devil, as a roaring lion, walketh about, seeking whom he may devour"*

"Is that from the Bible?" She still had the one her mother had given her. She'd kept it hidden at the bottom of her trunk.

"First Peter, chapter five, I think. I've somehow lost my Bible. I miss it." He didn't mention that his things had been ransacked the first week he'd been on this expedition. His Bible wasn't the only thing to come up missing. His best hunting knife and an extra pair of boots were pilfered too. He had reported the theft to Eric, but nothing had ever come of it.

Emma looked up and around the camp, then lowered her voice. "I have a Bible."

"Do you read it?"

"I've tried, but I don't understand it very well. Could you . . . could you teach me?"

Luke paused for a moment, his gaze thoughtful. "We could pass it back and forth. I could add notes and tuck them inside, what I think it means."

"Yes. I-I would like that very much."

"It would be risky."

She looked down at her clasped hands and then back into his concerned brown eyes. "Yes, it will." Some of the desperation buried deep inside her seeped out into her words. "I will find a way."

"All right then. I was reading in First Peter when my Bible disappeared. We can start there if you like."

"Emma? What's going on here?"

They both looked up to find Eric standing there, glaring at Luke. "What do you think you are doing with *my* wife?" The violence in his voice grew with each punctuated word.

Emma gasped and then winced as she set her foot on the ground. "I tripped and hurt my ankle. Mr. Bowen thinks it is sprained."

Luke stood to face Eric.

Eric stomped toward them. *"Mr. Bowen"*—his voice dripped with sarcasm—"has no business taking care of *my* wife."

"Did you want me to leave her on the ground? I do have some medical experience, you know. You've told me to use it when needed."

"For the men, yes. Not for my wife."

"I did what I would have done for any of our group. The swelling was immediate. She will have to stay off of it for a week or so."

"Next thing you will ask is if you may stay by her side, sit next to her on the boat while you draw birds, is that it?" Eric's narrow-eyed glare was utterly malicious, but Luke didn't seem in the least disturbed by it.

"If you'll excuse me, sir, I'll get back to my work. Unless, of course, there's some reason I shouldn't?"

"What is that supposed to mean?" Eric took another step toward Luke and grasped his upper arm. "Are you threatening me?"

Now it was Luke's eyes that narrowed. "Threatening you? No, sir." Luke pulled back hard, jerking his arm free of Eric's grip. He squared off with Eric. "I only meant that the judge's investigation could impact our expedition. But then I don't know that for certain. The judge and I did start to talk yesterday, but we didn't get far when we discovered he knows my mother. He is a good friend of her best friends, the Simmons. So we didn't get around to talking about the investigation much."

"But you will, I suppose?"

Luke's shrug was nonchalant. "My time with the judge ended when Ben Jenkins showed up for his turn to be questioned. But yes, the judge did say he would talk to me later today, after he is finished with everyone else. I guess by then he could know the journal exists."

"Why, you no good—" Eric reached out to grasp Luke again, but Luke sidestepped him. The move was clearly unexpected as Eric stumbled. He righted himself, looking as if he would like to plow into Luke.

Emma could stand no more. "Eric, please! The men are approaching. Stop this!"

Eric turned on her, his voice a hiss of rage. "Don't even *think* about trying to protect him, Emma." He looked to the men, then back at her. His tone dripped with scorn. "You can't even walk across the ground without stumbling."

He drew in a breath, straightened his coat, and directed a hard stare at Luke. "Stay away from my wife, do you understand? It will be . . . unpleasant if you don't heed my warning."

Luke just stared at him, feeling as solid as the ground he stood on.

Eric turned to go, then shot parting words over his shoulder. "Bring the journal to me. It's mine."

"I believe the journal is in a safe place for now."

Eric turned. "You think a journal is going to keep you safe? You can't blackmail me."

"I guess if you want it to remain hidden you're going to have to treat your wife better."

Emma gasped, and Eric's face turned thunderous. He glanced at Emma. "Whatever she's told you is nothing but a woman's imaginings. I treat her as she deserves, and it's no business of yours."

Luke looked at the man long and hard. "Your wife hasn't told me anything, but I've got eyes"—he glanced around the camp—"just like everybody else. If I see anything I don't like, that journal and everything I know about it will go to Judge Littleton."

Eric's mouth worked, as though words formed but wouldn't come out. Finally he grit his teeth. "We'll see about that."

Emma watched as her husband strode away, his footsteps an angry stomp, his arms swinging at his sides.

When Eric was out of earshot, Emma stood and looked up at Luke. "What are you thinking, baiting him like that? Eric will kill you. I know it."

"He might try. But as long as the judge is with us, he won't dare do anything to you or me." He looked down at her, and the fire in his eyes was replaced with another look. A far more gentle one. "God has mysterious ways of working, Mrs. Montclaire. We just have to keep trusting Him."

Emma's heart swelled with the first glimmer of hope she'd had since her wedding day.

Luke turned toward the group of approaching men. Emma heard him giving orders to bring her food and set her up a comfortable place to sit against the log. "And Josh"—he pointed to the barge—"would you go to the cabin and ask Judge Littleton if you could get some of Emma's books? Tell him about her fall."

"Yes, sir!" The young Josh looked over at Emma with a smile and a tip of his hat. She didn't tell Eric, couldn't tell Eric, but when he wasn't around, the men on this excursion treated her with a kind respect. But she was unable to acknowledge it. Eric hadn't had to tell her; she knew he wanted her to stay away from the men, any man for that matter.

Luke turned to her. "I'll bring you some drawing tools too."

Emma laughed and shook her head. "I can't draw."

Luke gave her a wink. "I'll include a lesson."

Something akin to peace settled on her, though there was no discernible reason to be at peace. In the next day or the next hour something horrible could happen, but she couldn't seem to worry. She looked up and saw the gentle swaying of the green-leafed trees. The sky peeked through, clear blue dotted with wispy, scattered clouds scudding across like they had somewhere to go, something to see.

Sitting there, she did what Luke said he did. She closed her eyes . . . and prayed.

Chapter Fourteen

*P*lease be seated, my boy."

Luke did as the judge bid, taking the seat facing the older man. He studied the judge's eyes, his face, and liked what he saw. This was a man of character. A good man.

The judge leaned back in his chair, his demeanor relaxed. But Luke knew there was steel behind the kindly exterior. He'd seen it several times since the judge had arrived. Heard it in the man's voice more than once.

As he heard it now when the judge finally spoke. "Now, it's time for you to tell me what you know, Luke." The judge gave him a small smile. "All of it, if you please."

For a moment Luke considered withholding, wondering if telling all, as he'd been bid, would cause Emma harm. But he knew what set one free was the truth, and with that sure knowledge, he once again did as the judge bid. He told the judge everything that had happened since he first met Emma and Eric Montclaire. He even told him of the events earlier that day, and of his threat to Eric about the journal.

"It seemed the only thing I had to hold the man back from continuing to abuse his wife, sir."

The judge's expression gave nothing away. "So you have the journal?"

Luke reached into his coat and pulled it out, then handed it to the judge.

Judge Littleton took the worn book into his hands and flipped through it, reading an entry here and there, remaining thoughtful and quiet.

Finally he looked up at Luke, set the journal aside, and in a gentle, quiet voice asked, "So you're in love with another man's wife?"

Shock jolted through Luke, like the kick of a mad mule. He started to deny it, to shake his head, but even as he did so, he found he couldn't hold the judge's wise but kind stare.

The judge let the silence sink through Luke's attempt at denial. And in that silence Luke faced the truth.

The judge was right. God help him, he had fallen in love with Emma Montclaire. *Lord, what have I done?*

"All right, then." The judge leaned forward. "If all you've said is true, then I can't blame you for wanting to protect Mrs. Montclaire, but what are you going to do? Follow them around the rest of their lives and watch over her? What happens once this journal business is settled? What then?"

Luke didn't know the answer to any of the judge's questions. "Can't you do something? Eric ordered that man killed."

The judge sighed and rubbed his knee as if it was paining him. "Maybe. But it's his word against yours and his wife's. Considering the current of emotions between you two, folks could find it easy to believe that the two of you are making up this story. Trying to get rid of the unwanted husband."

Outrage at such a suggestion flooded Luke, but when he met the judge's eyes, he realized, yet again, the man was right. "I hadn't thought of it like that."

"That's obvious to me, and it's why I believe you. That, and the fact that Eric Montclaire is the most deceitful man I've ever come across. But a jury might not see it that way. As I'm sure you're aware, Mr. Montclaire can be quite convincing."

That was true. He'd blinded all of them with his charismatic charm and good looks for a time—especially Emma. "What can we do?"

"Well, now, if I could get a confession out of the fella who did the killing, how Mr. Montclaire paid him to do it, well then, we'd have two fish to fry. Do you know the scoundrel's name?"

Luke shook his head. "Emma will know. She overheard Eric and the man talking about it."

The judge took a long, deep breath. "I was afraid of that. I'll have to talk to her then."

"Is that a problem?"

"It might alert Eric—show him our hand, so to speak."

And it could be dangerous for Emma. Though neither of them spoke the concern, Luke knew they shared it. There had to be some way around—wait! Of course! "Judge, Emma and I are sharing a book, passing it back and forth between us. I could slip in a note with the question. She could write me the answer, and then I will get it to you."

The judge rubbed his chin. "Might just work. How long do you think that would take?"

Luke shrugged. "A day or two."

"All right then. That'll be our plan for now. Have her write down her response and pass it back to you. I would like to have the killer's name in writing." He paused, then looked at Luke like a father might. "So you're hoping Eric will be punished for this crime and . . . then what?"

"He *deserves* to be punished?" Luke stated with heat. "He had a man killed for a journal!"

"Never mind that Mrs. Montclaire is so pretty. Why it hurts my eyes just to look at her!" The judge chuckled. "Let me ask you a question, Mr. Bowen. If Mrs. Montclaire was a big, old ugly woman, would you be going to all this trouble to help her?"

Luke could not remain sitting with all the pressure mounting in his chest at these truths. He stood and paced across the cabin to look out its tiny window. "I don't know; I suppose not." He hung his head, staring at the bare wood floor. "I suppose I'd think it was none of my business what a man did with his wife."

"Hmmm. I can see you're a good, God-fearing man. Now you go on and chew on those thoughts for awhile."

Luke nodded, almost choking on remorse. How could he have done it? How could he have allowed his emotions to dictate his actions where Emma was concerned? Maybe God did want him to help her, but it would have to be His way, not Luke's.

Luke turned back toward the judge, feeling like he was sitting in the presence of a backwoods angel. No wonder this man had such an amazing reputation. "What do I do now?"

"Just get me that name." The judge stood and patted Luke's shoulder. "And take it a day at a time. God won't leave you or forsake you in this."

Tears rose up into his eyes. He missed his father. He slapped his hat down on his head and blinked a few times. "Thank you, sir."

"Why, you're welcome, son. You can come and talk to me anytime. Anytime you need to."

Luke left the cabin not knowing where to go or what to do. All his motivations were stripped from him, and he felt useless and naked. *Lord, what am I doing here?*

If I recall, you are there to draw maps.

Luke let out a bark of laughter. God's voice sounded just like Judge Littleton's.

Emma slipped between the covers as Eric entered their tent.

She'd been dreading this moment. He would be beyond angry after what had happened this afternoon.

"How is your ankle?"

Emma started. He sounded genuinely caring. Her tense muscles relaxed a notch. "A little sore, but the swelling hasn't worsened. I expect it will be better in a few days."

Eric reached for the buttons on his coat. He didn't wear the buckskin that the other men of the expedition wore. No, he wore a gentleman's waistcoat of dark blue satin; tight-fitting, gray pantaloons; tall boots; and a crisp, white shirt and cravat.

Emma shifted on the hard bed of blankets on the ground, leaving her injured ankle hanging out on one side so that the heaviness of the blanket didn't cause her more pain. She watched as Eric tossed the coat on a chair he'd had brought in, then directed her gaze to the floor as he reached for the top button on his shirt.

"That's good news." Eric continued as if there hadn't been a long pause in their conversation. "I have plans for you tonight."

Emma's head jerked up. "Plans?" Eric chuckled, and understanding turned her cold. When would she learn? He thrived on her fear. She must not show it. Not let it color her tone.

Her chin lifted just a notch, she let a false sense of curiosity fill her eyes, "What sort of plans?"

He saw through the act. He always did. There was nothing she could do to stop the ebb and flow of his ever-changing moods. She was so tired of pretending! Tired of trying to make him feel right with the world. But even after her small success the other night, she was afraid, terrified of what would happen if she stopped.

"You seemed to like it when Bowen was playing doctor. I thought a little playacting of our own would be . . . diverting."

Despair filled her. "Eric, I'm tired. And my ankle aches so. Can't it wait?"

He came toward her in a slow move and yet too quick for her to think of a way to counteract it. He grasped her wrist in his hands and brought them up by her face. "You liked it today and you were in pain. You'll like it now."

Emma turned her head toward the side, away from him, saw the candle burning bright, saw their tent and the shadows they must be making. *Go along with it,* one part of her mind said. *Don't fight him, not here. Someone will hear you if you cry out.*

But that could be good. The judge was here. Maybe he would help her. She bit her lip, indecision pulling her in all directions.

"Don't even think about calling out." Ah, yes. Eric read her mind. He always did. "You are mine. There is nothing anyone can do about that."

Emma turned her face toward his and stared into eyes that had gone from smoky blue to dark gray. "Why? What do you want from me?"

Instead of answering Eric pressed her arms further back into the blanket, into the hard ground. The pain from her ankle receded as the pain screamed through her arms. He leaned toward her to kiss her, but it wasn't a kiss. He hadn't ever kissed her the way a husband should.

She fought, turning her head away and bucking a shoulder toward his chin.

He followed. His hot breath making a scalding path down her cheek and throat.

"No!" It wasn't a yell, but it was loud.

"There's nothing you can do." His confident tone made her want to scream. He reached for her nightgown, took the two sides where the buttons met in his hands and pulled.

Emma heard the fabric rip. She tried to turn, to rear up, but he was too strong.

"Please . . ." The horrified whisper filled the tent, and she turned her head as the trickle of tears fell into her hair.

Eric shook her hard. "You will *never*"—he gritted out—"make a fool out of me like that again." He shook her again, so hard her head snapped back and forth. "Not ever! Do you understand me, Emma?"

God help me! I can't do this anymore! I'm dying inside, . . . I want to die.

Just as Eric's face filled her vision, black rage in his eyes and taut energy in every muscle of his body, they heard shouts.

"Fire! *Fire!*"

Eric turned toward the shouts, cursed, and then shoved Emma away and rose to his feet. He stood over her shaking body, looked down at her with eyes black with hatred, and then turned and pulled on his clothes.

She sat up and stared, unblinking, her hand clasping together the edges of the torn nightgown as her husband rushed out the tent flap.

The men stood around the charred remains of one of the canoes. Judge Littleton walked over toward Eric and looked him in the eye.

"How can something sitting in water burn like that?" Eric asked, as if to himself.

The judge followed Eric's stare, taking in the remains of wood still floating in the water like a blackened blanket. It had been one of the supply boats. Food stores, trinkets for the Indians, and some tools they'd stored away—all gone.

The judge allowed himself a small chuckle at the sight. He'd been in the cabin, going over his notes and thinking about the charges he would make, when he heard the shouts. He glanced at Eric. "It doesn't seem you're having much success with this venture of yours, Mr. Montclaire."

The young man glared at him, but the judge went on. "I wonder, sir, if there might be a reason for that?"

Eric's lips pressed so hard together they turned white. "It's bad luck, and I think I know the cause of it."

This should be interesting. The judge arched a brow. "Oh?"

"Yes, actually. I should have told you sooner, but I believe one of my men stole the journal and killed the journal's author to have it."

"Is that so? Who is this character?"

Eric jerked his head toward the dark-haired man standing a stone's throw away by the shore. "Luke Bowen. I saw him with a leather-bound book." Eric turned toward the judge and shrugged.

"He claimed when I hired him that he could draw maps, that he was a cartographer. I haven't seen much proof of that yet."

"That's not much evidence, Mr. Montclaire. You got anything else?" Judge Littleton reached for his pipe and took his time lighting it. This man was snaky, twisting and turning wherever he could, and the judge had learned the value of long silences.

"The thought struck me that the journal might have some drawings in it . . . some maps. Maybe he wants to pass them off as his own . . . and collect my money as pay." Eric paused and then added, "He is probably the one who set fire to the canoe."

The judge pondered that. "But if he stole the journal, he wouldn't want to burn your boat, now would he? He'd be planning to pull out those maps later, down the trail, after he'd seen the land firsthand."

Eric nodded. "I thought of that. But there's been a turn of events since I hired him."

"Oh? What's that?"

"He thinks he's in love with my"—the man almost spat the last word—"wife."

The judge nodded, watching the men's efforts to haul the floating, charred remains of the boat onto the shore. "I see."

"Then you'll arrest him? Take him back to St. Louis?"

"Well, now, I'm not convinced so much as that." The judge patted Eric on the arm, and almost laughed when the young popinjay flinched. "I think I'll just stick around a few more days, find out what's really going on around here. I know you want the truth to come out, now don't you?"

When Eric didn't answer, just seethed beside him, the judge fought to restrain a smile. "What are your plans, son? Are you gonna build another boat or just give in and go home now?"

Eric turned toward the judge and looked him dead in the eye. "I never give in."

Yes, Judge Littleton could well believe that. He only hoped this man's deceit and evil came to an end soon. Before someone else paid the ultimate price.

Chapter Fifteen

*T*he early morning mist swirled over the gray-green waters of the Missouri River like a hovering cloak. A great bird flew overhead, stretched its wings and sounded a *caw, caw, caw.*

Emma looked up at the bird, wrapped the blanket tighter around her shoulders and inhaled the sweetness of the air. A smile lingered around her lips, and her fingers tightened the knot of blanket at her throat as she watched the bird soar and then, in an effortless turn, dip toward the river. She gripped the rail of the barge and leaned forward to see it dive, a sudden strike toward the frothing water, and then rise again before her next heartbeat, a fish grasped in its talons. She blinked back the response to such beauty and grace.

"He is really something, isn't he?"

The masculine voice made her jerk, and she felt all the pleasure drain from her face. Turning, she saw Luke and breathed a sigh of relief. Still, though she was glad it was Luke and not her husband, she could not relax. Just being here, talking to him . . . what if Eric saw them? She looked down, grasped the blanket tighter as if to ward off all men. Couldn't they just go away? Couldn't they just leave her alone?

She was tired.

So tired.

She drew a fortifying breath and answered him instead of doing what she wanted, turn and walk away. "Yes, it's something I've never seen before." She supposed that if she knew of a place to run, a safe place, she might do it. But she didn't. Her only alternative was to be shut back into the cabin, a place that had become as suffocating as her marriage. She would rather risk being caught talking to a man who had care and concern in his eyes than go back in there and sit alone.

"I have the lessons for you."

"Lessons?"

"You've been reading your Bible? I wrote down some notes on the first chapter of Peter." Luke glanced around at the men who were poling nearby and then leaned in. "And the art lesson I promised you." He thrust some folded sheets of paper toward her, his voice low. "And something else. A question from Judge Littleton."

"Oh." Emma looked down at the papers now clutched in her hand. She had been reading her Bible but not the Scripture Luke had asked her to read. Instead she had flipped it open and been struck by the words in Psalms.

> LORD, *how are they increased that trouble me!*
> *Many are they that rise up against me.*
> *Many there be which say of my soul,*
> *There is no help for him in God. Selah.*
>
> *But thou, O* LORD, *art a shield for me;*
> *My glory, and the lifter up of mine head*
> *I cried unto the* LORD *with my voice,*
> *And he heard me out of his holy hill. Selah.*

I laid me down and slept;
I awaked; for the LORD sustained me.
I will not be afraid of ten thousands of people,
That have set themselves against me round about.

Arise, O LORD;
Save me, O my God:
For thou hast smitten all mine enemies upon the cheek
bone; Thou hast broken the teeth of the ungodly.
Salvation belongeth unto the LORD:
Thy blessing is upon thy people. Selah.

She'd read the words over and over, memorizing them. She repeated them to herself as a prayer whenever she felt afraid. Which was often.

Emma shoved the papers inside her blanket. She swallowed hard, afraid but hopeful, then looked back up. Luke backed away, his hand to the brim of his hat. "Don't let your husband see it."

"No. I won't. Thank you." She turned back toward the water and gazed out over its wavy surface. The papers lay like red-hot irons against her chest. If Eric caught her with them . . . well . . . she didn't know what he would do, but it was certain he would do something terrible. To them both.

Luke watched, his stomach lurching within him as she made her way back to the cabin on the barge. He so rarely saw her outside it since they'd set sail again. He'd had to take the chance. But now he wondered if he should have waited and given her more time to enjoy the fresh air. His gaze roved over the men who were busy at the monumental task of rowing them up the Missouri. He'd been quiet and quick about talking with her, but any one of them could have noticed and tried to overhear. Any one of them could report back to Eric that Luke had been talking to his wife.

Speaking of Eric . . . Luke frowned. Where was the man? He rarely traveled on one of the canoes during the day, always keeping a close eye on the men aboard the barge and Emma.

Luke made his way over to the stern and looked out at the land. The fog lifted, leaving a glittering droplet effect on the surface of the land. And the land was changing. Forests and rocky outcroppings were giving way to stretches of land that the Corps of Discovery called prairie. He hadn't made it this far the last time—with Lewis and Clark. The last time he had gotten as far as the French village of La Charrette—the last white settlement this far west. The memory caused a tightness in his chest—the weight of his father's death announced in a letter, the curving, tear-stained handwriting of his mother. Then the despair at leaving the expedition.

But no. He could choose not to think of those things and so not to feel the feelings all over again. He was back on the river, heading west, entering the prairie lands, a place of wide open spaces filled with vegetation, flowering plants, and new animals to be seen like the prairie dogs and abounding grouse. Last night, as they'd set up camp in an area off the bank with tall, sweet-smelling grasses, he'd seen the famed prairie dog. Lewis and Clark had brought back sketches of the animal.

Luke smiled, remembering when he first saw some of the sketches brought back from that expedition. Those men had discovered a new world, a world that had waited for men like him to come and explore it. It looked like the kind of land a man could farm, rich soil without all the rock and tree clearing, but he wasn't a farmer. Was he? He didn't like the plowing and sowing and waiting and praying for rain. The harvesting and weighing and selling. The constant disappointments when the crop yields weren't as high as expected. The backbreaking work . . . did he?

As he probed for an answer, he found a surprising place in his heart. He looked out over the greens and yellows of fields of grassland and found the notion of a cabin here, with a woman to love, to provide for, not so very distasteful as he once thought.

The discovery shook him. Why did he no longer know what he was about? Drawing maps? Drawing birds and plants? Drawing anything?

He looked up and down the river's bank, saw it washing away into the water, and hung his head. That's what he felt like. Like everything inside him was washing away into a great current that he could neither comprehend nor control. He didn't know what would be left of him in the end.

Mid-afternoon the next day Emma appeared at his side. He had been sketching out the latest bend in the river, from an island about three miles back around the bend, and then up to the place where the bank rose to twenty feet on the larboard side. He reckoned that to be four miles and so made the river on the page four inches to scale.

From landmark to landmark, he scaled it to fit on the paper with notations on the side that gave more information about what he saw—the animals, the plants, rock formations, a salt lick, an abandoned Indian camp—anything he thought would help make a good map. Emma peered over his shoulder. Luke looked up, tried to shutter the gladness that sprung up as he saw her face.

Then he saw the new bruise just above her left cheek.

Her eyes were damp with unshed tears but strong, determined. She held the Bible out to him. The pages were hanging out from the binding, ripped and shredded.

"He found the Bible and the drawing lesson but not the judge's note. I"—she hesitated and then rushed the rest—"I kept that from him."

The cost was written over her whole being. Everything in him wanted to go and find the man who could do this to her. He didn't care what happened to him. He wanted nothing more than to shoot Eric Montclaire right between the eyes.

His fists curled against his thighs. *Lord, this isn't fair. I can't do anything!* "What did he do to you?"

She looked down and shook her head, a red flush filling her face. Some of her hair, glinting golden as the sunlight struck it, came loose from its knot and hid her face. "I've written out the name. Take it. Hurry. He's gone to check on the hunters, but he will be back any minute."

Luke shook his head. "No!" Everything in him shouted it. He didn't realize he'd said it aloud until her soft but firm voice corrected him.

"Yes." She looked up, the bright light of the sun full on her ravished face, and glared at him. *"Yes."* She pressed the book into his chest. "Give my answer to the judge. I—" She looked down at his chest, then reached out and touched his arm with a gentle touch.

Luke watched, feeling the crashing of his anger pound through his head as she turned away and limped back to the cabin.

He looked down at the torn Bible and then gripped it tight against his chest. The man had no fear. The thought penetrated, drove its truth home. Only someone who didn't believe in God could do this to His Word.

A deep chill made him shiver, and though this man was his enemy, for the first time he feared for Eric. With fumbling hands he opened the Bible, letting the pages fall where they may, to the place where the judge's note was tucked. The page the letter rested against had been pieced back together. He read the passage of Psalms, realizing that Emma wanted to give him a message of the strength she'd found in it, and then unfolded the note. There was a name written there. A single phrase.

"My husband admitted to me that his employee, Patrick Hardesty, murdered Robert Frazer for possession of the journal as the man would not sell it."

Luke tucked the note into his pocket as he scanned the men busy at their work. The judge had chosen to journey in his own canoe and was some distance behind them. But they would bank soon, camp for the night, and he would be ready.

Ready to watch them arrest Eric Montclaire.

Chapter Sixteen

*E*mma made her slow and painful walk back toward the cabin. Gladness and relief flooded her as her hair fell from its pins, hiding her face from the curious looks of the men sweating at their oars. She glanced up at them where they sat on their short rowing benches. Some looked at her in curiosity, some uneasy, others looked away, not able to meet her eyes. She turned away and let herself inside the cabin. Somehow she knew they wouldn't tell Eric she'd been out on the deck this afternoon. They would protect her with silence.

The cabin was dim and tidy. Even here Eric didn't allow anything out of place. Her gaze swung to the wooden chair and the bindings that had been around her waist, tying her to it. She still wasn't sure how she'd so easily gotten free of those knots.

She swallowed hard and made her way back to the chair. Sitting down, she pulled the loops of ragged cloth back over her head and the back of the chair. With gritted teeth, she retied the knots, tight, and then slid them around to the back, just as her husband had placed them. Now to wait.

She dozed off, the heat of a warm autumn day making the cabin stifling. Sweat dripped from her neck and soaked her dress.

Her hair lay plastered to her face, her head leaning on the back of the chair. Deep thirst ravaged her as she sat there, drifting in and out of miserable sleep.

A sudden noise startled her awake, and she lifted her head. Her heart pounded. Yes, God had promised to rescue her. He'd promised. He'd given her that Scripture to cling to. Hadn't He? It was hard to remember when she looked at Eric's face. The words jumbled in her brain, making her panic. She pressed her lips together and forced herself to meet Eric's eyes, judging his mood with the long honed skill of survival.

"For heaven's sake, Emma. You look red as an Indian."

She'd never seen an Indian. She'd heard people called them red skins, but she didn't know why. "I'm thirsty." The words croaked from a dry, cracking throat.

A vein pulsed between his eyebrows—he didn't look so beautiful now. Her mind skittered to and fro. How had she not seen the real him? How had she been so blinded? He wasn't lovely in any way. . . . She could only see his darkness now, that thing that lived and breathed inside of him. That thing that came out most forcefully when she drew near.

"This is *your* fault." He stalked toward the water pitcher, fury in his every movement, and poured a drink. But as he brought the water to her, she watched another mercurial mood shift as he softened. He gazed down at her with possessive love. "You must stop this foolishness, my dear. You know I don't like punishing you like this."

"I'm sorry," Emma whispered.

He grasped her chin, gently this time, and raised her face toward his, waiting until her eyes locked with his. "You know I don't enjoy hurting you, don't you? You know how much I love you."

He sounded like a forlorn little boy. Emma looked him square in the eyes and nodded. "I will be good. I promise."

Eric reached around and untied the knots, then handed her the cup. "Of course you will." His voice broke a little as he knelt down at her feet and rested his hands in her lap. Emma gulped from the cup, feeling the cool relief slide down her throat. Eric grasped her hands as soon as she lowered it. "You love me, don't you, Emma? Only me?"

She reached out and touched his hair as she would a child's, struggling to still the nausea rising to her throat, and nodded. "Of course." It was the best she could do. She could not say the words.

Eric stood and pulled her into his arms. He buried his face in her hair, taking the remaining pins out and running his hands through the long golden length. He pulled her head back with her hair, gently, trying to show her, she knew, how very sorry he was. He leaned in and kissed her on her trembling lips. "Don't be afraid. I am sure this is behind us now. I should have never brought you. We should have never left St. Louis. I should have had the men do this expedition on their own."

"You had to lead them. They wouldn't have known what to do without you."

Eric smiled, and Emma saw a glimpse of the man she thought she'd married. "Yes, you're right. You know the truth, don't you? They wouldn't get very far without me." He kissed her again. Emma fought not to turn away, to run. Everything inside her screamed that this was wrong, all wrong.

Just as Eric grasped hold of the top button on her dress, a loud knock sounded on the door. Irritation turned Eric's face into a scowl as he reared back and flung open the door.

"We've arrived at the camping spot the hunters spoke of, sir." The man took a quick glance at Emma and then slapped his hat on his head and backed away.

"Yes, well good. I will be right out." Eric seemed to be coming out of a fog as he turned back to her. He squinted his eyes at her as if she had something to do with the timing of their arrival, then reached for his hat. "It seems we will have to pick this moment up later, my dear. I hope you are not too disappointed." He laughed as if he'd made a great joke.

Emma tried to stop the waves of relief from reaching her face. She must distract him before he noticed. "Will you need me to help cook tonight?"

A stupid question. He never allowed her that kind of contact with the men, but it did turn his mind from the intent he'd had a few moments ago.

"You're neither a maid nor a cook, Emma." Annoyance filled his tone, and he motioned around the cabin. "Tidy up the cabin for your husband like a good wife. And . . . take a sponge bath. You've been overheated."

Emma suppressed a crazed bubble of laughter. She hadn't thought of that. What if she stank? Would that deter him? Ducking her head as if in embarrassment, but really to hide her smile, she murmured, "Yes, of course."

The next sound she heard was the slamming of the door.

She made quick work of the water left in the water pitcher. She did pour a little on a cloth and dab it onto her hot face, but she didn't touch her body with it. She instead pulled off her clothes, careful to hang them up on the hooks on the wall, and then she collapsed back on the bed, clad in only her chemise. Stretching the aches from her arms and shoulders, she closed her eyes and allowed herself to fall into an exhausted sleep.

Luke saw the judge at the campfire eating from a small metal plate and nodding to something Michael Hennessey, one of the more intelligent members of their expedition, was saying. Luke approached, the note from Emma tucked inside his pocket. Instead of joining them right away, he stopped for his own dinner from the cook and then wandered over, eating casually, to the other side of the fire. Judge Littleton looked up, caught his eye; Luke gave him a small nod.

The judge lifted his chin, a movement that said he understood, and then continued his conversation with Michael while Luke scanned the campsite for Eric. There, speaking with the men who were assigned to hunt for the group. And right in the middle of those men stood the man named in Emma's note—Patrick Hardesty. He should have known. Hardesty was a meaty, quick-to-anger sort. His arms bulged with muscles when he towed the boat or rowed. He wasn't too smart, but he had the brawn to be the muscle for an intelligent schemer like Eric. The two made a formidable pair.

A sudden hand on his shoulder had him turning to see Judge Littleton at his side.

"How are you doing, son?" The judge's warm grin was as welcome as sunshine on a rain-laden day.

Luke turned away from Eric and faced the judge. With slow, easy movements he reached for the note and hid it under his plate. "Trying to remember what you said, truth be told."

The judge looked him in the eyes, and Luke saw so much in that steady gaze. Compassion . . . a man who knew long-suffering.

Luke reached out and passed the note to the judge's big hand. The judge motioned toward a small stand of trees some distance away as he slipped the paper into his coat pocket. Judge Littleton wasn't a small man. His frame stood tall and broad with a bit of a belly hanging over his waistband. His face was weathered, his once-black hair peppered with enough gray to make it mostly that shade now. But his eyes shone with wisdom, discernment. These were the eyes of someone who had fought and won battles of his own.

Luke nodded. "Have you seen Mrs. Montclaire today?"

"Haven't had the pleasure . . . no. How is she?"

A knot rose to Luke's throat as he pictured her face. "Not too good." Luke stopped talking for a moment to regain his composure. Then, angry all over again, he told the judge what he'd seen this afternoon. "He beat her up pretty bad. Bruised face, then there's her ankle, so I don't imagine she can fight back much." His anger seeped into his tone. "Isn't there something in the law that forbids a man to beat his wife? Isn't there something you can do?"

They had reached the trees, and Luke leaned back against one of them. The judge pulled out his pipe and took his time lighting it, leaning back and puffing little rings of smoke while he seemed to be considering the question.

Luke grew impatient. "I don't understand. I don't want to care so much, but"—he looked up at the darkening sky—"where is God if you or I can't do anything?"

The judge nodded. "I been wondering that same thing, son. Sometimes God takes a mighty long time in answering our questions and our prayers. I reckon He knows what He is doing though. It's just hard to figure sometimes."

Luke turned his head toward this man who said such profound but simple things. "But it's not right. I would have been good to her. I would have treated her like a queen."

"Maybe being treated like a queen wouldn't do her any good. Maybe she's gaining something in all this." The judge blew out another smoke ring, seeming to admire it. "You haven't been married before, have you, son?"

"No." Luke knew he sounded frustrated, but he couldn't seem to help it.

"Well, let me tell you something about marriage, my boy. There's this period of time"—he chuckled—"well, it's real nice. She's your queen, and you are some hero to her. Can't wait to see each other at the end of the day. Can't wait to touch her, hold her." He looked down at the grasses that were waving in the breeze, and Luke sensed a sadness in him. Luke grew very still waiting for the rest of this story.

Judge Littleton looked toward the river that glistened in the rising moonlight. "But something happens to most folks. It's not a sudden thing, mind you, not like Mr. and Mrs. Montclaire. That there is a true tragedy. No, it's more of a slow wearing away, wearing down."

He smiled and looked over toward Luke. "It doesn't always happen, but often enough to be common. After a few years her crown is looking pretty tarnished, and your armor is a bit rusty. Too many mistakes. Too much sin."

"Did that happen to you?"

The judge nodded. "Biggest regret of my life. My wife, Martha, she died, oh, about five years ago now. We had five children, three of which are still living and have given me some fine grandchildren, but—"

Luke nodded, encouraging him to continue.

"But I don't think she liked me much the last dozen or so years we were together. I don't think we liked each other very much, and I regret it. I let it happen. I let her quit on me."

Luke looked down at his loosely clasped hands and nodded. "I'm sorry to hear that, sir. But what Eric is doing to Emma is much worse." In a low voice, he spoke his worst fear. "He isn't right, in the head, I mean. I fear he will kill her someday."

The judge put his hand on Luke's shoulder. He looked him square in the eyes and stated, "I'm not excusing Montclaire's actions, not at all. What he is doing is pure evil, and I'm praying with you for God's salvation for her. But we've got to love our enemies as hard and impossible as that might seem. We've got to see them through Christ's eyes. You might be surprised how easy it is to hurt the one closest to you when you are hurt or angry or in pain, my boy. You might be real surprised how fragile your goodness is."

He turned and walked back to the camp leaving Luke stunned and grasping for the full meaning.

Was there hope for any of them?

Chapter Seventeen

*E*ric watched, teeth gritted together, as the judge left Luke's side. What a cozy little encounter they'd had. What were those two plotting? He turned away from his men and strode over toward the campfire. The time had come to take back control of this expedition. To rid himself of any and all dissenters who lay in the way of his plans.

The tall grasses irritated him, making his steps uneven and not as fluid of an approach as he would have liked. The irritation turned into a simmering burn as he watched the judge pull a piece of paper from his coat and glance at it. Had Luke given him that? What might it say?

He slowed—both his steps and his racing heart—took a long breath, and commanded his world to right in his mind. Calm returned. There was nothing he couldn't handle. Nothing he hadn't coped with to this point. This investigation presented a small hurdle, a hiccup in his plans. Nothing more.

He would succeed. This was only the first step to building the most powerful trading company in the West. What immense wealth and power he would wield when he'd accomplished that. And his wife? Well, she would come to heel and realize that if she only obeyed, he would give her everything a man could offer.

At the thought of Emma, his heart started pounding again. He paused, slowing down even more until he had those emotions, too, under control. His wife didn't know what she fought against. He wanted to give her the world. She was silly and clumsy and had to be taught. She didn't yet realize the cost of all he longed to give her. But she would. She would.

His steps brought him to Judge Littleton. He almost laughed looking at the man. He was anything but little. But getting on in age, never mind that he seemed to move and ride a horse like a much younger man. He would have a weakness. They all did.

Eric gestured to the note in the man's hands. "Something important?"

The judge stuffed the note back into his pocket. He looked over at Eric as if just discovering he stood there. "Yes. It is important."

Eric resisted the urge to snatch the note from the man's pocket. He had dealt with men like this before. Men with power and authority. They thought they were special. They thought they could beat him. But they never had. And they never would.

Eric nodded, feigning disinterest with a flick of his hand. "How long do you think you will continue on with us? The excursion"—he looked over at the judge's physique—"must be trying."

The judge patted his belly and laughed, a real, hearty laugh that made Eric's blood boil through his veins.

"No, not at all, son." The judge took a deep breath of the clear air, put his big hands on his waist, and rocked back and forth from heel to toe. "Nothing like getting out into this great country of ours to put a little spring in the step. You enjoying the journey?"

Eric didn't know how to answer such a question. He would enjoy it when he had several trading posts set up along Lewis and Clark's trail. He would enjoy the money and power of owning such a trading company. This was only an inconvenience.

Judge Littleton chuckled. "That was an unfair question, son."

Why did the blasted man always call everyone *son?* Rage hovered, prickling at the surface of Eric's skin . . . his face, his neck. He could feel the anger pulsing all the way through him.

I am not anyone's son.

"Unfair?" Eric questioned with just the right amount of amused condescension.

The judge took his hat off and slapped it against his thigh, looking out over the campfire toward the cabin on the barge. "It can't be easy . . ."

Eric followed his gaze toward the cabin, toward Emma.

Eric's voice dropped, low and quiet. "What are you trying to say?"

"Oh, just that it can't be easy being newly wedded, hauling your wife out here, having to do this now."

Eric turned toward the judge and pierced him with his most intense gaze, the kind that usually made men look away. "Let's dispense with the games. What do you want, and when will you leave? That is the only conversing I want from you."

The judge's face grew equally serious. He turned toward Eric and lifted a brow. "All right, then. I have a witness that says you paid Patrick Hardesty to kill Robert Frazer in cold blood for the journal. I also have evidence to back up the witness. And"—

the judge paused as everything in Eric stopped—"I have Hardesty's confession. He admitted to it and your part in it."

"That is a lie."

"That will be decided by a court of law."

Eric shook his head. He didn't believe him. He'd just spoken to Hardesty this morning, and the man had assured him that he'd said nothing to anyone.

"You're lying. I don't know why . . . maybe to support the intentions of Luke Bowen, whom you've grown so friendly with these last days? Or maybe something else, some jealousy. But you have been trying to destroy me since you joined this expedition."

The judge rocked back on his heels. His piercing eyes impaled Eric as his voice grew low and authoritative. "But that's not the real problem here, is it?"

Eric's breath grew tight in his chest. It was as if the man had just stripped him of every brick and stone, every piece of mortar that held him in one piece. This man knew something else.

"What are you referring to?" Eric had to gain some foothold, some grounding in this sinking sand.

"Why, sir. I'm referring to your father."

Eric's heart clogged his throat and he hated it. He hated himself and this man in front of him. A man so like his father. A man with such power . . .

No one would ever have such power over him again. Never again.

An image of his mother cowering down, her thin arms up over her head to protect her from the club his father wielded flashed across his mind. He'd rushed, screaming and crying and full of a frustrated agony. He'd pushed against his father, but he'd only been eleven years old! There was nothing he could do to stop him.

And then his father had turned the club on him and spent his pain on Eric's small frame, beating him black and blue. His mother had sobbed in the corner, blood coming from her head, her face turning a livid shade of blue-tinged purple. But they'd both lived through it. His father had worn himself out, and his mother had escaped more beatings for that night. He had saved her for one day, one evening, that one time.

As quick as a blink, another image followed that one.

Hiding in the barn as soon as he could walk again. He hid there all the next day, and then when darkness came, he'd started walking from their Ohio farm. He'd walked and walked and walked, across fields and streams, across farms where good fathers hired him for an odd job or two and the mothers looked at him with worry in their eyes, giving him food and clothing and a bed for as long as he liked.

They said he was a beautiful child. The most beautiful child they had ever seen. It had been a curse at his home, something his father chided him about. "You can't be mine . . . too pretty for a girl, even." But out on the open trail, it became something of a charm. It made people want to help him. It didn't take him long to realize the power of it. A smile, his round cap clutched in his hand, a waver in his voice. It melted just about every woman of the house. Then, for the men, a ducking of his head and a hearty "yes, sir," a mumbling when asked where his parents were, what he was doing out on his own. Usually the wife stopped the questioning and brought out some food.

After a while, he had come up with a story, something about his folks dying and leaving him alone. About his being small for his age, he convinced them he was sixteen, about the scars on his back that time he'd been caught without a shirt. He became very, very good at making people love him.

He shook himself from his recollections and looked at the judge. He'd become sloppy, he realized with sudden clarity. Where was his legendary charm? His profound likability? Why did this man, of all men, make him feel so out of control?

He needed time . . . time to figure this man out. He needed to remember what he was and how good he could be at it. He halted the judge's words with a lifted hand. "Stop."

The judge paused. "Not ready yet? To hear the truth?"

"I just wouldn't want you to say something you regret." Eric looked the man dead in the eye and smiled. "How about some dinner? In the cabin? Emma would love to see you again."

The judge stared back, clearly not flattered in the least by Eric's magnanimous gesture. "All right, son. If that's the way you want this to go. I'll give you an evening."

Eric nodded and touched the brim of his hat, then turned to go.

He could feel the judge's gaze on his neck like the hottest ray of the sun, like a target, like a mark of the guilty.

A single bead of sweat rolled down Eric's neck and down the center of his back.

He couldn't remember the last time that had happened.

Chapter Eighteen

*E*mma jerked upright as the door to the cabin swung open. It had become a common trait of hers, this startle reflex. She looked down at the coverlet on the bed and hurried to smooth out the invisible wrinkles, hating the blanket, hating Eric, hating herself and what she had become.

They had been on this particular bank for two days now, and everyone wondered when and if they would continue on their journey. She knew better. She knew Eric had something going on that no one knew about. The two becoming one . . . it went both ways. She sensed he had a plan.

She turned from the tidying up as her husband entered the room. Her skirts felt wrinkled and dirty even though she knew they were clean and straight. She smoothed them down and wondered if she had a hair out of place. As she brushed back the silken strands into the knot at her nape, she glanced about the room to see if anything else seemed untidy. "Hello, Eric."

He didn't answer her, just moved over and brushed his knuckles against her jawline. She concentrated on a point on the wall above his shoulder so as not to flinch.

"Judge Littleton is coming to dinner. Put on something pretty, my dear. Your best gown. And for goodness sake, Emma, clean this cabin. I will have a larger table moved in"—he turned and pointed—"there."

She glanced around the immaculate cabin. What was she to change? Nothing was dirty or out of place. She turned her attention back to her husband's disapproving face. Oh, how she'd dreamed of touching that face. Of letting her fingers trail along that straight jaw, caress those beautiful lips. But she never got the chance.

A stab of grief shot through her.

Rallying from her despair, she made do with what she had. Acting the devoted wife. "The judge is coming? That will be nice." Eric had some plan for this secluded dinner, but she had no choice but to go along with it. "Shall I cook something?"

They both knew she wouldn't be allowed to cook, especially with the kind of food they had to work with on the frontier, but she didn't know what else to offer.

He laughed—an unpleasant, mocking sound that reverberated across the room. "I'll have Billy cook us something special. You just look pretty. Entertain the man with the charm I knew you had when I married you."

Charm? No one who knew her would ever call her charming. Shy maybe, a bit clumsy. Pretty, she'd been called on occasion. Someone else had remarked upon her as dignified. Pale was certainly accurate, with her ivory skin and blonde hair. Emma knew if not for her blue eyes, she would fade into the background of any setting. Charming, though, she most certainly was not.

Which brought the old question to mind. She hesitated, not wanting to risk Eric losing his temper. He noticed her mood though. He always seemed to read her down into her very soul.

"What is it? You only have to dress the part. You can *act* the part of my wife, can't you?"

He thought her acting? Well, yes, now. But not at first. Everything she did, every effort she expended . . . she'd tried so hard to make him happy. She knew better now. He would never be happy. She laughed a little and shrugged one shoulder. "I was wondering why you married me, Eric. You could have had any woman you wanted."

Eric's boots rang across the wood planks as he came over to her and took her face in his hands. He grasped the sides of her head in a rough caress that delved into her hair. "How can you ask such a thing—again?"

Emma stared up into his wide blue eyes. "How can I not? You seem to despise me."

Eric leaned down and kissed her forehead, then squeezed her head a little harder beneath his palms. "Of course I don't despise you. Do you think I would choose anyone but the best? You don't know, do you?"

"Know what?" She looked up into his face and dared to allow her need to hear the answer, to unlock the puzzle, flash across her face. She didn't need—or even want—to hear him proclaim his undying love for her. She didn't need compliments. She wanted answers, clues, reasons she was here. *Something* to explain what had happened to her.

Eric chuckled. "I've been remiss, I suppose. I should have told you."

She looked up, afraid but determined not to show it; she swallowed hard and did not blink. "Yes?"

"When you look at a man, at me, I feel"—she inhaled and then held it deep in her lungs—"I feel whole."

She shook her head. How could she make any man feel whole? There wasn't anything in her, any great strength or faith. He must be making it up, trying to pacify her. No one who felt whole would treat her the way her husband treated her, would he?

He stepped away and turned his back on her. "I'll see to the dinner preparations and direct a table and three chairs to be set up. Light some candles, my dear. You will see. The judge will respond to you as every man who comes into contact with you does. You make men feel like men."

After he left, she sagged into a chair and leaned her head into her hands, her elbows braced on the small, spindly desk. What if she failed tonight? What if Judge Littleton found her . . . ordinary?

What would Eric do to her then?

The candles were lit, their soft, flickering glow a counterpoint to the thudding of Emma's heart as she opened the door to Judge Littleton.

He'd come with flowers. Wildflowers of yellow and tiny blue petals that he thrust out toward her as he tipped his hat.

"Oh, my!" Emma didn't try to hide her surprise and delight. The time and effort to find them along the muddy bank and tall grassy area of their camp wasn't lost on her. "Thank you, sir."

"Not a'tall. Not a'tall," he repeated as he walked into the room. She smiled, trying her best to put him at ease.

"Please, sit down." She gestured to the candlelit table. "Eric has gone for our meal and should be back soon." She buried her nose in the bouquet and then turned to find something to put them in. Seeing nothing but the pitcher of water that they used to wash their hands, she stuffed the green stems in and carried the blue pottery over to the table, arranging the candles so that the happy bouquet fit in the center.

"Would you like some tea?" A nervous smile hovered on her lips. Had he read her note? Did he know the answers to his questions?

"That would be nice." The judge paused, seeming to take in his surroundings in an instant—the tidy cabin, their belongings neatly stored, the tablecloth and dishes set out. "I see Eric has done his best to make you comfortable on such a trip."

Emma paused. Comfortable? How was she to answer to such a statement? She started to nod, then decided against it. This man had the authority to make something else of her life. But what could she say?

Only the truth. "Appearances aren't always what they seem, sir."

The judge's face turned solemn as he looked down at his empty plate. "No. I suppose not." He looked up at her. "Are you unhappy, Emma?"

A bark of laughter escaped her throat. She had never thought to be happy. Not every day, not every week even, but occasionally. Yes, occasionally. She lifted her face toward his and allowed her ravished heart to reach her eyes, reach the tight skin around her eyes and mouth, reach the stiffness of her throat and then her shoulders and then her stance. She swallowed, nearing tears but commanding them away. "I'm stronger than I ever thought to be." She smiled and lifted her chin. "I suppose I've grown up, and there is something worthy in that, I think."

The judge nodded, but his mouth was set in a grim line. "Emma, there is nothing in the law that prohibits a man from, well, hurting his wife, physically or otherwise. Now, if he has committed adultery, then we might have something. We would have to prove it, of course, and you would be left with nothing. But you would be free and might remarry one day."

Emma looked down feeling the flush of heat reach her cheeks at such open talk. "No. He has never done anything like that."

"You certain about that, ma'am?"

Emma peeked up at him and then looked back at the floor. "Yes. I'm sure."

"Well, then. The only other reason I've heard of that gives a woman the right to divorce her husband is if he has abandoned her for a great length of time. Years. And those cases are very rare."

Emma stared at the judge, shocked into momentary silence. She let the judge's words sink in—and suddenly the reason Eric demanded she go on this trip was very, very clear. "There is nothing I can do."

At her low whisper the judge remained silent for a moment. "If it's beyond bearing, well, ma'am, some women run away. You couldn't take anything with you so as not to be accused of stealing. It would require a great deal of faith, I'd imagine."

Emma looked up with huge eyes. "Don't you think I have thought of that? I've lain awake after . . . afterward and thought of nothing else for hours. But I know my husband, sir. He would come after me. He would find me. He would never let me humiliate him that way."

"That may be true, but don't forget your Father in heaven. He's watching you, watching over you though it doesn't seem much like that right now. And He promises He won't leave us nor forsake us. You might have to be brave, Emma, but I'm thinking an opportunity—a way—is being made for you. When it happens, you're going to have to act . . . act in faith."

"What is faith?"

"Faith is believing in something that seems impossible, like Eric not finding you if you ran away. See, God knows everything. And He's a lick smarter than even your husband. Why, God could keep you hidden from him for the rest of your life if He had a mind to. Or there might be some other way God has for you to get free of this, some way we haven't even thought of, 'cause we can't think like Him, you see. We see what we think we know. God sees all the possibilities of every situation and has a million creative ways to go about helping you. Our job is to keep watching, praying, and sometimes I like to call out to God and remind Him that I am still waitin' on an answer. Oh, He knows, but it just makes me feel better. Emma, you got to find your way of looking to God and then believe with all your heart that He has a plan for you, a plan that is good."

Bursts of hope and a hundred questions flooded Emma's heart and mind. She opened her mouth, but a sound from the door handle had them both turning toward it and stilled their conversation. Eric entered with two trays laden with dishes of steaming food.

"Excellent." Eric gave them his blessing as he walked toward the table and deposited the dishes. "I hoped you had arrived. The food is hot."

Emma swallowed back her questions and went forward to help serve, but Eric shook his head. "No, dear. Sit down and allow me."

Emma shot the judge a glance and then sat at the side; Eric and Judge Littleton sat at the head and foot of the table.

"I've pulled from deep within the food stores for this feast," Eric said with a flash of white teeth to them both. "No venison tonight. We have beef, biscuits, potatoes and carrots, some corn pone that has been sweetened with real sugar, and"—he paused for effect and then took the cover off a dish—"pie for dessert."

Emma smiled, happy to be able to give the judge such a feast. "It's almost like Christmas."

Eric looked at her, an intense gladness in his eyes, like he loved her, like he was having a wonderful, normal time that any couple would have while entertaining an honored guest. "Just like Christmas." He turned toward the judge and smiled, "Is she not beautiful when she's delighted?"

Judge Littleton cast an amused gaze in her direction. In a gentle voice of a father, he agreed, "She is quite something when she smiles."

Emma looked down, tears close.

Eric took the judge's plate and, with careful precision, as if choosing the best parts of the beef and potatoes, dished out a portion. He portioned out a small amount for Emma, then passed her the dish with a small but confident smile.

Emma took the plate, fighting the nervous concern filling her. Eric should be nervous. Every movement should be abrupt, tense. If Eric had the slightest inkling that she'd told the killer's name . . . that she'd given away his part in the murder . . . he should be as he was when most threatened. Yet he seemed calm. He seemed in perfect control.

A terrifying thought, indeed.

"Who will say the grace?" Judge Littleton's question interrupted her thoughts.

Emma looked at the judge, eyes wide, and then guilt washed over her at her response to his question. She had always said grace at her parents' home. It might have been a mindless routine. It might have been a mere formality, but she realized in that moment, she missed it. Eric never said grace—just stared overlong at her waistline and then her plate before plunging in.

"Please"—Emma cut in before Eric could make a comment—"Judge Littleton, would you do us the honor?"

"Of course, Emma." He bowed his head and stretched out his hands to each of them. Right before she closed her eyes, she saw his graying head and wondered about his life. What had brought him to this moment with them? She bowed her head and clasped hands with Eric on one side, Judge Littleton on the other.

"Our heavenly Father," he began in a deep baritone voice, "we give thanks for this food and ask Your blessing upon it. We give thanks for our very lives. You. The giver of life, life eternal, have rescued us from death. Not death in this life but a death that lasts forever. You." He paused, and Emma had the sense there was some still, powerful presence in the room with them. Her chest wanted to burst with a resounding *yes,* but she didn't let it. She gave a small nod of agreement instead.

"You." He repeated the word as if it were a name. "You are the hope of our salvation."

"Amen." Eric's tone had the effect of a heavy stone hefted into a peaceful pool. Her husband's cold, snide tone crashed into her and reached out, annihilating the sense she'd had of that wonderful, pure presence. All she could do was press her knees tight together and try to restrain the sobs struggling to break free.

She would go on as always.

She would pretend.

Eric made small talk as they began eating. He asked about the judge's life, his journey into law, his cases.

Judge Littleton answered all Eric's questions with candor and humor. He was the perfect guest, causing Emma to laugh out loud and then quiet and try to discern his every meaning behind his words. But still she feared for him. She wasn't sure that he understood Eric's ability to overpower anyone he came into contact with. Had anyone?

Halfway through their meal, the judge paused. His face paled and he looked toward her. "Some more water, please, ma'am?"

She rushed to the water pitcher. Was he choking? He didn't sound like it, but the look on his face was so . . . odd. A spark of panic sprang to life and grew within her. She poured the water into his cup and thrust it out toward him.

His face went from the color of chalk to bright red.

"Please, Judge, drink this. Are you all right?"

The judge downed the water, only to choke on it and go into a coughing fit. Emma looked from the judge's mottled face to her husband's.

Eric sat very still. Watching. Waiting.

The spark exploded into a raging fire. "What have you *done?* Eric! Help him!"

Eric's gaze swung to hers and locked on. The truth was easy to read in his stunningly smug features. He was responsible.

Emma turned toward the judge and began beating him on the back. "Cough it up, sir. Vomit it up!" She beat as hard as her fist would allow.

The judge turned a strangled expression on her. He reached for her, tried to say something, and then fell from his chair to the floor, wheezing and gasping. Emma threw herself to the floor beside him.

"No! Not you!" Her gaze shot to her husband and then back toward the dying man. She took the judge by the shoulders. "I'm sorry. I don't know what to do."

He suddenly went still.

"No . . ." She stared into the judge's empty, glazed eyes. "No, please sir, *no.*" Her voice was tiny against the cold silence of the room. She held onto the judge's broad shoulders as he shuddered against the floor of the cabin.

Emma leaned toward him and sobbed into the man's neck as he heaved his last words into her ear.

"Emmanuel. Remember. God . . . with . . . you."

Emma screamed then, rocking back and forth, the judge's head pulled toward her chest. "No!"

She looked up into the blank, beautiful, stone-solid eyes of her husband. "What have you done?"

Eric looked like he'd conquered the world.

But Emma, for the first time, looked at the monster that was her husband and knew.

She would conquer him.

Chapter Nineteen

A clanking sound from the judge's body startled her. Eric remained rooted, strong and confident, on his chair. He watched her, gloating. As if there wasn't a thing in the world she could do.

But there was. She saw it.

Her chance.

Pretending to lean over the judge in grief—though, indeed, grief screamed real in her heart—she reached for it. She grasped her fingers around the cold, hard metal of the judge's loaded pistol.

It slipped from his holster as easy as butter. It was heavier than she'd thought, but she must not let it tremble. She raised the weapon and swung the barrel toward her husband's face.

His lips pressed together; his eyes hardened like diamonds. "Emma, don't be foolish. Put that down. You are overwrought. Stop this nonsense right now."

A laugh-cry escaped her throat. She cocked the gun. "Do you think so? Do you think I couldn't do it?"

"I *know* so. Emma, stop this. Everything will be all right."

She laughed outright then. *"Now?* Now will it be all right, all perfect? What of the next time you are threatened? What of minutes from now when they find his body? You are a fool, Eric." She took a slow side step, intent on keeping the gun trained toward her husband's chest.

"You wouldn't know how to shoot it even if you could. Now stop this. I will make everything right."

Emma moved a step closer, her voice low and sure. "I know how to shoot a gun, Eric." She jutted out her chin and shook her head a little, a confident smile rising in secretive knowledge to her lips. "Maybe you don't know me as well as you think. Maybe there are things you haven't yet discovered about me. Such as a pastime I enjoyed a few years back. My father took me. We shot at targets. I became good at it. Very good."

It wasn't true. She had never held a gun before. But if she needed to, she could shoot him. And she would. "Now listen to me, *my dear*"—her tone dripped poison, just as he had said the phrase to her so many times before. She took a step closer, raised the heavy metal with outstretched arms and, shutting one eye as she'd seen men do, she trained the sights of the pistol at his chest.

It felt powerful.

God help me . . .

It felt so powerful.

Her throat tightened, but she forced the words out. Words she hadn't even known she'd dreamed of saying to him until they broke free. "Stay right where you are. Don't move for a very long time. Don't follow me." Emma edged toward a pack that she had kept ready with a few clothes, a few supplies, some food and water, just in case. She lifted up the bag, hefted it onto her shoulder, and edged toward the door.

"Don't come for me, Eric. Don't follow me. If you do"—she focused the gun back on his chest—"I will kill you."

"You could never shoot me."

Emma kept the gun trained on his chest. "I think I could. I think I could right now. Just move toward me, Eric. Make it easy for me. Make it about defending myself."

He leaned forward just a bit, as if he would stand.

The gun shook in her hand. "I dare you. Please."

"Emma, stop this nonsense. Stop it right now!"

She stood at the door . . . at the threshold of her new life. "I'm going to tell you something, Eric. And I want you to try and really hear me. You will never touch me again. If you try, I will kill you." She paused and looked at the gun. "And if I fail"—she lifted the gun to her own head.

Eric went very still. He looked at her as if he'd never seen her before.

"You will never touch me again, Eric. Do you understand?" She turned the door handle and took that first step out the door—

Eric lunged toward her!

She pulled the trigger. The sound reverberated against the building. Eric fell to the floor, blood seeping from his shoulder. He started to rise.

"No." She shook her head at him like all the times she had wanted to say that one word. *"No!"*

Get out! The cry echoed in her mind. To where she didn't know. How, she couldn't fathom. But she believed the chance the judge had told her to watch for had appeared.

And she was taking it.

Luke heard shouts coming from the barge and turned from the campfire to run toward the riverbank. The crack of a gunshot jolted shock through him. He broke through a stand of trees just in time to see Emma burst from the cabin. She didn't even see him. He watched, startled energy pulsing through him, as she ran across the deck, a smoking pistol in her hand. She leapt over the railing of the barge. His mouth fell open as she plunged into the shallow water of the shore, her skirts gathered up in one fist, the pistol raised high in her other.

What had happened?

His mind grappled, trying to understand what he saw as he ran the short distance to her side. He reached her just as she set foot upon the bank.

"Emma, wait!" He grasped her shoulder and turned her toward him. "Where are you going?"

She shook her head and gave him a blank stare. "I am leaving."

"Leaving? Where?"

"Leaving him." She pulled out of Luke's grasp, turned, and ran toward the distant, rolling prairie land that looked to have no end.

Luke watched her retreating back for a long moment and then snapped into action. He dashed toward his tent, gathered up his belongings: his sleeping roll, the maps, his journal, the shredded Bible, his hidden food stores, his money. Then he exited the tent and grasped hold of it too. He tore the canvas from its stakes sunk in the fine, sandy earth and dragged it after him as he ran to catch up with Emma.

He expected a shot in the back at any moment. He saw the men of the excursion in a blur as he raced by them. They stood silent, unmoving, and he realized that they, at least, would not stop them.

He raced up a slight hill as far as his provisions would allow. He knew he should dump the tent. He knew he should unburden himself so that they might escape before Eric came after them. But they would not get very far in this land without provisions. They would need food and shelter to survive. So he hoisted the heavy tent onto his shoulder and dragged the rest behind him. Like an anchor against a strong current, his burden dragged him down to a slow moving jog.

The grasses grabbed at the tent, making a chopping movement of his gait. He heard shouts, heard Eric's voice in the distance. A bellow that echoed behind him. And Emma? She grew further and further ahead of him.

"I will supply all of your needs, according to My riches in glory."

He stopped and turned, at first not recognizing the voice. He paused, turned round and round in the twilight of an open, grassy prairie. Then he stopped cold. The voice . . .

God?

He brought his hand to his forehead, a brief, fleeting movement before he dropped to his knees. He didn't believe it at first. But he'd heard it.

He had heard the voice of God.

Loud and yet quiet at the same time, it reverberated inside his chest. It turned him, sudden and sure, inside out.

God had talked to him!

His chest heaved with the meaning of it. He stood and looked toward the sky. He looked up and then back and saw the men of the campsite rallying under their leader's direction.

But he wasn't afraid. He turned and saw Emma's swishing skirts in the distance, on a rise, almost out of sight. Tears clogged his throat.

But he wasn't afraid!

Luke looked toward the heavens. "What do You want me to do?"

The question exploded from his core into the glory of a fiery red sunset. The sky brightened. He watched as the hues of pink and red and orange grew deeper and throbbed against a green-gray horizon. To the West. Westward. His heart's cry.

Luke looked down at the paltry provisions he'd gathered. He saw them, a few day's provisions and a ragged tent, grasped in his hands and slung across his shoulder. A laugh escaped his throat. It was caught up into the wind where it whistled away into nothing.

It *was* nothing.

He was nothing.

Only God could save them from this darkness. This evil.

With an abrupt movement, he dropped everything he held dear except the Bible, everything that the world's wisdom said they needed to make it one more day.

And then he ran.

After Emma.

Chapter Twenty

She was limping. The pack she had taken with her dragged on the ground behind her, bumping up and down over the mounds of half-flattened grass. Energy filled Luke as he raced toward her. Within seconds he was at her side, scooping her up into his arms, taking the pack from her hand and slinging it over his shoulder.

She gasped when he lifted her from the ground but swung her arms up and around his neck, gazing at him with wide eyes. "You came."

Her face was mere inches across from his, but he didn't look down into those wide blue eyes. No. He set his sights toward the western horizon. *Where now, God? What now?*

He knew if he looked at her he would falter. He would think of the impossibility of what they were doing and the fear of such failure would ruin him. He knew he could not look to the right or the left. He had to keep walking.

A gentle breeze blew into their faces, blowing his hair back, sending hers fluttering against his arm and then wrapping around his back and waist, tying them together more than his arms holding her close against his chest.

She was light. Lighter than she should have been. With the voluminous dresses she wore, he hadn't realized she'd lost so much weight, but he could feel the difference from the time he carried her in St. Louis.

She said nothing more, just leaned against his shoulder and gave in. As the mantle of protector settled over him, he knew they were connected. Not in a physical way but on some level he didn't even understand. Couldn't explain. He only knew he would follow that voice within and trust that God had everything figured out.

A small grouping of trees stood in the distance. The twilight hovered over the leaves, giving the sense of a washed-out world of reds and oranges. He turned toward the grove, silent but determined. He walked quickly and sure now, his breathing easy but fast against her hair. He stopped when they were under the cover of trees, big and small, their leafy roof a comfort.

He set her feet down, a gentle sliding movement of letting her go. "We will stop here a bit, rest, and get our bearings." He slung down the pack, realizing for the first time how heavy it was. "What do you have in there?"

She shrugged. "Some food and water. There wasn't time for anything else."

Luke nodded and reached into the pack. He pulled out a water canteen, uncorked it, and held it out to her. She shook her head. "I'm not thirsty yet. You've been running. You drink."

Luke took a small pull from the neck and then eased the cork back into place. Truth be known, he wasn't very thirsty either.

"Why did you come? You know they will chase us." Emma's face was pale in the last rays of twilight as she looked up at him. He gazed into those eyes and fought the emotions washing over him. Heart-pounding, head-spinning, hands-sweating, misery-ecstasy.

Why had he come? Such a simple question, so simple it made him admit the truth.

He loved her.

He was in love with her.

He wanted to spend the rest of his days on Earth with her.

And he could admit none of it. She was not his. Could not be his. Not so long as she and Eric were married. And so he would fight against those feelings. He would simply be what God called him to be: her protector.

For as long as she needed him.

"You needed me."

Emma blinked. She took a step back and then another. From out of nowhere came a pistol. She must have had a tight grip on it this entire time. She raised it toward Luke's chest.

"I don't need you or any man."

Luke didn't spare a glance at the pistol; he stared into Emma's eyes. "All right, then." He looked down at his hands, watched them open and close as if grasping something as frail and invisible as her heart. He looked back up into her eyes and allowed a self-derisive smile. "Maybe I need you."

The words stopped her. She turned her face to one side, pressed her lips together tight and trembling. The gun lowered, inch by inch, to the front of her dress. Both of her hands clasped together, still tight around the handle.

"If you come with me, Eric will kill you too. I only wounded him." She looked down at the gun again and then back up at his face, her lips pursed. "You shouldn't try to save me."

"So you are running toward your death? Is that what you want?"

She swallowed and looked down at the moss green earth at their feet. "At this moment I am free." A small laugh escaped her. She lifted the gun to her chest and cradled it, stroking the shining metal. Her voice dropped to a whisper. "I will never go back. I will never go back to any man."

Pain pierced Luke's heart, a knife-stab of grief, tearing, rending. But he understood. If Eric ever tried to take her back, she would use the gun on him and, if that failed, on herself. She would never be Eric's wife again.

Or possibly any man's.

That truth struck so deep, he couldn't breathe for a moment. But then the memory of the voice echoed in his mind, setting him aright. He mustn't look at what was happening before his eyes. God had a purpose he didn't fully know or comprehend. And a purpose for Luke in this story unfolding around him. That was what he must focus on.

God's will and purpose.

So, God . . . what now?

The answer flooded him, body and soul. It lifted him from what man's eyes saw to what God saw. "It's a sin, you know."

Those glittering eyes fastened on him. "What is?"

"You . . . taking comfort in that gun. Thinking you could kill yourself before ever allowing him to touch you again."

She shook her head, a brief denial, not wanting to see the truth of his words. But he had to help her understand. Help her gain God's eyes. "God will provide another way out for you, Emma. *He* will save you."

"That's what the judge said . . . and that's why, when this chance to run came, I took it. But I'll never go back. I can't face going back to him. Ever."

Luke held out his hand. "Give me the gun, Emma. Give me your false hope."

She tightened her grasp and drew it close to her chest, almost like a long-lost love she had recently found again. "I can't." Tears reached her eyes. She blinked, and two round teardrops slipped down her cheeks.

In the fading twilight, with the wind whistling all around them, she stared, her blue eyes as hard and glittering as crystal, into his eyes, and shook her head back and forth. "You don't understand. I *need* it." A sob broke from her throat. "I have to have it."

He wanted to gather her up into his arms. He wanted to say that everything would be all right. But he didn't know that. All he knew was that they were on a journey together, and that their only hope of survival was in hearing His voice.

He kept his hand outstretched. Waited. "Trust me." He caught himself then. That wasn't right. "No, don't trust me."

Her eyes flew to his face.

"Emma, trust God."

Her face tightened. Time revolved around them, the light growing darker by the minute. It was strange. As if he could hear the sweet-toned church bell from his childhood home, ringing in the distance to herald some occasion, be it a wedding or a birth or a . . . funeral.

He watched in the stillness as she looked down at the shiny object clutched to her chest. He held his breath as she held it out a little and looked at it. He saw in the turmoil on her features all that it meant to her and felt his heart leap when, with a sudden movement, she thrust the weapon out to him.

Luke took the gun, relief and gratitude filling him as he grasped it, then stilled at her low voice.

"He killed the judge, you know. Eric poisoned him at my table."

Shock rendered Luke mute. He lowered the gun, tucked it into the back waistband of his pants, saying nothing.

"I held him as he died."

Luke just stared at her, letting the pain in his eyes tell her how sorry he was. How he wished he could have done something.

"The judge's body . . . it shook, spasmodic in my arms. He couldn't get his breath. Eric just sat there and watched. He was so confident. So sure. He doesn't think anything can hurt him. And Luke, nothing can but a bullet." She pointed to the gun he'd tucked away. "A bullet from that gun."

Her despair loosed his tongue at last. "As much as I would like to use that gun on your husband, Emma, we can't. The Lord will avenge Judge Littleton."

"Why didn't God stop Eric if He is so able to take care of us?"

As those tragic, troubled eyes looked into Luke's face, a moment of doubt swirled through him. Why *hadn't* God intervened? The judge was good. Better than any of them. Surely God would protect a man like that. And who was Luke to think he had heard the voice of God? Why would God allow so fine a man as the judge to be murdered and then speak to one such as he?

A sudden gust of wind blew right at them. It gusted so strong that Emma clung to him and he to her. Sensations washed over him—her arms wrapped around his waist; the cold, hard steel of the gun against his back; and the Voice, a resonant echo inside his chest.

I will make a way for the righteous. I will not fail the upright of heart. I will not fail you of heavy laden burdens. I will remember you. I will carry you. I will save. I will save.

"We will keep moving." Luke pulled Emma from his chest. His voice was soft and reassuring as he grasped her shoulders in a tight grip and looked directly into her eyes.

His soul was restored to peace. His spirit revived. "Emma. Trust me. We will follow God together."

Chapter Twenty-One

*E*ric lay bleeding on the floor, fighting dizziness, as soldiers burst into the room. They stopped just over the threshold, their gazes searching the room. Lieutenant Arthur rushed to the judge's side while Lieutenant Eisler turned toward Eric.

"What happened?" He demanded, squatting beside Eric, taking in his bleeding shoulder.

"Emma . . ." Eric gasped out. "She shot me."

The man's eyes widened. "Your wife shot you?"

Before Eric could answer, Lieutenant Arthur yelled out, "John, come quick! The judge isn't breathing."

Lieutenant Eisler rushed to the judge's side. Eric scooted a little to one side, wincing as he moved, so that he could see what was happening. There were so many wonderful ways he could manipulate the situation to his advantage. One of the soldiers waved his hand in front of the judge's mouth to check for breath.

"I see no wound," Lieutenant Arthur murmured. He stood and shot Eric an accusatory glare. "What happened to the judge?"

Eric shrugged with his good shoulder. "I don't know. During dinner he began to wheeze, his face turned red. I think he was choking. Before I could do anything, he fell off his chair to the floor."

The two lieutenants stared at each other. "What do we do?" Lieutenant Arthur asked in a low voice. "He's dead, isn't he?"

Eisler nodded and swung back toward Eric. "We have to question Mr. and Mrs. Montclaire. But first we have to get Mr. Montclaire some medical help."

The other soldier nodded. "I will round up some men to go after Mrs. Montclaire."

"Good. I'll see to Mr. Montclaire—probably have to take the bullet out myself as Mr. Bowen did most of the doctoring. Now it seems he's gone off chasing after Mrs. Montclaire."

Lieutenant Arthur's voice lowered even more. "You think Mrs. Montclaire is behind this? You think she wanted out of the marriage that bad?"

The other man shook his head. "It's hard to believe it of her. She didn't seem the type. And then there is Mr. Bowen; he will have to be questioned too. You make sure to bring him back."

"What about the judge?" Lieutenant Arthur looked down toward the still body. Eric could just make out what Eisler replied—something about taking him back to St. Louis, and then a remark about length of the trip, rot and stench, and burying him here instead.

They both stood and came toward Eric. He would have liked to have taken charge of the situation, but he couldn't move his head without the room spinning. It was only a shoulder wound, shouldn't be too serious, but he had never been shot before, and the pain and blood loss made his mind reel. In a daze he realized the men were hauling him up. A black fuzziness loomed at the edges of his vision as they carried him to the bed. When they moved his dangling arm to his side, the pain grew so intense he found no matter how hard he tried to concentrate it away, the blackness engulfed him.

The next morning found that fall had given up its grasp on the land to a greater force of breath-robbing wind, a portent of coming ice and snow. As Luke and Emma woke from their few hours of sleep, frost covered the tall grasses. When they walked, their breath made a fog against their faces.

"In the journal"—Luke paused, gauging Emma's stride and making his steps even with hers—"Frazer wrote about a post set up somewhere near here. I think it's coming up soon."

"Do you think it's still there?"

Luke looked toward the rise of a hill. "Something should still be there."

Emma blew on her hands. If only he could give her some mittens. "We need to find some sort of shelter."

"Why do you think they haven't found us yet?" Emma voiced the question he knew they'd both been pondering.

Luke shook his head. "Either God has a protective shield around us, or maybe the whole expedition has been stymied due to the judge's death. I pray it's one of those two. Otherwise they're still coming and can't be far behind on the river."

"They'll catch up with us eventually, won't they?"

"Yes. If we could move further from the river, we could lose them, but that's too risky. Nobody knows the land out there. And nobody would be there to help. We'd be living in the wilderness with the wild animals, one gun, and only a couple more days' worth of food. No"—Luke slapped his hat back on his head—"we have to stay near the river."

It was fascinating. Emma seemed to have lost her fear of Eric. And now, whenever Luke talked, she listened with an intense and curious gaze. As a result he also found himself looking at the land in a new way, pointing it out to her when something of interest caught his eye. For the first time in his life, he told someone else his thoughts. It was strange and comforting at the same time.

Sometimes, when he pointed out a bird or a flower, described the textures he saw, the way it moved and how he would capture the feel that it was moving and alive, well, those were times he wished he could draw for her. But there was no paper, no ink and quill—nothing beyond the little food they had on his back and the gun in his belt. And his voice. He found a profound contentment well within him as he described to her how he saw the world.

An hour later they were sitting on a ridge overlooking the river. It was covered with trees and high up. Safe.

Emma pointed to a tree on the other side of the river that bent at an angle over the water. Its leaves drooped from white barked branches. She sat close to him and looked up at him with expectation. "Mr. Bowen, how would you draw that?"

Luke laughed. "I think it's about time you called me Luke, don't you?"

Emma nodded. "All right. But only if you call me Emma."

Luke thought about it for a moment. Calling her Emma made her feel closer, and he wasn't sure that was a good idea, but it seems too distant and chilly to keep calling her Mrs. Montclaire. "All right then, Emma." He nodded toward the tree in question.

"That's a cottonwood. Nothing special." But then he paused and studied it. He pointed to the roots. "Do you see how the roots are coming up on the surface? How the bank has washed away and left some of them bare?"

Emma nodded.

That one glance at her. It only took that one second in time for his mind to memorize every detail: the small smile on her nearly closed lips, white teeth showing from behind the small gap of her pink lips, the way the sun and wind had kissed a rosy glow onto her pale cheeks and nose, the loosened strands of wheat-colored hair framing intelligent eyes—blue flecked with gray. And then there was the way she looked at him, hanging on his words, waiting for him to explain the mysteries of the world to her.

And she didn't know! She didn't have any idea what that warm smile in her eyes did to his insides.

Once again he loved and hated his gift.

He cleared his throat and gestured toward the tree. "That is where I would start. Drawing those roots. I would think about how long they've been there and how long they might yet last. See the different colors of the bark?"

"Yes, there are many different colors. Are they weakened? Being exposed like that?"

"Yes, they're weakening." Luke pointed up to the tops of the branches. "See the leaves?"

Emma nodded.

"Now see the leaves of the trees near them?" His hand gestured toward the stronger trees.

Emma paused and then said in a voice of growing wonder. "The leaves are smaller, though the tree itself seems as big as the others."

"Yes. Exactly." Luke grinned at her. "The other trees are getting more from the soil, through the roots, so their leaves are bigger and healthier." He pointed toward the tree in question. "That tree is failing. It's hanging on. But it's failing because the roots are exposed, shrinking. It won't be too long before the whole thing falls into the river."

"As the river washes away the banks, little by little." Emma replied, her brows pulled together in thought. "It gives life and it takes life away."

Luke nodded. "Yes. That is what I would try to capture the feel of in a drawing."

Emma turned toward Luke. Her gaze roved his face like a sunlit kiss, like a caressing hand, like his all-seeing glance that brought him up short and naked and happy. "I think people are like that."

He stared into her sky-blue eyes, letting his silence encourage her thoughts.

"Some are just hanging on, hoping life won't sweep them away."

"Is that how you feel?"

Emma nodded. "Until you came into my life. You are like . . ." She looked up, her eyes squinting into the sun. "You are like a great rope around that tree, holding it, hauling it back up so that it's straight. But"—she touched his arm with feather-light fingers. "I'm afraid that I am on the bank that is washing away, and it will take too much to pull me up. I'm afraid the roots are still eroding. That unless I have a full transplant to some other place, some place far, far from such a river, I am only being given a reprieve."

Her words cut him, delved in, and showed him her place and his. He had no answer for her.

She stood and nodded. "Let's find this trading post."

Her voice sounded brisk with forced cheerfulness, and that briskness tore through his heart. He finally realized how it had been for her—every day, another piece of her dropping, falling, as life seeped away. That kind of person couldn't love anything. Anyone. She'd just been waiting to succumb to the river's flow.

That she'd been reduced to such a place tore at his soul. *Almighty God, have mercy on this woman.*

They hiked back down to the weed-clogged path that strained their strength. Most times Luke led, but sometimes Emma took the fore. From time to time they stopped to rest a moment, take a drink from the canteen they shared, and listen for sounds of pursuit. Then they moved onward . . . forward . . . west.

The sun sank and the cold settled in. They had nothing but a pack with dwindling food, a river full of muddy water to drink, and God. Luke attempted to build a lean-to to break the sharp edge of wind while Emma gathered firewood.

They sat around the small fire, eating the last of their provisions.

Luke savored his final bite, then sighed. "I'll have to hunt tomorrow. We need fresh meat."

Emma looked up at him, chewing the last of the dried venison and nodded. "That would be good."

They sat in silence, contemplating their next move. Finally she looked up at him. "Do you think we're close? To the post, I mean?"

"It's hard to say. The journal mentioned it but not the exact location."

"You don't think we've missed it? Could we have passed it by and not known?"

Luke didn't want to say it, but he wondered the same thing. "Might be, but I don't think so."

Emma nodded and took a deep breath. "Well. Time for some sleep then." She nodded once and then rose. He watched as she made her way to the lean-to that had no bed, no blanket, no comfort. He turned away and heard her curl up on the leafy bed of spruce boughs he'd cut for her. For a moment he could not stop the images that came, thoughts of her at home in Kentucky. The two of them together in their own warm, comfortable home . . .

Then, steeling his resolve, he pushed the images aside. Such thoughts were not for him. Not now.

Maybe not ever.

Chapter Twenty-Two

*L*ook!"

Luke squinted in the direction Emma pointed out, studying the structure ahead of them. "Might be the post I told you about. The one in the journal."

"It has to be. No one else besides the Indians live out here, and they wouldn't build a trading post."

Luke gave her a sideways grin, letting a hint of admiration for her show. But the confused wariness of her reaction told him she didn't quite trust what she saw. "Let's go and see if anyone is home, shall we?"

A path wound its way toward the building. Luke took in the tramped-down ground. Someone traveled here often. Indians must come here to trade on a regular basis.

Luke knocked on the door, and they waited in the chill afternoon air for a response. When none was forthcoming, he took a step back and studied the roof. "There isn't any smoke coming from the chimney. Maybe the place is abandoned."

"Is the door locked?"

Luke reached out and pressed down on the rusted latch. It squeaked as it moved, but the door had swelled and was stuck in the frame. He took a step back then plowed his shoulder against the wood. The door gave way causing Luke to stumble inside. Emma hurried to follow him.

"Ew!" Emma held her hand to her nose.

Luke didn't disagree. The interior was dark and smelled stale and musty. He cleared away cobwebs with his arm, leading her further inside. "What a mess."

Clothing and dirty blankets lay on the floor, ashes overflowed in the fireplace below an iron cooking pot hanging on a spit. Emma lifted the lid, and recoiled at what she found inside. Her nose wrinkled, she took the pot off the spit, carried it out the door, and set it aside. When she came back in, she shook her head. "What happened to whoever was here, do you think?"

Luke shrugged, turning from the inspection of a rifle hanging above the fireplace. "Hard to tell. This place looks abandoned, so it might have been a forced, sudden sort of departure."

"Well, at least the furniture seems sound."

Indeed, it did. There was a scarred wooden table with two chairs, a four-poster bed with a thin but serviceable straw ticking mattress, some cooking utensils near the cupboard. Further inspection revealed dishes and spoons in the cupboard. There was also a long counter at one end of the cabin with shelves built in it where the trader must have attended to his business. Low, on one of the bottom shelves, Luke found a forgotten beaver pelt, still dark brown, shiny, and perfect. It gave credence to their supposition.

"Maybe the trader went for supplies and will be back," Emma ventured.

"Could be. Either way, this is a good place for us to rest up, decide what we're going to do."

Emma's eyes were tight with strain but hopeful in the dim light. "I think I would like to clean it up a bit first."

He grinned. "I reckon so."

Emma pointed to the dusty, dirty bedding. "Help me haul this monstrosity outside, will you?"

Luke ducked his head, hiding the smile lifting the corners of his mouth, and did whatever she asked.

They hauled the mattress out into the open sunshine where Emma directed he prop it up against the side of the post. She found two stout sticks to beat it with while she pulled off a blanket and dust-coated quilt. "Beat that thing like—well, like you hate it. I'm going to the river to wash the bedding."

A shaft of fear lanced through Luke when he thought of what could happen to her at the river, but he suppressed it. She was not a child, and he must not treat her as one. "Just be careful." She was enjoying bossing him a little too much, but he grinned at the thought. He would beat this old straw tick. He would pretend it was someone he didn't much like . . .

That face wouldn't be hard to imagine.

The first stick didn't last very long. It snapped from the force of his pounding. With the second stick he took his time, concentrating on every square, dusty inch until the mattress sprang back like a fresh-stuffed bed. That Emma would have such a wonderful surface to sleep on tonight pleased him deeply.

A little later his rumbling belly told him it was time to rustle up some dinner. He headed back into the house for the rifle he had found, loaded it with shot, and then stepped outside again and surveyed their surroundings.

A wooded area nearby looked the most promising, so he headed that way, hoping Emma wouldn't come back and worry about where he'd gone. If he could have, he would have written her a note to explain. He just had to hope he made quick work of the task and got back before she did.

The half-stock rifle he'd found in the post felt foreign in his hands. He hadn't picked one up for weeks. He crept around the trees, looking for prey, which seemed to be everywhere. He could hear birds, scurrying animals, buzzing insects—then he realized he had trained his ears to hear them so that he could sit close by to draw them.

A noise caught his ear and he turned. There. A squirrel busy nibbling on a nut. A chuckle threatened his chest as he watched it. He knew in an instant how to sketch it, the cheeks stuffed and moving, the little mouth that opened and closed over the torn shell and the big, round eyes. His fur bushed out around his head and tail. His head darted back and forth as if he'd been expecting Luke and his gun.

Speaking of which . . . he'd best take care of business before the squirrel ran off!

Luke puffed out a big breath and then raised his rifle. Looking down the sights he pointed it at the furry creature—and pulled the trigger.

The shot was good. The squirrel fell back into the long grass. Luke sprinted forward and nodded over it. Now if he could just find another one. Not more than twenty minutes later he spied a big, brown rabbit. Wanting to hurry, he didn't waste any time—just aimed and fired.

He hurried back toward the post, and when he reached the little clearing, he saw that Emma was spreading the blankets over some scraggly bushes. She struggled to get the sodden blankets up and over the tall bushes, so he rushed over to help.

"Those aren't going to be dry anytime soon," Luke remarked with raised eyebrows at her.

"Well, maybe not. Maybe not for tonight, but when they do dry, they will be clean. I can assure you of that."

Luke hid his grin. This was a side of Emma he'd never seen. She seemed to enjoy housewifely chores and henpecking him and feeling like she was taking care of someone. Odds were good Eric didn't allow her that role in their home and she'd felt painfully unneeded there. Emma needed to feel needed. To look after her husband each day . . . to raise and cherish children. He could see her now, the tender smile she'd offer her children, ruffling the hair of one while directing another to some daily task. . . .

"What do you have there?"

Luke started, Emma's question jerking him from his thoughts. He lifted the squirrel. His raised eyebrows matched hers. "Dinner?"

Emma laughed, her eyes sparkling with something he didn't think he'd ever seen there: happiness. "Looks fine. But I'm surprised it stood still long enough for you to shoot it. I'll bet you were sketching it in your mind for a good couple of minutes, weren't you?"

How did she know that? How did she know him so well as that? Luke shrugged, trying for gravity. "I figured you were hungry."

Emma pushed a hand against his shoulder, laughter still lingering in her eyes. "I guess I am. Shall we fry him up?"

Luke turned to go and do the task of skinning the animal. Emma called over her shoulder as he walked away. "I found some dried food stores in the post. Maybe I can come up with something to go with your feast."

She was teasing him, and it tore at his heart like the ripping of a sail in whipping wind. He blinked and then nodded. "That would be nice."

She smiled, and Luke marveled how real it looked—not something she had to hide and worry someone would see. No, this was a full-blown, the sun shining on her face, contented smile. He must have been gaping because all of a sudden her eyelids dropped over her happiness, and she turned back toward the post, the column of her back erect, her head held high, her golden hair twisted up like a crown.

Luke sighed. *Did she have any idea how much his heart twisted up over her?*

They ate in a companionable silence. Emma had found some cornmeal and made corn cakes that were just right—crisp on the outside and soft and sweet on the inside. She rose up after eating and dusted off her skirts. Then she busied herself in the cabin: setting things to rights, cleaning the dishes and making up the bed with the surprisingly dry quilt. She wouldn't have a blanket as it was still damp, but she had something at least to cover the straw ticking.

"Luke?"

"Yes?"

"We should get some sleep." She said it as a soft, practical command.

He rose, dusted the dirt off his pants, and ducked under the low frame of the doorway that led to the one other room of the post.

"I'll sleep on the floor." He said it in a sudden way that sounded choked.

She lifted her face toward him and stared at him for a long silent moment. "You'll take the blanket."

"No need for that—"

The protest died on his lips as she shook her head hard at him. "If I am having the comfort of a mattress, you will have the blanket."

"Well, all right then." There was no use arguing with her when she had her lips all compressed and her eyes flashing determination. He hid a smile at the thought that he could always cover her with the blanket later, after she fell asleep.

"Thank you, Luke."

She was so strong. Had she always been so? He didn't think so. He remembered the judge's words about God being slow to act sometimes so that this human clay could be molded, formed into what He wanted—that was the message, and he'd agreed, seen it in his own life.

He turned away as they both took off their shoes. Luke grasped the blanket and laid it out on the floor between the door and the bed. He could hear a rustling sound and glanced over toward her.

She was taking down her hair.

He swallowed hard, then made himself look away.

Tired as he was, it was a long time before he was able to fall asleep.

Emma woke to the sound of soft snores. She blinked up at the unfamiliar ceiling, anxiety filling her. Where was she? Was Eric awake yet?

Turning onto her side, she looked around the room and saw Luke on the floor beside her. A relieved breath whooshed from her chest. She was here with Luke. She was safe.

He stirred and turned his face toward her. He looked so peaceful, relaxed in sleep. The antithesis of Eric. Where Eric was light in features, Luke was dark. But on the inside . . .

Eric was dark, and Luke was filled with light. Shame filled her as she remembered all Eric had done to her in the darkness of their nights together. She would never be worthy of a man like Luke.

He stirred again, awakening. She liked the feel of it, the knowledge that she knew the moment when he awakened enough to remember his surroundings—and her. He turned his face toward her and smiled. Emma drifted on a blissful wave of peace when another feeling impeded on her moment of heaven.

Eric was coming.

She felt it before they heard it.

Hoofbeats. Horses. Headed right for them.

Chapter Twenty-Three

*L*uke and Emma jumped up at the same time. "We have to go. Now." Luke hurried into his boots.

Emma threw on her shoes and grasped the hair pins off the bureau, twisting her hair into a loose bun as she ran from the room.

"You go." Luke gestured to the door. "I will hold them off."

Emma shook her head. How could he say such a thing?

Luke pulled the gun from the back waist of his pants and held it out to her. "You can do it."

"I won't go without you."

They stared at each other for a heartbeat. Then they moved.

Luke grasped her hand and pulled her outside. They ran through the tall grasses toward the river. They both heard the pounding of hooves and looked back. The horses stopped in front of the trading post and a soldier dismounted.

"Get down. Hide."

Luke's whisper brushed Emma's ear as they dropped low, crouching in the tall grass. She caught her breath. "We can't stay here. They will figure out that we've just left and search the entire area for us."

"I know." Luke rose but stayed crouched so that the grasses still hid him. "Try to run like this until we're out of sight."

Emma copied his action and they were off. A few minutes later the grasses thinned, doing little good as a cover, so they stood and ran as fast as they could. They came to a small cliff edge that led to a narrow shoreline of the riverbank.

"Oh, no!" Emma wanted to weep. "How are we going to get down there?"

Luke took her hand and ran with her along the top of the cliff. "Come on. It's not as steep this way." Both of them were out of breath.

The cliff edge finally descended enough that they were able climb down toward the choppy flow of the water. "Now comes the hard part."

He didn't need to say it. Emma knew what he had planned.

They plunged into the water, waded deeper and deeper until the bottom gave way and they had to swim to the opposite shore. The other side was rock. Pure elevation, up and up, ending in a cliff edge that reached into the sky. There was no shore to land on.

Emma pointed ahead, west. "There."

Luke followed her pointing finger to the small crop of land, then took Emma's hand and pulled her along, both of them fighting the strong current.

The water dragged at her skirts, and the rock of the riverbank left little to grasp hold of. Luke's strong hand pulled her along, and she concentrated on holding it as tight as she could, a lifeline in the swirling undercurrent that could easily sweep them both away. Her feet stumbled on the rock and mud bottom, the sucking current making every step a near impossibility.

She concentrated on two things—the pull of Luke's hand and the spot of land that lay ahead against sandstone.

They finally reached it, and he pulled her like a sodden rag doll from the water. They stumbled across the narrow shore to the edge of the stone cliff face. From every appearance they'd reached a dead end.

They would have to turn and face their enemy.

"Wait." Luke's grip on her hand tightened. "Look. Do you see it?"

There, in the rock, was an entrance. A cave.

"Come on."

Luke led her into the recesses of nature's hiding place. They groped their way through the ensuing darkness, back and further back, knowing that an end would come at any moment, but it didn't. Soon they were on their hands and knees, feeling the hard rock, the solidness beneath them, seeing next to nothing, going by feel alone.

Emma shivered. "It's so dark. I'm afraid."

"It won't be this dark for long." Excitement rang in his voice. "Do you hear that?"

Emma stopped and listened. In the distance ahead of them, she heard a rushing sound. "A waterfall."

They crawled through the winding tunnel, and soon she saw a shaft of light in the distance. It grew ever brighter until they found themselves at a ledge. The sound of roaring water overwhelmed her as she edged out onto the ledge in the cliff wall. She stood beside Luke, pressing back against the stone, seeing the falls from the mountain's point of view.

Astonishment filled Emma's chest. "It's amazing!" She took a step forward and reached out her hand. If only she could touch the cascading waters. . . .

Luke pulled her back against his chest. "No. It will carry you down and away."

"But we can't go forward." She pointed to what they both saw was a dead end.

"We wait."

"What if they track us?" She turned and gripped his arm. "They will know we were at the cabin. We left so many signs."

Luke pulled her down, nestling her against his chest even as he pulled the gun from his belt. He held it ready, saying nothing.

She shivered against him, feeling the mist from the cold water and the chill of her fear. They both faced the cave and waited.

Was *this* it, then?

Was this what he'd been born to do? He would die protecting her. But, dear God, please God, don't let him die protecting her only to have her taken back into that slavery. Surely God wouldn't force him to watch from heaven what her husband did to her for the rest of her life.

He gripped Emma's thin body to his and wanted nothing more than to make them both disappear—and suddenly understood. This was what drove Emma to the rail on the boat. This was what had her holding so fast to that gun. She had wanted, *needed* to make it all go away with a leap into the river or a bullet. And he had saved her from it. Twice.

He'd stopped her. Commanded her to give up her hope of freedom. He'd told her to trust him. To let go of her gun and trust God. But would God show up? Would He save them?

A flickering light caught his attention. Torches. He eased to his feet, and Emma followed in silence. They both stared at the falls. Both knew they could throw themselves into those waters and hope they didn't crash to river rock. . . .

But Luke knew. Their chances of surviving the jump were slim.

He let her go and turned. Emma moved away from Luke as if to shield him. She took a step toward the flickering lights coming nearer and nearer. Luke held the gun ready by his side.

A few moments later shadowy forms flickered against the cave wall. A uniformed soldier—one of the men who had accompanied Judge Littleton—came into view first.

"They're here!" He pointed his rifle at Luke as three more men from the expedition came from behind him. Luke stood beside Emma, his pistol pointing at their pursuers.

"Drop your weapon, Mr. Bowen," the soldier stated as all four of them lifted their guns.

Luke gave the man a long stare. *God . . . what do I do? What do You call me to?* One moment . . . two . . . and Luke knew the answer. He lowered the gun to the rocky ledge floor.

"But where is Eric?" Emma's sorrowful voice came from behind him. "He didn't come himself?"

The soldier fixed a look on Emma. "Mr. Montclaire was injured, if you recall, and is being escorted back to St. Louis to be tried for the murder of Judge Littleton." He came closer, his gaze now on Luke. "Step back from the gun, Mr. Bowen. You and Mrs. Montclaire will also be escorted back to St. Louis. Mr. Montclaire is claiming the two of you plotted to kill the judge."

Emma gasped. "That's a *lie!*"

The soldier stared at her, and Luke had no trouble recognizing the accusation and judgment in his eyes. "Possibly. But it doesn't look good that you shot your husband and then the two of you ran off together."

Despair and now a little fear filled Luke's chest. He had never thought how it might look to all of them. That they might not understand why they'd run. *God, forgive me. Have I only made matters worse?* "What happens in St. Louis?"

"The three of you will stand trial for the death of Robert Frazer, the journal's author, and for the death of Judge Littleton. The courts will decide which man"—his gaze landed on Emma again—"or woman is responsible. And then the guilty party will be punished."

The soldier picked up Luke's gun and slid it into the waist of his pants, then moved so that Luke and Emma could pass by him, back into the cave to follow the other soldiers to the outside.

"Punished?"

Luke's heart ached at the fear in Emma's soft question, but the soldier's answer came sure and cold.

"Hung, ma'am. The guilty party will hang."

Emma stood with a blanket wrapped around her shoulders against the bracing wind on the quick moving barge. The colors of the sky were bright this morning—a pink sunrise shimmered over the hills and pure yellow rays of sunshine bathed the land in what promised to be a beautiful day, their final day. The trip back to St. Louis had gone much faster than the way west as now they were traveling with the current and not against it.

They rounded a bend, and she saw the city of her birth, St. Louis, for the first time in months. A bubble of hysterical laughter fought the tears in her throat as they passed the mill and the buildings came into view. After everything she had been through . . . everything she had endured since that "perfect day" . . . she was now being accused of murdering a man who had tried to help them all.

A tear seeped out, and she dashed it away with the wadded-up blanket. She wouldn't cry. She was done with crying. She would be strong, take whatever came next, and prove her innocence.

She thought of the Bible, the shredded pages that were left . . . pages she read each day, trying to piece together the words to make a full verse and chapter. Bits of the story of Genesis, mankind's beginning. Some of Isaiah's words were left whole. He was a prophet on fire, she thought with a smile. Whether condemning the Israelites' ways or holding out hope for their salvation, he led the people with a burning conviction. And then there was Daniel. She loved the words of a man who had been a slave, a captive in a pagan society so different from his own. Daniel's faith remained strong throughout it all. And now . . . she wished to be like him.

"I'm off to the lion's den, Lord," she said quietly. "I pray You will be with me like You were with Daniel."

"It will take more than prayer to get you free of this charge, Mrs. Montclaire."

Lieutenant Arthur's voice startled her. She turned toward him and raked back the strands of hair in her face. She met his gaze unblinking. "You truly think I killed the judge?"

He flushed at her challenge and looked away, then turned brisk. "It won't matter what I think, ma'am. That will be decided by a jury."

Would the jury be made up of the citizens of St. Louis? Citizens that remembered her as an awkward, shy child? They had celebrated with her parents at her amazing match. They loved Eric. They revered Eric. They thought Eric was one of the best things that could have happened to their city, to them, and especially to her. She wrapped the blanket tighter around her shoulders. "Well, then. All we can do is tell the truth. Only the truth can set us free."

He looked away from her, an abrupt move that put them both on edge. The awkward moment was saved by Luke coming around the corner of the cabin. He walked up to them and motioned ahead. "Looks like we are almost there."

The lieutenant nodded, turned, and walked away. Emma supposed he was giving them a last moment of privacy before they would be marched like criminals through the town's streets.

Luke came up to the railing of the barge and leaned in. "How are you holding up?"

She turned toward the town and gazed at it. "I'm afraid but trying not to be. I am trying to trust God. We are headed for a fight. Lies will come against me—us." She turned her face toward his, saw the strain around his mouth. Oh, how she wished he had never had to be involved in her life and problems. "We go to the lion's den, Luke. I pray God will save us."

A small smile lit Luke's features. "You've been reading that torn-up Bible, haven't you?"

Emma couldn't help her laugh. "As best I can."

Luke reached out and touched her cheek, a tiny brush of his fingertips, and then lowered his hand. "That's good."

Emma pulled back from his touch. "Luke, you must not look at me like that. You must not reach for me, ever. I fear their greatest evidence against us is that we ran away together. I fear it will look as if we planned it."

Pain tinged Luke's eyes as he took off his hat and ran his fingers through his straight, black hair. His gaze skittered away to rove the bank of the Missouri. "I'm sorry, Emma. Maybe if I had never spoken to you . . ."

"You have nothing to be sorry for," Emma stated, low and determined. "We could be hung! *I'm* the sorry one." She fought back the tears she'd vowed never to shed again. "You didn't deserve any of this."

"And you did?" Luke's voice grew heated. "Don't believe it, Emma. Don't ever believe any of this was your fault. You are the victim here."

He stepped back, staring hard at her face as if memorizing it so that he could hold it close for the days to come.

She pressed her hand to her mouth and blinked hard. And then she stiffened her spine and turned toward the shore and St. Louis where the men on board this craft were preparing to bank.

She had always dreamed of the future—of being a wife and mother and living out her days in a home that she kept warm and comfortable for her family. She'd never in her wildest fearful imaginings thought she would be entering the town where she grew up as a prisoner. But then she'd never been wise enough, jaded enough, strong enough to even consider such a thing. Like Eve, she found the fruit of the knowledge of good and evil to be a rotten thing indeed.

Chapter Twenty-Four

*L*ieutenant Arthur approached her as the barge docked. He held a length of rope in one hand. His mouth had thinned into a flat line, but his face flushed scarlet as he neared. Emma didn't wait for him to command her. She lifted her chin and held out her arms. She stood as tall as she could and thought of those gone before her—Joan of Arc, the sister queens who fought for England's crown, and Daniel—Daniel of the Bible. She decided to believe God would save her. It was a choice—fear or faith.

She chose faith.

Lieutenant Arthur flushed brighter, if that was possible, as he tied the length around her wrists. "It's what's expected."

That he had bothered to explain was surprising. "You are only doing your job, sir, and I thank you for the kindness you have shown me on this journey."

His gaze jerked up from her hands, and she smiled at his startled look. "Shall we?"

Emma followed the lieutenant to the shore where Luke was waiting for them with the other men. They walked, the two of them in the center, hands tied in front of them. Men flanked them on each side, with the lieutenant leading their small party along the Great Trail into town. Down First Street they walked, toward the small, wooden structure that served this newly won Louisiana Territory as the government house and sometimes, when the circuit preacher was in town, a church.

When would the trial start? Before Judge Littleton, Emma had never heard of a judge coming regularly to St. Louis. After the Louisiana Purchase, over five years ago, the soldiers transported prisoners to the territory capitol in Vincennes, where Governor William Henry Harrison and his magistrates would hear the case. Now that Judge Littleton was dead, who would act as judge?

The thought of Judge Littleton brought an aching pain to her chest. The lieutenant had told them that he had been buried in the wilderness as the trip back to St. Louis was too long to preserve the body. The thought that she was somehow responsible pricked at her, but she pushed it aside as foolishness. She'd only been in the room. Eric had poisoned the man, and she would do her best to prove it.

They must be making quite an entrance, Emma thought, keeping her gaze to the ground as the townsfolk streamed from their houses and shops to gawk. She heard their excited chatter, the noise like dark waves washing over her, threatening to drown her under the shame.

God . . . give me strength.

Luke did as Emma asked and didn't look at her. He kept his gaze straight ahead and focused on the plain, wooden building they neared.

A crowd followed them as they came into the square yard. The door to the government building opened, and Lieutenant Eisler stepped out with another uniformed man who appeared to be of higher rank.

They stopped, but Lieutenant Arthur walked to meet them and saluted to the commander. Luke strained to hear what they were saying.

"She's been through enough, sir."

Luke saw the other commander stop and consider Arthur's words. "Very well, but post a guard. She won't be allowed to leave for any reason."

The commander came up to Luke and regarded him with stern, narrowed eyes. He glanced at Emma, his lips pressing into a thin line, and then back at Luke again. Luke could feel Emma's body quivering beside him. He wanted to look at her, to encourage her, but he restrained the urge and stared, instead, at the man in front of them.

Lieutenant Arthur stated loud enough for the entire crowd to hear. "Captain Davis has decided that you, Mrs. Montclaire"—he glanced at Emma—"will be allowed to house with your parents during the trial, which will start tomorrow, as soon as Judge Griffin arrives from Vincennes."

Captain Davis took a step toward Emma. "A guard will be posted at the door. Do not attempt to leave the house. Do you understand, ma'am?"

"Yes, sir."

Looking toward Luke, the captain paused. "Mr. Bowen will be taken to the stockade at Fort Belle Fontaine."

"Where is my husband?" Emma's question, though asked in a shaky voice, startled all of them.

"Eric Montclaire is at the fort recovering from his injury." The captain stressed the last word, clearly reminding Emma she was the cause of it.

Luke ducked his head and hid a smile as he saw that Emma, as frightened as she was, didn't flinch. She stared right back at the captain.

Lieutenant Arthur went over to Emma and grasped her by the arm.

A loud female cry came from the onlookers. *"Emma!"*

They turned and saw Emma's mother barrel across the street, her skirts grasped in fists at either side.

"Momma!" Emma's voice was tear clogged, and Luke saw her eyes fill as her mother came to a stop and pressed her hand to her mouth.

"Good heavens, Emma, what has happened?"

At a nod from the captain, Lieutenant Arthur led Emma to her mother. When Mrs. Daring saw the rope tied around her daughter's wrists, she wailed anew. Mr. Daring soon caught up with his wife and took her in hand, demanding she stand still and wait. But Mrs. Daring shrugged him off, took the steps that separated her from her daughter, and took Emma into her arms.

Lieutenant Arthur looked away, fidgeting and shuffling his feet; but he allowed the embrace, saying in a loud voice, "Go back to your homes, citizens. This scene is over." To Mr. and Mrs. Daring he stated, "Emma is to stay with you until the trial. A guard will be posted outside your door. She is not to leave for any reason."

"A guard at my door!" Mrs. Daring's outraged shock rang in her tone. "What is the *meaning* of all this?"

Lieutenant Arthur peered at Emma's mother, then drew himself up to his full height and huffed. "Your daughter stands accused of the murder of Judge Littleton, along with that man."

He turned and pointed back to Luke. "If you will not agree to the terms of her imprisonment, she will be taken to Fort Belle Fontaine along with Mr. Bowen."

"Murder? The judge?" Mrs. Daring shrieked. "Are you *mad?*" Her voice dropped to a low growl. "Emma could *never* do such a thing."

The lieutenant walked over and stood staring down his nose at Emma's parents. "Compose yourselves. We are doing a great favor to allow her the comfort of your home while we await the trial and—"

Mr. Daring cut in. "Yes, yes of course. Sir, my wife is overwrought. You must understand the shock of a mother. Forgive us. We will take Emma straight home."

Mrs. Daring swayed on her feet, her eyes blinked in a rapid but dazed way that said she might faint. Mr. Daring pulled some smelling salts from his pocket and held them out to her. That seemed to revive her enough to start wailing again.

Mrs. Daring clung to Emma as they all turned and headed toward their home. Emma gave Luke a sad look over her shoulder and then turned away. When next he saw her, they would be facing a judge. Luke took a deep breath and turned toward the approaching lieutenant.

Now for the long walk north. For imprisonment . . .

And Fort Belle Fontaine.

Lieutenant Arthur shoved Luke into a small cell of the stockade and slammed the iron bars shut. The next sound was the metal click of the lock sliding into place.

"You think I'm guilty, don't you?"

Lieutenant Arthur met his gaze. "I think you had the journal. I think Mrs. Montclaire ran out on her husband to be with you." He leaned into Luke's face, the bars separating them. "I think you want things that aren't yours."

Luke took that in as he stared back at the man. Prickles of unease mounted inside him as he realized how everything looked to others. How had he . . . they . . . come to this? He was having a hard time acknowledging that this was his new reality, that the evidence was stacked against them.

He turned away from the lieutenant, hoping he would leave. Luke would save his answers for the trial. He wouldn't talk about it before he had a judge and jury to hear the evidence.

The lieutenant made a scoffing laugh, and then the outer door to the stockade slammed shut. Darkness flooded the room. There was no window, no fire, just thin, pale light coming from under the outer door of the large room.

A sudden thought occurred. Was Eric here? There *were* other holding cells. "Anybody here?" He squinted through the dim light. When no one answered, he turned to explore the small space that would be his home for the next few days. He stretched his arms out in front of him and took a few slow steps.

There was a cot with a straw mattress, no blanket or pillow, and an old chamber pot. That was it. He lay back on the prickly mattress, hearing the rustle and smelling the mustiness of old hay. He placed his hands, fingers crossed, behind his head and closed his aching eyes. Behind his closed lids he saw Emma's face—her sunlit hair tumbling over her shoulders, her blue eyes intense and flashing at him.

He swallowed, feeling thirsty. His throat tightened. Then he saw the rope they would lower over his head. Saw the moment they would push him forward so that he hung, suspended . . .

His eyes flashed open. He gritted his teeth together and turned onto his side. He wanted to cry out to God, but he was tired, so tired. He had cried out to Him so many times already, and here he was, locked in a stockade. He'd tried to rid himself of his love for Emma, and it hadn't worked. The judge had warned him. He could have left her. He could have chosen not to follow her when she ran away. He could have left her in God's hands, . . . but he hadn't.

Confusion roared within him. Had his need to save her done more harm than good? Had his decisions led to this? What might have happened if he had forced himself to turn his back on her, ignored her need—*Lord, she couldn't have gotten a mile without me!* He curled into his upraised knees, his head bowed. *Am I right?*

I will make a way for the righteous. I will not fail the upright of heart. I will not fail you of heavy laden burdens. I will remember you. I will carry you. I will save. I will save.

The same words he'd heard before, but now he heard the message in a new way. God was not saying He would make a way for them *together.* He had promised only to save them both.

Holy Spirit revelation crashed into his mind like a crushing wave. He hadn't given her up. Hadn't ever really tried. All the times he'd let his mind imagine . . . let himself see the two of them together . . .

But Emma was not his. He'd gone after her, convinced she needed him. Sure he was right to do so. Hadn't God spoken to him? But now . . . truth struck deep and sure.

God had spoken to remind Luke that Emma was God's daughter, and God was strong enough, sure enough, loving enough, and good enough to take care of her all by Himself.

Luke bent further over his legs, quivering like a frightened child. All his efforts, for naught. All he'd done by stepping in was make things more complicated. Worse for both of them.

He was ready. Give it up. All of it.

Take it all, Lord. I can't hold on to any of it. Take the good and bad and everything I am. Take it all. And forgive me, Father. Forgive me. . . .

As the prayers poured out of him, Luke's heart seemed to be breaking. All the anger and frustration buried deep within flowed free. And even as he begged for forgiveness, he forgave his own father for never really seeing him. He forgave himself for failing, over and over again, in not trusting God with his future and depending on his feelings. He let go of his dream of seeing the Pacific, watched it burn into nothing behind his closed eyes as waves roared and crashed in his imagination, then faded into nothing. He saw Emma's face, saw his drawing of her, remembered her hair, the way it had tied them together that night he had rescued her from throwing herself over the edge into the heaving storm. He took a deep, shuddering breath and let the memory go, saw it fade away . . . away . . . away . . . until there was nothing left but him and God.

A deep peace flooded him. Behind his closed eyes he saw a picture of heaven. He saw God on a throne, a blinding white light with . . . no, not the color white, he realized. It was a brightness that defied anything he had ever seen. It shone down on him, each ray, each particle of it, filled with God's provision.

His peace.

His love.

A glimpse of Jehovah, Yahweh, the Beginning and the End.

Luke clung to the mattress, burying his face into the prickly straw. He welcomed the sensation. Turning, he lay on his back and lifted his bound hands toward heaven.

So be it, my Lord.

I am Yours.

Only Yours.

Chapter Twenty-Five

They sat down to dinner. Emma, her mother and father, and a hovering servant whom Emma's father soon banned from the room. They arranged themselves in the familiar places.

As she scooted her chair up to the gleaming wood of the table, Emma closed her eyes for a long moment, smelled the familiar fragrances of the wood polish, the spices in the dishes her parents loved . . . and childhood memories washed over her like a sought-for rain.

It was good to be home.

Emma bowed her head as her father said the blessing. It was the same blessing he had always prayed over their food, except at the end he said a simple plea. "God have mercy upon us all." *Yes, God . . . please.*

Her mother was now somewhat composed, her smelling salts in a pretty little box by the side of her dinner plate. Just in case.

With an abrupt move her father pushed his plate aside and buried his face in his hands. "Tell us what has happened, Emma."

"Let her eat, John. She looks half-starved."

Her father looked up at her thin face. He nodded, the realization an added burden that weighed down his face. "When you are ready, Emma."

She reached across the table and grasped his thin, aged-spotted hand. "It won't take long, Papa. This stomach can't hold much." The statement, one that she had hoped would bring a lightness to the conversation, made both of her parents wail.

Her mother pushed her plate away and brought the smelling salts to her nose. She closed her eyes and breathed in and out above the tiny box. Emma wanted to say she was sorry, but the mound of roasted beef in her mouth, tasting like heaven itself, was too big to say anything at all.

When at last she took a long, deep drink of the sugared tea and sat back with a contented groan, she knew it was time.

Her fingers lingered over the handle of the delicate teacup. She stared at it for a long minute and then blurted out. "Eric beat me."

She looked up into her parents' eyes, knowing that what she was going to tell them was almost unimaginable to them. They would blame themselves for not seeing Eric's true nature, if they even believed her. Nothing was ever going to be the same between them after this night.

Her fingers tightened around the handle of the cup. "It started right after the wedding. He . . . was angry, often and for no reason that I could ascertain." She looked up at her mother. "The luncheon? You thought I ran away due to shyness, a new bride's nerves? Do you remember?"

Her mother nodded, her brows pulled tight together, her lips pressed tight.

"I ran away because I had a bruise on my cheek." She took a deep breath. "And Momma"—her throat clogged, worked to get the words out—"the powder didn't cover it. Not that time."

"Oh!" Her mother pressed her hands against her mouth, blinked fast as tears raced down her paper-thin cheeks.

"I tried to please him. I tried not to rile him or upset him or do anything—except exactly what he wanted. But I never knew for sure what that was!" How to explain it? That something settled over her, that burden of his that gradually became something *she* had to do . . . and yet she'd had no idea how to fulfill his needs. "Nothing I did was right, or enough. Nothing was good enough to please him. He was unappeasable."

Her father rose and paced back and forth as the words came to her. "I never choose the right dress. I never said the right thing. I was never where I was supposed to be, doing the exact thing I was supposed do, at the exact time. I was never *enough*. Sometimes I gave him a moment's relief, but it never lasted."

"Why didn't you come to us? Why didn't you tell us? Why didn't you come *home?*" Her father's voice rose in volume with each question.

Emma's eyes filled with tears that she dashed away. She'd vowed not to cry over Eric, and just look at her—so weak. "I was afraid. For a long time I thought he would change. And I thought I would learn to be a better wife. Eric was so . . . prized. So . . . sought after. How could I disappoint you with my failure?"

Emma's father hung his head. He slumped back into his chair as his shoulders shook. Emma reached across the table and squeezed his hand. "Papa, it's not your fault. Don't blame yourself. You didn't know."

Her father shook his head. "I did. I knew something was wrong with him. I felt it. But I ignored it. I didn't want to see it."

Emma's mother rushed out. "No, it's my fault! I pushed for the match. I wanted the best for her, and he looked like the best thing that would ever come along."

They sat in a long silence, knowing that there was no sense in blaming anyone or even taking the blame. Finally her father poured them all a fresh cup of tea from the teapot. He sat down and took a deep breath, then turned to Emma. "What happened next? What happened on this journey that would make anyone accuse you of Judge Littleton's murder? I cannot fathom it."

Emma spent the rest of the evening explaining what had occurred during the expedition. She left out the details that would cause them more pain—how she'd nearly thrown herself overboard, how she'd felt a prisoner aboard the barge—but she did tell of the journal, about Judge Littleton showing up and investigating the murder of Robert Frazer, and about the dinner with the judge. She told them how he died in her arms.

She didn't mention Luke, and they didn't ask.

And anyway, she thought as she went off to bed, they would hear it all come out at the trial.

Luke turned at the grating sound of a key in the lock. He rose up from the cot and stood, walked over to the bars of his cell and wrapped his fingers around them. There had been some water and a plate of cold food shoved at him earlier in the day, and he thought this might be the same. But as soon as he saw the tall shadows of two men entering the dim light of the stockade, he knew . . .

It was Eric Montclaire.

A soldier, dressed like the others in black boots, a white tucked-in shirt, and a blue-and-red tailcoat with gold braiding, walked in. The man beside him wore a worn and dirty coat, but there was authority in his bearing, and a disdain toward anyone else . . .

Who else could it be but Eric.

The soldier didn't acknowledge Luke. He marched Eric to the cell next to his and motioned him in. Luke watched, eyes hooded. The soldier shrank back as if intimidated by Eric even though he had a loaded rifle resting on his right arm. Luke wanted to put his fist through the wall.

What power did this man have over others?

Eric entered the cell and turned, facing Luke. He let out a low chuckle. "Looks like she got to us both." The soldier backed out and rammed the lock in place.

Luke ignored the remark. He directed his question to the soldier. "When is the trial? Do you know?"

"The judge arrived this afternoon. I think it will begin tomorrow."

"Thank you." Luke meant it. It was good to know the timing, what would happen next. It gave him a little peace.

As the soldier hurried out, the light faded away. Luke felt Eric's presence—a dark, heavy presence.

"So you think you love my wife?" Eric's silky voice floated in the darkness.

Luke turned toward his cot, sat down, and tried to ignore Eric.

But Eric had other means to torture him—a long recounting of every encounter he had ever had with Emma and how he had conquered her.

"When I first saw her, it was only a glimpse really. A glimpse of gold and blue, a stunning blue dress, her hair all piled up underneath a dark velvet hat." Eric chuckled. "It was at the bakery. She was wearing gloves. Oh, how I remember those silken hands as she reached out for the bread. How graceful and"—he breathed hard out his nose—"sweet she was."

Luke lay down and pulled his arms over his head, trying to block out his voice. He didn't want to hear this, and yet he did. Eric might tell him something to make him understand if he listened around and between the words . . . if he asked the right questions . . .

"I wanted nothing more than her at that moment." He chuckled, and the malevolence of it turned Luke's stomach. "I envisioned taking those gloves off her hands, unpinning the hat and her hair, watching it cascade down her back, and then taking those lovely, slim wrists in one of my hands and pressing her arms up over her head as I—"

Lord, help me. I can't do this. Luke blocked the next words and turned his head away on his thin mattress.

"I orchestrated a chance meeting at the next Sunday service. Her parents were so . . . easily convinced. New in town. A lonely bachelor staying at a boarding house. They offered me a home-cooked meal and"—he let out a pleased sigh—"that was the beginning of their slow slide into my hands."

"Why are you telling me this?"

"Oh, you will get your turn, never fear." Eric chuckled. "You do want to know, don't you? I know you do. How such a *good,* innocent woman could have fallen into the hands of such evil." Eric didn't give him time to answer. He plunged on.

"I soon discovered that the way to Emma's heart would not be through flowers and declarations of love. Not even my apparent good looks had its usual effect, which only made me want her more. No, my Emma, my future wife—for I had decided to make her that after our first conversation—was a dreamer. She hung on every detail of my travels. She was more educated than any woman I'd known, more hungry for knowledge, more interesting. She wanted to know all about my business and how it worked. It wasn't too hard to make myself out the humble businessman in search of his fortune. I hinted at my wealth but more, told her of my ambition. I described what my perfect life would be, my wife and children living in their white-stone mansion while I provided every comfort, every need. She was as easy as plucking a ripe plum from a tree, her eyes so big and blue and believing in me."

"Why break her then?" Luke asked the question through gritted teeth. "She would have loved you forever if you hadn't—"

Eric rose up from his cot and came to the bars that separated their cells. He wrapped his hands like claws around the iron as Luke looked over at him for the first time. Eric's face was hard-edged, enraged. "Because it was all a fairy tale!" He pulled and pushed against the bars. "It would have ended soon enough! I would have destroyed it eventually!"

Luke sat up. He looked at Eric's face, so ravished, so pain racked. Suddenly, incomprehensibly, something he never dreamed he could feel for this man overwhelmed him.

Compassion.

"So instead of waiting on it to happen, you took matters into your own hands so that you could control the timing of it. Is that it?"

Eric stopped. He stared at Luke and didn't move. "Yes, that's it." His voice sounded strangely normal again. He turned away and lay down, careful of his injured shoulder, wrapped in a white bandage.

God . . . his mind is broken, isn't it?

Luke looked up at the wood ceiling and then down at his clasped hands. *Lord, I don't trust him. But if You have a purpose here, well, You are going to have to fill me in on it.* It was as though Luke walked a tightrope, one that might lead to answers or to his death. God knew he didn't want to die. But there was something Luke wanted even more than life itself.

To follow God. No matter where it led.

Luke let out a long breath, letting the burden of confusion and uncertainty leave him. He lay back on the cot and clasped his hands behind his head.

One day at a time. One moment at a time. It was as Emma said. They were going into the lion's den and, like Daniel, they had to cling to God for the next words, for the next breath.

Chapter Twenty-Six

A pounding knock from the front door woke Emma with a jerk. She jumped from the bed, wide awake. The trial. It was time.

She threw on one of her best dresses, then sat at her three-mirrored dressing table and coiled her hair into a simple chignon at her nape. It felt heavy against the back of her neck. Heaviness. All heavy.

She reached for the powder to cover the dark circles under her eyes, eyes that attested to her lack of sleep, but then she put it down. Let nothing cover truth this day.

She reached for a velvet, green-hued hat. It was adorned with a wide ribbon of striped green and gold satin and a single peacock feather that draped to one side. Emma tilted her chin up. She leaned forward and peered in the mirror, but her show of bravado did not stop the quivering, flip-flop of her stomach. Her gloved hands squeezed together in her lap.

The knock she had been expecting sounded at her door. She stood, smoothed down the cream-colored skirt, the underskirt of pale green and gold showing at the bottom and in the front.

Well, she looked as good as she could under the circumstances. She walked toward the door and pulled it open.

A soldier stood with her mother and father on either side. "It is time."

She didn't look at her mother. Couldn't risk it. It was all too unbearable. What had she done to deserve this? Nothing.

But that didn't matter. All that mattered was the truth. Letting the truth come out.

She nodded to the soldier, then noted the rope in his hands. "Sir, I will not try to fight you or flee. Must you tie my hands?"

He was a young man and looked down at the rope as if it were a foreign thing that had suddenly appeared in his hands. "Sorry, ma'am. I was told to do so."

Emma held out her wrists. It wasn't the first time she had given up the mobility of her hands, but she hoped this day would prove the last.

The four of them walked down the cold, windswept road to the courthouse. As they turned a corner, Emma paused, causing her guard to stop beside her. She felt her breath give way as she took in the scene. It looked as if the whole town had turned out to gawk. The soldier plunged forward, the rope pulling on her like a lead line, an animal being led to the slaughter. They entered the crowded courtroom. She looked back and forth and side to side, panic rising. Was there anyone here she knew? All she saw were strangers . . . and a territory of people who wanted one answer.

Who killed the honorable Judge Littleton?

She was ushered down the center aisle; and then, before she could think what was happening, she was directed to sit down beside Luke at a long, dark table. She dared not look at him. If she looked at him, she would fall apart in front of them all.

Soldiers from the fort were standing at different stations, their uniform proclaiming the importance of this trial. Emma glanced to her side. Beside Luke sat a serious-looking man with small eyes, mutton-chop sideburns, a long face that was pock-marked from some previous battle with smallpox. He looked over at her, and she knew by the shrewd intelligence in his eyes that he was very good at defending those he believed in. He leaned across Luke and stretched out his hand. "Linus Barthom, of the territorial capital of Vincennes, ma'am. I would be happy to be your lawyer."

Emma gulped, nodded. "Thank you, sir." She looked at Luke for the first time. She searched his eyes but only for a moment. That was all—just a moment to gauge how he was, if they had mistreated him. It was all she could risk with everyone watching them.

Her gaze swung to the other side of the aisle where Eric sat with a tall, reed-thin man with dark hair and a thin mustache. Eric's lawyer, she guessed. Emma studied her husband. . . . His golden-brown hair was brushed back from his forehead, just as he liked it. He looked exactly as he always did.

Flawless.

A creaking of a door turned her attention to the front of the room, toward the wooden platform and hastily constructed witness stand, the judge's high desk, and in the right corner of the small room, two rows of chairs with townsfolk on them. Emma took a bracing breath. The jury.

She scanned the faces and recognized four of the twelve men. Ron Crosby was one of the town's blacksmiths. Gilbert Murphey was a farmer who lived just outside of town. Then there was Mitchell Patterson. Her heart sank as she looked at him. He was a jack-of-all-trades, everything from barber to repairman to undertaker. But what made him frightening was that he was always in the middle of any catastrophe. He had loudly stated opinions on everything.

The fourth man she recognized was John Sumner, a slim, quiet man who made the most elegant furniture and jewelry boxes. Her mother had ordered several pieces from him over the years, and Emma had loved going into his shop, smelling the fresh-cut wood and running her fingers through the curling wood shavings. He had a daughter too, Maggie Sumner, but she had been several years older than Emma. Emma didn't know where the woman was, but she didn't think she was in St. Louis any longer.

Everyone rose and quieted as the judge entered the crowded room. She watched his face, saw the stern set to his mouth and the scanning, narrowed eyes. Emma tried not to shrink from his direct stare. He was angry, she realized, and determined. He had probably known Judge Littleton, might have even been his good friend. He would not stop until someone was punished for this crime. Everything in her wanted to bolt from the room. But she forced herself to stand up straight and not look away.

After the judge called the restless crowd into order and they were settled back upon their benches, the lawyer from Eric's side stood and called Eric to the stand. Eric rose from his seat, the action smooth, graceful. A confident unbending that reminded Emma why she had said yes when he asked her to marry him. He was everything any man would want to be—on the outside anyway. She bit down on her bottom lip as she saw it again. Could anyone blame her for her blindness? If they only knew.

Eric placed his hand on the Bible and swore to tell the truth. Emma barely restrained a humorless laugh.

"Mr. Montclaire, would you please state your full name for the court, sir?"

Eric looked at the jury, gave them a polite nod. "Eric Benjamin Montclaire."

"And what is your occupation, sir?"

"I was hired by the Ohio Fur Company to explore the West and set up trading posts along the route the Corps of Discovery discovered to the Pacific."

"Is it true that you are also a part owner in the Ohio Fur Company?"

"Upon the success of the venture, yes, that would be true."

Eric had never told her that. But then he had never told her much of anything about his business dealings.

"And when you began to gather supplies and men for the journey, is it true that you found you needed a journal written by one Robert Frazer?"

Eric paused and considered the question. "I learned of the possibility of an existing journal. But when one of my men asked Mr. Frazer about it, he said there was no journal."

"Did you believe him, Mr. Montclaire?"

"I wasn't sure he was telling the truth. Mr. Hardesty, one of my hired men, and I discussed approaching him with a large sum of money."

"And what happened next, sir?"

"Mr. Hardesty revisited him, and Mr. Frazer admitted he had written one but couldn't sell it."

"Did he say why he wouldn't sell it?"

"I believe he said it was poorly written. I think he was embarrassed by it."

"Objection!" At her attorney's bellow, Emma jerked in her chair. "Speculation, Your Honor."

The judge beat his gavel down on the desk with a thump. "Yes, yes. Counsel, advise your client not to speculate on the feelings and thoughts of others." He turned toward Eric. "Mr. Montclaire. Stick to the facts, sir. Do you understand?"

Eric nodded. "Of course, Your Honor."

The judge directed his hand toward the lawyer. "Proceed, Mr. Reynolds."

Mr. Reynolds approached Eric. "Sir, did you have any contact with the author of the journal after that."

"No. I did not."

"So you continued with your plans for the expedition without the journal?"

"That is correct."

Emma stifled a gasp. How could he lie boldfaced when she and Luke had seen the journal? She was brought up short as she realized that they might have been the only two. What if it came down to their word against his?

"Mr. Montclaire, did you hire a cartographer to accompany you on the expedition?"

"Yes."

"And is that man in this courtroom, sir?"

"Yes." Eric pointed at Luke. "Luke Bowen was hired to draw maps and help us find our way. He was on the Corps of Discovery expedition for some of the route, and I thought he would be the best candidate for our success."

"And how did Mr. Bowen perform as a cartographer?"

"He did an exemplary job. He knew the way and became our key navigator as well as cartographer."

"But there was something about Mr. Bowen that didn't set well with you, wasn't there?"

Eric's face changed. He looked down at his hands and flushed. "Yes." One word. How could one word carry such anger and resentment?

"Would you share with the court what it was about Mr. Bowen that you didn't care for?"

Eric looked up and stared hard at Luke. "He fell in love with my wife."

Growing murmurs came from the agitated crowd, and Emma felt all eyes on Luke and then her. The judge pounded his gavel. "Order! Order in the court."

When everyone stilled, Reynolds continued. "So your wife accompanied you on this expedition?"

Eric looked down at his hands again. "Yes."

"Now, Mr. Montclaire, that might seem strange to some folks. Can you explain why you would take your new bride on a dangerous excursion all the way to the Pacific? Why, some might even call it foolhardy."

Eric looked up and gazed at Emma. She forced herself to look back and show no emotion.

"At first, when the opportunity came to me, I had thought to leave her here. But we were newly married, and the thought of leaving her for two years or more"—he paused and looked toward the jury—"I built a small cabin on the keelboat for her privacy and protection. I purchased better provisions so that she would be well taken care of." He turned back toward Emma, his lovesick look a masterful deception. "I just couldn't do it. I couldn't leave her."

Eric's lawyer paused; the room fell quiet as the grave. Emma knew what everyone saw when they looked at the man on the stand—a man who loved his wife *so much* he couldn't bear to be apart from her.

Emma's head ached from the numbing success Eric was having as a witness. Surely someone else knew about the journal! After all, the original reason Judge Littleton tracked them down was because of the journal and Mr. Frazer's death. When would the questioning begin about the one thing she was sure of? That her husband, Eric Montclaire, had killed Judge Littleton with a poisoned—

A heavy chill washed over her. A poisoned meal. Eric had used a poisoned meal. But how was she to prove that? From the known facts—and that was all the judge said they were allowed to say—Eric had sat at the table and watched a man choke to death on his food. Yes, Eric had reacted strangely to the scene, didn't rush to the judge's side to help, didn't show any compassion as the judge fell to the floor . . .

But those facts could be interpreted as many different emotions. What if Eric was in shock? What if he said he was frozen, unable to move because he didn't know what to do?

Emma looked down at her clasped, gloved hands and realized for the first time that while she knew he had done this thing, she couldn't prove it.

She swallowed hard, seeing the night play back in her mind. She saw herself run to the judge's side and cradle his head in her lap. She saw Eric sit and stare at them. She'd known he was gloating, but there was nothing he'd said aloud to support her supposition. No, she'd known as a wife knows her husband's every move, every motive. But no one would recognize that. That was no proof that Eric poisoned the judge. She needed evidence.

And she didn't have it.

Emma lifted her head, her brows arching, her mouth tight. She looked at Eric on the stand as he looked up at her.

Their gazes locked.

Eric's lips twitched ever so slightly. But she saw it. A small, victory smile. The words of the lawyers, the words of the judge faded into a dim background as she saw the truth: she had no evidence that Eric had killed anyone.

An overheard conversation? He'd explained it away with silken ease. He wanted to pay the man for the journal, and no one would fault him for that. When later she would tell them he had told Mr. Hardesty to do whatever it takes to get the journal, the jury would think what Eric intended: that he'd meant to pay the man. They would believe the successful and wealthy Eric Montclaire over the silly imaginings of a wife.

A poisoned meal? Of course not! It was a gracious meal with the judge, a gesture of cooperation. Eric had only wanted to help in the investigation. He had only been a bystander, in shock, when he'd sat doing nothing while his emotional, hysterical wife cradled the judge's head in her lap as the poor man died.

And then . . . ah yes, and then.

Emma shot her husband. She . . . had . . . shot . . . her . . . husband. That fact was undeniable.

Emma squeezed her eyes shut. *God . . . please, God . . .* She shivered as she realized that they, the judge, the jury, this home-town audience of friends and strangers, would be stunned when Eric told of his shoulder wound, of the way she ran away, Luke Bowen hot on her heels. Especially now that everyone believed Luke was in love with her.

She took a deep, silent breath. Had Eric masterminded the whole thing? Was he capable of such . . . evil? She didn't know. But she did know that as he told his version of the story, he would appear the wounded one.

Eric Montclaire, the monster and murderer, had made himself the victim.

Unless she did something, something he thought certain she wouldn't do, he would win. Eric didn't need his beauty, his charisma, his overpowering charm to win against them. No. Unless Emma bared the truth, nothing but the truth and prayed they all would believe the truth . . .

She and Luke would hang.

Chapter Twenty-Seven

*L*uke felt as sick as he had ever been in his life.

Nothing matched this horrific feeling. Not the bouts with influenza, when he leaned over and spilled out the contents of his stomach into a bowl his mother gave him, her hand pressing a cool cloth on his forehead as he leaned back onto his pillow and thought for sure that he would die. Not even the one serious brush with death when he had contracted typhoid and the whole family with him. The neighbors nursed them all back to health, but it had left him weak and in a mental, cloudy haze for months.

No, none of that could begin to compare. His body felt soul-sick. His emotions were stretched to the breaking point. His gut knotted and churned. His skin felt hot and cold at the same time. But what frightened him the most was the hum of rage he felt toward the beautiful face in that witness box.

Never before had Luke met such a consummate liar. He almost believed Eric himself. And that thought led to more stomach-twisting nausea. They must all believe him. The jury believed him; he could see it in their eyes . . . except one. There was one man who looked on the whole proceedings with a thoughtful countenance. Luke had the sense he'd seen that man before—

Of course. It was the carpenter, the man to whose shop he had taken Emma when she collapsed. The man who gave him the jewelry box.

Finally, mercifully, the proceedings broke for the noon meal. Their attorney, Mr. Barthom, brought out a basket of food cooked, he explained, by Maggie Sumner.

Another name Luke recognized.

Luke turned to his attorney. "Who are you? Who appointed you our lawyer?"

"A man in Vincennes came to visit me. His name is James Therone. He is the husband of your mother's friend and was a good friend of Judge Littleton's." He paused as Luke made the connection.

"Yes, my mother's friend, Hattie Therone, knew the judge very well. He told me so himself."

"Mr. Therone came and asked me to take your case. He said that you were both innocent of any wrongdoing and that Eric Montclaire was a man not as he appears."

Luke huffed out a breath as he made the mental connection. "We are being tried, aren't we? Emma and I? You are the defending attorney?"

"Yes. If you are both acquitted and enough evidence points to Mr. Montclaire, I believe they will retry the judge's murder with Montclaire as the suspect."

Luke met Emma's gaze. They stared for a long minute as the meaning of those words sank in.

Emma was the first to break the silence with a whisper. "I'm afraid."

Luke couldn't blame her. "It looks bad, doesn't it?"

"He's convinced them."

Her voice was so thin it broke his heart anew. "We still get our turn, Emma. Stay strong. You are the one who said we should trust God, remember? Daniel and the lion's den?"

"Yes, but I think I was wrong, Luke. It's not a lion's den. It's an angel's den. He looks like an angel to them."

Mr. Barthom turned brisk with questions for both of them. They explained everything that had happened since they met. Toward the end of their noon hour, Mr. Barthom turned toward Emma and asked the one question Luke thought no one would ever come right out and ask her. "Mrs. Montclaire, did your husband beat you?"

She looked down, blinked rapidly, and smoothed her skirt. As they waited, she drew in a deep breath and nodded. "Yes, and more."

"What more? If I am to truly help you, I must know everything."

She swallowed hard and then spilled it out in a rush. "He held me down. Took me, you know, in the marriage way, but not that way at all. I-I would have given him anything. I loved him when we married. But . . . but he didn't want me to give it. . . . He wanted to have to take it." She looked up at them both, cheeks painfully flushed. "Does that make sense?"

Luke was boiling mad again. To hear her put it like that— aloud. He wanted to kill Eric. He wanted to hurt him first and then kill him. *God, forgive me. God, help me!*

"I tried to make everything . . . all right. I tried to make him happy. No. Not happy, something inside me knew I could never do that. But I tried to keep the darkness away from the both of us." She shrugged. "I was quiet when he wanted quiet. I was there when he needed me, body or mind or soul, listening and watching and waiting. I could tell when he wanted me to be something and . . . and I tried to be that at the time. But . . . it was never enough. It would always turn and then"—she took a great breath—"then I would know it was time."

Mr. Barthom's tone was remarkably calm. "Time for what?"

"Time to be his whipping boy." She pressed her lips together, and Luke realized she was trying to explain the unexplainable. "Time to take his punishment onto myself."

The two men sat in dead silence. They looked at each other, and Luke knew that Emma had made them feel, for a moment, some of what Eric had burdened her with. And in that moment Luke knew that whoever Mr. Barthom was, whatever force of man or God had convinced him to represent them, that Emma had just won him to their side.

"Well, then." Mr. Barthom cleared his throat and looked down at his hastily pulled pocket watch. "They will be back at any moment. We don't have time to go over our plan, but know"—he paused and looked at Emma and then Luke—"know that what happens during the rest of this afternoon is not going to look good. It won't encourage either of you. But I have a plan." He reached over and gave Emma's hand a squeeze and then Luke's shoulder a couple of strong pats.

The door swung open, and the crowd filtered back in. Luke turned in his seat toward the front, but before he gave his full attention to the next hours of testimony, he reached his hand under the table and found Emma's.

For a moment. A long, throat-clogging moment, he grasped her hand in his and squeezed tight.

How much longer would this torture go on?

Emma watched, her heart pounding, as Eric's attorney continued his questioning.

"Mr. Montclaire, you were hailed on October 13 by a canoe while on the Missouri River, is that correct?"

Eric nodded at the man, looking as calm as a puddle. "Yes."

"Who was aboard that canoe?"

"Judge Littleton and two soldiers, Lieutenant Eisler and Lieutenant Arthur from Fort Belle Fontaine."

"And what did the judge and these men want, Mr. Montclaire?"

"They said the author of the journal had been murdered. They wanted to question us and, I suppose, learn if we had the journal."

"Did the judge question you, sir?"

"Yes, he questioned me first."

"Why do you think he questioned you first? Were you under suspicion?"

Eric shifted in his chair, but his eyes and voice were clear of any emotion except calm. "I was the leader of the expedition, so it stands to reason that I would be questioned first. I think he suspected any of us but started with me as I had the most to gain by having the journal."

"Ah. The most to gain. Yes, it stands to reason you would gain valuable information if in possession of the journal, but there was someone else who stood to gain much, isn't there?"

"Yes." Eric looked at Luke. Emma seethed, her teeth clamped tight together to keep herself from yelling out *liar.*

"And who would that person be, sir?"

"Mr. Bowen. He was the guide and cartographer. He was the one who needed the journal the most."

"Did you ever see Mr. Bowen in possession of the journal?"

Eric nodded. "I can't be sure, as I didn't see it opened. But I did on occasion see him studying a brown, leather-bound book."

"Did you tell the judge this?"

"Yes, yes, I did."

"And what did Judge Littleton say to that?"

Eric shrugged. "He didn't say much. Just that he would stay on for a few days and question all of the men."

"Was that the last conversation you had with the judge about the journal, Mr. Montclaire?"

"Yes. He spent the next couple of days questioning my men. Everyone cooperated."

"When did you next see the judge?"

"Judge Littleton was talking to Mr. Bowen at the campfire. They seemed deep in conversation. After Mr. Bowen walked away, I approached the judge and asked him if he would like to have dinner with my wife and me. He accepted."

"Why did you invite the judge to dinner?"

Eric looked surprised by the question, then he shrugged and smiled a little. "Good manners, I guess. I thought the man looked tired."

There was a chuckle or two from the crowd. It was all Emma could do not to turn around and glare at them. Couldn't they see beyond his smooth, charming facade? Then she remembered that she hadn't. How could she expect them to see it?

After the crowd had settled down and the judge nodded to Eric's lawyer to continue, the man went on. "Mr. Montclaire"—he paused, clearly for effect—"tell the jury what happened that evening at dinner."

Eric shifted again in his chair, as if uncomfortable. The look he directed to Emma was perfectly balanced between shame and reluctance. Emma returned his look steadily, remaining as still as her heaving chest would allow.

"I instructed our cook, Billy Lang, to prepare a nice meal for the three of us. Emma cleaned the cabin and made the table look nice. I was gone fetching the meal when the judge arrived. When I got back, Emma was putting some flowers the judge brought into a pitcher of water, and they were talking. Everything seemed fine."

"So, you didn't notice anything amiss with Mrs. Montclaire or Judge Littleton?"

Eric hesitated. "Not really, though Emma seemed skittish and easily startled."

"Can you give us an example of that, sir?"

One side of Eric's mouth lifted, as though it pained him to remember. "She jumped when I came in with the food. Her hand was shaking when we held hands for the prayer. Things like that."

Emma couldn't hold in her tiny gasp. If she had done those things, it was because she was always nervous around her husband. That night had been no different.

"So the three of you said grace and then began to eat?"

"Yes, sir. We were about halfway through the meal having an enjoyable time when the judge grabbed his throat and his face turned red. It all happened so fast. Before I knew it, he had fallen out of his chair to the floor, wheezing for air."

"So he was breathing? He was wheezing?"

"Yes, I could hear the wheezing."

"What did your wife do, sir?"

"Emma threw herself down by his side and placed her hands on his chest."

"What do you think she was trying to do?"

"I thought she was trying to help him. I didn't think putting pressure on his chest was the best idea, but I didn't know what to do, so I just stayed back. I was going to go for help when the judge said something to Emma and then stopped breathing. Next thing I knew, Emma was screaming, and then she pointed his gun at me."

The crowd was stone silent as they digested this information. The jury was sitting up in their seats, necks craned forward, giving every appearance of being spellbound by the tale.

"Where did you say she got the gun, Mr. Montclaire?"

A look of shocked comprehension spread across Eric's face, as though he suddenly understood something. "From-from the judge's holster." He paused and cast a wide-eyed look at Emma. "If she . . . if she wanted that gun, then she'd have to kill him—"

"Objection!" shouted Mr. Barthom.

The judge gave Eric a stern look. "Sustained. Keep your opinions to yourself, Mr. Montclaire."

"What happened next?" His lawyer hurried to ask.

Eric looked pained. "She pointed the gun at me. She became hysterical, telling me not to come near her or she would shoot. I tried to reason with her, but she wouldn't listen. She picked up a pack—it was already packed and ready—and then she went to the door. I lunged for the gun thinking I could disarm her. But she"—he looked down a moment at his sling and then back up, staring at Emma with a look of bewildered hurt—"she shot me."

The room burst into cries of shock and outrage. People stared at Emma in wide-eyed disbelief. The judge had to beat the gavel on the desk several times before everyone calmed back down.

"Mr. Montclaire, one final question. When was the last time you saw your wife before today, sir?"

Eric made a great sigh and looked at Emma with shattered eyes. "She fled the room and disappeared. I later heard that she and Mr. Bowen had run away."

Emma could feel the outrage of the crowd behind her and see the looks of scorn in the jury before her. Everyone was quiet as the lawyer turned to Mr. Barthom. "Your witness, Mr. Barthom."

Emma watched, feeling her pulse throb in her clasped hands, as their lawyer approached the witness box. He cleared his throat and spoke in a calm tone. "Mr. Montclaire, is it true that you beat your wife?"

Emma froze. The crowd gasped. And Eric's lawyer jumped to his feet.

"Objection! *Objection!*"

The judge stared at Eric's lawyer and then looked at Mr. Barthom. "Sir, I hope you have good cause to ask such a question."

Mr. Barthom extended his head toward the judge. "Of course, Your Honor. I plan to give just cause why Mrs. Montclaire would shoot her husband and flee from him."

The judge paused, blinked his hooded eyes, and then inclined his head. "While there is no law to keep a man from beating his wife, I will allow it."

Mr. Barthom turned back to Eric. "Sir, is it true that you beat your wife throughout your marriage?"

Eric's face was red and thunderous. "Where did you hear such a thing? That is preposterous!"

"Sir, may I remind you of your oath before God. Did you ever strike your wife?"

"No!" Eric growled out. "She was clumsy, as anyone who knows her well can attest. There were bruises on her at times that appalled me, but I tried to remain patient with all of her accidents. That is all they were, accidents."

"We shall see," Mr. Barthom said with a smile. "That will be all, Mr. Montclaire."

Eric's lawyer unfolded from his chair like a snake slipping from under a rock. A shiver skittered down Emma's back. "Would Mrs. Emma Montclaire please take the witness stand?"

Emma's knees shook under her skirts as she walked to the box, waited while they untied her hands, and then held up one hand and placed the other one on the Bible and took the oath. The room was pin-drop quiet as she took her seat and looked up at the lawyer.

"Mrs. Montclaire, let's start with the journal." Could the man's voice be any more stern? "Did you ever see the journal in your husband's possession?"

"No, but I know he had it."

"You know he had it. Hmm." Mr. Reynolds rubbed his thin chin with a hand. "When is the first time you saw the journal with your own eyes."

Emma looked at Luke and swallowed hard. "Mr. Bowen had it. The day Judge Littleton came. Eric told Mr. Bowen to stay with me in the cabin—to keep out of sight, you know—but I knew Eric wanted Mr. Bowen to keep the *journal* out of sight until he could find out what was going on."

"So you are saying that your husband knew before ever speaking to Judge Littleton that the judge was on a hunt for the journal."

Emma nodded. "Yes. Eric needed that journal. I overheard him telling Mr. Hardesty to get the journal no matter the cost, and I knew he meant to have the author killed if need be to get it."

"Really? Mrs. Montclaire, couldn't 'at any cost' have meant money? That Mr. Montclaire planned to offer a great sum to have it? Why did you think he planned to have Mr. Frazer murdered?"

Emma took a deep breath and plunged on. "Because Eric saw me outside the door and knew I had overheard. After Mr. Hardesty left, he demanded I tell him what I heard and then what I thought about it. When I didn't answer him, Eric hit me, knocked me to the floor. I finally told him I thought he meant to kill Mr. Frazer, and he laughed and said I was the only one that really knew him. It was as good as a confession to me."

Emma heard the crowd grow restless on the benches.

"But it wasn't a confession, was it? He never said he achieved his goal of getting the journal, did he? And you never saw it in anyone's hands except for Luke Bowen's, isn't that right?"

"Luke had it because Eric gave it to him to study."

"How do you know that?"

"Because that is what Luke—Mr. Bowen—told me." She fought to control her tone, to hold back her frustration. Why was this odious man making Luke out to be a liar?

"And you believed a stranger, this *Luke* Bowen, over your own husband."

Emma scarcely had time for her mouth to drop open and then clamp down shut before the lawyer continued. "Mrs. Montclaire, what exactly is your relationship with Mr. Bowen?"

"He's a friend."

"A friend. A very close friend?"

235

Emma wanted to deny it, but she couldn't; she had taken the oath. "Yes, a good friend."

"Did Mr. Bowen ever kiss you?"

"Objection!"

The word startled her, and her gaze flew to Mr. Barthom.

"Withdrawn, Your Honor." Mr. Reynolds focused again on Emma, drew a breath, and shot out one question after another. "You love Mr. Bowen, isn't that right, Mrs. Montclaire? You would do anything, *say* anything, to save him?"

Emma shook her head. "I am telling the truth."

"Then tell us the truth, Mrs. Montclaire. Are you in love with Luke Bowen?"

Emma's eyes shot toward Luke's.

The lawyer leaned in; the crowd leaned forward as well. The judge turned grave eyes toward her.

"Mrs. Emma Montclaire"—she saw the triumph in the lawyer's eyes as he made each word pointed and clear—"Do— you—love—Luke—Bowen?"

She shook her head, but the truth she'd been denying beat loud and strong from her heart.

The lawyer turned and pointed at Luke and then pierced her with his eyes and all but shouted at her. "Do you love that man?"

A sob escaped Emma's throat. "Yes." God forgive her, she could lie to herself no longer. "Yes . . . I love him."

Chapter Twenty-Eight

*L*uke lay on his cot and tried to block out the low, dark chuckles from the next cell. Tomorrow, he was sure, he would be called to the stand. What was he to do?

Emma loved him.

He still couldn't quite believe everything that had happened that day.

She'd said she loved him.

How had he gone from plowing that field to being locked in this cell?

She'd had to tell the truth, and the truth was . . . she loved him.

A part of him rejoiced, but another part despaired. With those four words Emma had given Eric everything he needed to win.

He sighed and pulled a piece of paper from his pocket to reread the letter Mr. Barthom had given him before soldiers had hauled him back to Fort Belle Fontaine. His mother and sisters were coming. They should be here tomorrow.

He didn't know if he was glad or not. He needed their support, but the thought of them seeing him like this—

He rolled over and closed his eyes, not even knowing how to pray.

A clanging noise from the door jarred him awake moments later. One of the soldiers and another man, though the light was too dim to make out who it was, walked in.

"Mr. Bowen, you have a visitor."

Luke sat up and ran his fingers through his hair. A glance at Eric showed he was also trying to identify the visitor.

"This way, Mr. Bowen."

As Luke approached the bars, he saw that the other man was John Sumner, the carpenter he had met when he'd first met Emma. Luke frowned. Was he allowed to talk with a member of the jury?

The soldier cleared Luke's confusion, stating loud enough for Eric to hear as well, "I will be in the room while Mr. Sumner has a word with you. You may not discuss the trial in any way."

"The judge will hear about this," Eric growled from his cell.

Luke nodded to the soldier and followed him to a small room toward the front of the fort. The room was bare except for three chairs and a long wooden table. The soldier, a man Luke had not seen before, dragged a chair toward the door, sat down, and laid his gun across his lap, easy and ready.

Luke shook John's hand. "John, I must say I'm surprised to see you."

They took seats across from each other as John Sumner explained, "I had to thank you, in case I didn't have the chance later . . ."

Luke knew he meant in the case of Luke being found guilty. He swallowed hard. That statement alone coming from one of the jurors didn't bode well. "Thank me? For what?"

"You remember the music box that I made for Mrs. Montclaire? The one you took to Maggie at the saloon?"

Luke nodded. "I gave it to her. Told her it was from you, but that's all I did."

Sumner continued, joy on his face. "It did something for her. I don't understand it myself, but she"—he swallowed hard and smiled at Luke—"she came home. She left that life and came back home."

Luke smiled, his eyes growing wide. "John, I'm so glad."

"I never would have thought to give her a gift if it hadn't been for you. I begged her in letters now and then. I told her to come back and that I would never stop loving her, but something happened to her heart with that jewelry box. She won't speak of it, but she is back and trying to pick up a normal life again. We are thinking, after the trial, to move on. To give her a fresh start somewhere where no one knows her."

"Are the folks unforgiving, then?"

"They will always see her as a fallen woman. She is all I have. We could go anywhere."

"Stay in touch. Please write if—"

John took a sudden breath and nodded. "I know, I know. These are difficult times. I'm praying for you."

The soldier cleared his throat in warning. "Five more minutes."

Luke studied the man sitting across from him. "John, could you do me a favor?"

"Of course."

The soldier glared at them.

"My mother and three sisters are coming into town. They won't know anyone or have any idea where to stay. Could you be on the lookout for them? Help them find Emma's parents or somewhere to stay?"

"Of course. They can stay with Maggie and me. What is your mother's name?"

"Lenora Bowen. The girls are Torrance, Sophie, and Callie."

John grinned at him. "Four more females in the house. Maggie will be glad to have someone to dote on besides me."

Luke chuckled, and for a fleeting moment life felt almost normal. "Thank you, sir."

They stared at each other for a long moment, and something inside Luke clicked with surety. If he died, if they hanged him, this man would look out for his family.

Luke ducked his head to hide the emotions, but he knew John felt it too. They understood each other.

"Time's up." The soldier stood, and Luke and Sumner followed suit.

Back on his cot, Luke found some of his burden lifted. He even felt a little hopeful. That he could pray—which he did for much of the night.

Luke entered the packed courtroom escorted by Lieutenant Arthur. He followed the soldier to the table where Emma and Mr. Barthom already sat. As he passed a row in the front, just behind them he saw his mother and three sisters. The strain on his mother's face made her look older; her eyes were tight with fear as she lifted her chin toward Luke. Her hand went up to cover her mouth, but Luke could still hear the little sob as he walked past his family to his seat.

As he sat down next to Emma, she leaned over. "Is that your family? Behind us?"

"Yes."

"Oh, Luke. I'm so sorry."

"I would like to introduce you."

Emma's jaw grew taut, but she nodded.

Luke turned Emma toward his mother. "Emma, this is Lenora Bowen, my mother, and this is Callie, Sophie, and Torrie."

Emma nodded at each. "I'm honored to meet you," she said in a shaky voice.

"Our prayers are with you," his mother murmured, taking Emma's hand. When Emma turned back to face the front, Luke's mother looked at him, and he could feel her questions . . . no, one question: how could you have gotten yourself involved in this, son?

He wished he could explain it to her, but he couldn't. Not yet.

He turned back to the front, waiting. Mr. Barthom stood, hands on the table, and began. "I would call my next witness—"

Luke readied himself. It was time. Time to tell his side—

"Would Miss Sara Ward please come forward."

Sara Ward? Why was their attorney calling her?

Emma glanced at Eric and saw him pale as their cook and maid-of-all-work rose from the back of the room and walked to the stand. Sara didn't look at Eric, but Emma was sure the young woman felt the threat as he glared at her. Sara's voice shook as she took the oath, and she looked ghost-white as she sat on the chair in the witness box.

Mr. Barthom asked her name and job duties, then tilted his head. "Miss Ward, tell us your observations of Mr. and Mrs. Montclaire's marriage. Did they seem happy?"

Sara's voice could hardly be heard as she looked, wide-eyed, at the crowd of people, her gaze skittering over toward Eric. "Not as happy as some, I'm sure."

"What makes you say that?"

"Well, Mrs. Montclaire seemed afraid of Mr. Montclaire. Always tiptoeing around him, if you know what I mean."

"Did you see any evidence that Mrs. Montclaire was being harmed physically by her husband?"

Emma held her breath, but Sara didn't hesitate. She nodded. "She had bruises on her arms and face sometimes. I-I heard them fighting a lot."

"Fighting." Mr. Barthom paused. "Do you mean shouting at each other or did you hear more?"

Sara looked down at her lap and stated so low that the crowd leaned forward to hear her. "I heard some scuffling sometimes, upstairs. I heard the mistress cry out on more than one occasion. Once I heard a slapping sound, and then Mrs. Montclaire was crying. He told her to stay upstairs most of the time."

"What did you think of this, Miss Ward?"

She shrugged her slim shoulders. "I was sad for Mrs. Montclaire, but there wasn't much I could do to help her. One time I brought her a cool rag to lay on her face after Mr. Montclaire left. He always left in the afternoons."

"Do you know where he went in the afternoons, Miss Ward?"

"No, sir. I thought on some business thing. He was always having men come to the house for meetings. That expedition of his, you know."

Mr. Barthom nodded. "Thank you, Miss Ward." He turned to Eric's lawyer and indicated with a nod that he was finished with the witness.

Mr. Reynolds walked over to stand in front of poor Sara, who was looking ready to drop to the floor in a puddle. "Miss Ward, your testimony is filled with words like 'I guessed.' Let's do as the honorable judge asked and stick to the facts, shall we?"

Sara nodded. "Yes, sir."

"Did you ever see Mr. Montclaire strike his wife?"

"No, sir."

"Did you ever hear him threaten to harm her?"

Sara paused as if thinking back. "No, sir."

"So the fact that Mrs. Montclaire had bruises and the fact that you overheard some sounds that could be attributed to any number of causes"—he paused and smiled at her—"those things led you to think Mr. Montclaire was this monster that the accused wants us to believe. Is that right?"

Sara's forehead creased. "I guess so. It just didn't seem right, the two of them. She was always so jumpy around him."

"Did he give her any reason that you saw or heard to be so 'jumpy'?"

Sara's features went blank for a moment, then she shook her head. "Not that I saw or heard directly, I guess."

"Thank you, Miss Ward." Mr. Reynolds looked at the judge, who turned toward Sara, disquiet in his eyes, then said to the young woman, "You may step down, Miss."

Sara scrambled out of the witness box, making a dash down the aisle and out the front door.

Emma's heart sank. Of course Sara had never seen such things herself. Eric had always made sure they were alone when he struck her. But couldn't they see? Couldn't they understand what Sara heard?

Despair washed over her. She'd let herself believe something was finally going their way, but she'd been wrong. The situation was as bleak as ever.

Mr. Barthom stood and walked toward the witness stand, then turned and announced to the staring crowd, "Will Mr. Luke Bowen please take the stand?"

Emma wanted to reach out and grasp Luke's hand for luck. She wanted to communicate something to him, some encouragement or help, but she didn't. She looked straight ahead and lifted her chin.

Luke walked forward with his easy gait, his dark hair gleaming. She noted, almost in a daze, that it was longer than when she had first met him and brushed back from his face with a slight waviness. His face was clean shaven again, showing his strong jaw and chin. He stated his oath in a sure voice and took his seat.

Mr. Barthom turned toward him, the movement abrupt, and his words came loud and distinct. "Mr. Bowen, let's get something out of the way in the minds of these good people right now. Do you love Emma Montclaire?"

Emma couldn't help her gasp. What was their lawyer doing?

"Yes, I love her." Luke didn't look surprised by the question at all. He sat very still and upright, his face set, his eyes clear of any fear or guilt. He just looked . . . determined.

"And did you and Mrs. Montclaire commit adultery at any time or place?"

"No, we did not."

"Thank you, sir." He turned toward the jury and gave them a little smile. "It must have been difficult, loving a woman you couldn't have."

Luke nodded, glancing at Emma. "Yes, it is."

"And how did you cope with it, being her friend?"

Luke shrugged one shoulder. "Not very well sometimes, but mostly I just prayed. Judge Littleton pointed it out to me. Told me God wouldn't forsake me in the trial of seeing her every day but not able to love her."

Mr. Barthom's brows rose. "Judge Littleton knew of your love for Mrs. Montclaire? Well, sir, how is that possible?"

Luke chuckled. "He knew it before I had admitted it to myself. He was a very . . . wise man."

"So Judge Littleton advised you to pray? Anything else the judge said to you?"

Luke inclined his head. "Not about Emma so much. He told me about some of his own failings in his marriage and how life was, well, hard sometimes. He made me see the situation as a cross I had to bear. Mrs. Montclaire was not mine to love that way. But I could be her friend and support her against a"—he looked hard at Eric—"a husband who abused her. I had to do what I could for Mrs. Montclaire knowing I would never get anything in return."

"And what did you want in return?"

"To have her as my wife. To love her all the days of her life."

Emma felt the color drain and then flood her face. All their neighbors, relatives, the townsfolk . . . all were hearing this. She would never be able to lift her head in this town again. And yet . . .

Deep within she felt a rush of pleasure and pride in Luke. He'd fallen in love with her, yes, but he'd stayed honorable. As had she. And what Luke endured had been as great as what she had suffered.

Her throat choked for a moment. Why? Why had this happened to them? Likely, she would never know, but she was glad she had known *him*. She was still glad he had been there, was there now.

"Did the judge talk to you about anything else, Mr. Bowen?"

"Yes. We discussed the journal, and I told him everything I knew about it."

"Tell us about the journal."

"Mr. Montclaire gave it to me at our first meeting and told me to memorize it. He said that the journal had come at a great price and that I wasn't to let anything happen to it. I had the journal for the first weeks of the journey. It was sketchy, lots of missing information, but it had some helpful land descriptions in it. To be honest, I don't think we really needed it at all. But I didn't say anything. I just studied it."

"Go on."

"I told the judge what Emma told me the day Mr. Montclaire ordered us in the cabin together. That she believed Mr. Montclaire had murdered the author, or had him murdered, in order to obtain the journal. The judge wanted the name of the man who had committed the actual murder. He said without that name, all he had was our word against Mr. Montclaire's." Luke gave a small, weary chuckle. "I guess he saw this trial unfolding exactly as it has. Folks saying that Emma and me being in love with each other gave us reason to try to pin the murder on Mr. Montclaire and . . . well, get rid of him."

"Is that what is happening here?"

Luke gave a firm shake of his head. "No, sir, it is not. In fact, I asked Emma to write down the name, which she did. We'd been passing a Bible back and forth, reading it, praying for each other. She was going to put the paper with the name on it in the Bible as she passed it back to me. But the day she gave it to me, I could see that Mr. Montclaire had beaten her up pretty bad. She'd managed to keep the note from him, but he tore up the Bible. I gave the note to the judge, and that was the last time I saw him."

"You say Mr. Montclaire beat her so that he left marks? Right there on the trail, where everyone could see?"

"I figured that was why he rarely let her out of the cabin."

Mr. Barthom turned, wide-eyed toward the jury. "The law may not say anything about a man beating his wife, but gentlemen, what is the character of a man who locks his wife in a cabin like a prisoner and beats her and rapes her? I ask you, is that not the kind of man who would *murder* for something he wants? And then murder again to conceal his crime?"

"Objection!" Mr. Reynolds was on his feet as the crowd burst into loud murmurs. "Objection! Your Honor, we are not addressing the jury with closing arguments at this time!"

Outwardly Emma remained calm and unemotional. Inwardly, she was clapping her hands! Their lawyer was brilliant.

"Objection sustained!" The judge slammed the gavel down on his desk. "Mr. Barthom, are you finished with this witness?"

Emma's lawyer nodded, turned to Mr. Reynolds, and offered him a polite nod. "My apologies, sir. Your witness."

Mr. Reynolds walked to the witness stand, and Emma almost smiled at his agitated, hurried gait. "Mr. Bowen"—he said Luke's name like it was a dirty rag that he held by his fingertips—"did you ever see Mr. Montclaire raise a hand to his wife?"

"No, just the results of it."

"That was a yes-or-no question, sir. You are speculating on the cause of any bruises. Now, let me ask it again. Did you ever *see* Mr. Montclaire commit a violent, physical act toward his wife?"

"No." Luke ground the word out, clearly mad as a box of rattlesnakes.

"So when you saw bruises on Mrs. Montclaire's face, as her very dear friend," his voice oozed sarcasm, "you just assumed Mr. Montclaire was responsible?"

"The first time I didn't know what to think. She had a big bruise on her cheek that looked like a handprint. The second time I was suspicious. By the third time I was pretty sure what was going on. No one is *that* clumsy."

"Really? Are you an expert on matters of clumsiness?"

Luke took a short breath. Emma knew he was growing more and more angry at the lawyer, which was exactly what the man wanted. *Lord, please . . . give Luke strength and peace.*

When at last Luke answered, his tone was low, calm. "She's testified that he beat her. I believe her."

"You believe her because she said so. And why would you believe such a thing when no one has ever seen Mr. Montclaire raise a hand against his wife? Oh, wait. Because you love her and wanted her as your own. Isn't that right, Mr. Bowen?"

"I would have believed any woman with evidence like that."

"Really? And what would you have done for any woman? Would you have followed any woman when she ran off from her husband? Would you have poisoned the judge for any woman?"

"I did not poison the judge." Luke's voice hardened. "We don't know that anyone poisoned him. He could have had heart problems. That's what happened to my father."

At the depth of emotion—and rising frustration—in Luke's voice, a supercilious smile crawled across Mr. Reynolds's face. He went to the table where Eric was sitting and lifted up a corner of a folded cloth. He brought it to the judge's stand. "We have evidence from the scene of this monstrous crime that Judge Littleton was, indeed, poisoned, Your Honor. The apothecary, Mr. Williams, found high doses of strychnine in the beef."

Mr. Reynolds lifted the cloth, and the judge peered at the rotting, putrid beef beneath it. The front rows of the crowd and jury raised hands and sleeves to their noses at the stench. The judge waved it away. "Sir, remove that from my courtroom immediately. We will hear the testimony of the apothecary, I presume."

Mr. Reynolds looked to be holding back a smile as he directed someone to take the spoiled meat outside.

"I never saw that food or touched it!"

Emma couldn't blame Luke for his heated tone, but she knew it would only hurt him. She tried to catch his eye, to caution him, but he just went on.

"If the judge was poisoned, it wasn't by me. I was with the other men that night. You can ask any one of them."

Mr. Reynolds walked back over and nodded. "I did ask someone, Mr. Bowen. Someone named Billy Lang, the cook. Mr. Lang is willing to testify that you actually *were* near the food that night. That you helped him dish it onto serving plates right before Mr. Montclaire came for it."

"That's a lie. Ask the other men. I was with them around the campfire that whole night."

"You never left it? Even for a few minutes?"

Luke hesitated . . . and Emma's heart sank at his expression. *Lord . . . please . . .*

"I did leave for a few minutes at one point to, well, you know, relieve myself. I couldn't have been gone for more than five minutes."

Mr. Reynolds smiled his triumph. "Five minutes is more than enough time to plant poison inside the meat."

Luke shook his head. "But why would I do that if I love Emma so much? I could have killed all three of them."

The lawyer rounded on Luke. "Exactly! You and Emma planned this together, didn't you? Emma didn't eat any meat that night, as Mr. Montclaire will testify. Mr. Montclaire himself is here today only because he hadn't begun eating his beef yet. He prefers to eat one item on his plate in its entirety before beginning another. A lucky man, indeed, that he saved the beef for last." He fixed Luke with an accusatory glare. "Or *un*lucky, for you. Isn't that right, Mr. Bowen?"

Luke's face turned red and his jaw clenched shut. Emma was so stunned by the turn of events that she could barely breathe.

Everyone seemed to be waiting for Luke's response. If he gave way to the anger so evident on his features, they were done for. Emma wanted to look away, to close her eyes and put her hands over her ears. Instead, she kept her gaze fixed on him, willing him to look at her. No . . . to look to God.

One heartbeat, two. And then it happened. Luke's jaw eased, and the tension in his body seemed to melt away. His hands, which had been gripping the front of the witness box, relaxed; and he sat back in the seat. And then . . . he chuckled.

"I have to give it to you, sir, that is the most trumped-up, preposterous falsity I have ever heard in my life. Do you write novels? If not, you should consider it. Because, clearly, your imagination has no bounds."

Laughter rippled through the crowd, but they quickly sobered as Eric's lawyer turned to glare at them. When he turned back to Luke, his tone was as confident as ever.

"We shall see, Mr. Bowen. You may step down."

Chapter Twenty-Nine

The rest of the afternoon sped by as Mr. Barthom called the cook, Billy Lang, and then several of the men aboard the barge to the stand as character witnesses for Luke. They all agreed that Luke was a good man, one of the best they knew, but they admitted he had disappeared for a little while the night the judge died. And Billy said he'd had his back turned several times while Luke dished out the food for the Montclaires and the judge, giving him the opportunity to poison it.

Luke leaned over and whispered to Emma and Mr. Barthom. "I swear to you, I did not come close to Billy or the food that night."

"Why would Billy lie?" But even as Emma asked the question, she knew. Eric must have gotten to him, convinced him somehow to do it.

Exhaustion and the strain of the day made Emma's spine weak and her stomach tremble as the judge asked the lawyers for their closing statements. Mr. Reynolds went first.

"Gentlemen of the jury. I implore you to look at the facts. Luke Bowen wanted a job, a job he was unable to complete with the Corp of Discovery with Lewis and Clark. Imagine it, sirs. Your dearest dream cut short. You can see how he would do anything to have another chance at it, including murder Robert Frazer for the last known journal and therein cement his employment with Mr. Montclaire's expedition. What he didn't plan for was meeting and falling in love with Mrs. Montclaire. But fall in love he did.

"Blinded by his need to have another man's wife, he convinced himself that Mrs. Montclaire was being abused, giving him reason to hope for an opportunity to be rid of Mr. Montclaire. And Mrs. Montclaire? She loved him back, as she has admitted. When Judge Littleton arrived on the scene, imagine their fear that he would find Mr. Bowen guilty of murdering Robert Frazer. They knew the only way to stop the judge was to kill him. What more perfect plan than to pin the murder on the one man who stood in the way of their love? Mr. Eric Montclaire. It was a masterful plan.

"But Mr. Montclaire is no fool. He realized at that dinner with the judge, after seeing him poisoned at his own table, the length these two would go to be together. He tried to stop Mrs. Montclaire, but she shot him. She fired on an unarmed man, her own husband, to have what she wanted"—Mr. Reynolds turned and pointed, his finger like the barrel of a pistol— "Mr. Luke Bowen."

He fell silent, and Emma wanted to scream at him, "Just finish it! Finish your lies!"

After what seemed an eternity, he did so. "Gentlemen, take into account all the evidence you have heard and make the right decision. Luke Bowen stands guilty of the murder of Robert Frazer and Judge Littleton. Emma Montclaire stands guilty as an accomplice to the murder of Judge Littleton. I ask that you do the right thing, the hard thing where a woman is concerned, but the only thing your conscience will allow. . . . Rule guilty on all charges."

Nausea chewed at Emma's stomach as she scanned the somber faces of the men on the jury. Most were unreadable, except for Mitchell Patterson, who looked back and forth between Luke and her with narrowed eyes and a gloating glare. Looking away from the horrid man, she saw the one person who had compassion in his gaze. John Sumner. He gave her a short nod, and joy sparked within her. He was on their side! But would he be enough?

When Mr. Reynolds was once again seated beside Eric, Mr. Barthom rose and approached the jury. "Dear sirs, I, too, beg you to look at the evidence. The evidence of two good people caught in a web of deceit and evil. A woman, beaten and abused in a controlling marriage. And a man, yes, who wanted to finish the journey with Lewis and Clark he had been forced to abandon when his father died. But a man, as so many attest, of sterling character. A man who would never take another life to accomplish his dream, no matter how dear.

"Luke Bowen did not break the law by murdering Judge Littleton, nor did he plot to pin the murder on Eric Montclaire. No, Eric Montclaire poisoned the judge to keep his foul secret, that he ordered Robert Frazer's murder to attain the journal. Eric Montclaire beat, tied up, and raped his wife. Eric Montclaire is an evil, deceitful man who will do anything to have what he wants. He is the villain here. Not Luke Bowen. Not Emma Montclaire. Check your consciences, dear sirs, and you will see what I have seen."

He turned to rest his compassionate gaze on Emma. "A woman married to a man who would control her every move, demand her every thought, and take from her anything he wanted when he wanted it. And a good man who had the misfortune to be employed by such a monster. Caught in the middle, but devoted to doing what is right. A man who took the moral high ground for another's sake, even when he knew it could spell disaster for him."

Mr. Barthom paused, then took out a handkerchief and wiped at his perspiring brow. "Good sirs, I plead with you to vote Luke Bowen not guilty for the murder of Robert Frazer, and vote Luke Bowen and Emma Montclaire not guilty for the murder of Judge Littleton. Then let us try the true guilty parties—Eric Montclaire and Mr. Patrick Hardesty. Thank you, gentlemen."

As Mr. Barthom made his way back to the table and sat down next to Luke, the judge folded his hands in front of him and looked at the crowd. "We will break for the jury's deliberations." He brought down his gavel twice and stood.

Mr. Barthom leaned in and spoke in a low tone. "Emma is to go back to her parent's home. Luke, you will go with me to the trading post. When you hear the bell ring ten times, that will be the sign that the jury has decided, and you need to return here. Emma, a soldier will come to your home and escort you here. Be ready."

She clutched her hands in her lap. "Will it happen yet today, do you think?"

"Possibly." Mr. Barthom looked up at the jury who was leaving by a side door. "They will have a dinner break, and then the bell will ring three times to call them back in to deliberate. It could take a short time, or it could take a long time. One never knows."

So all that was left to them was to wait. Emma lifted her eyes to her lawyer's. "I understand. Thank you, Mr. Barthom, for everything you have done for us."

"Yes." Luke reached out to shake Mr. Barthom's hand. "We can't thank you enough."

Mr. Barthom's grave countenance wasn't encouraging. Nor were his words. "Save your thanks until we have heard the verdict."

Swallowing back her apprehension, Emma turned toward the middle aisle. It looked as though they were the last people to leave . . .

No. Eric and his lawyer stood across the aisle from her. Her gaze went to her husband's and locked there. What she saw in his eyes—the rage, the hatred—it took her breath away. Her hand rose to her throat. She watched as in slow motion Eric took a step toward her. He leaned in, placing his hat on his head as he hissed out his venom. "Good riddance."

Tears sprang to her eyes as he turned and walked away from her, making his way down the aisle toward the door, his back straight and slim in his perfectly tailored coat, his arm swinging easy and confident at his sides. His hat brim brushed against the back of the burnished curls on his neck.

A knot of grief formed in her throat. She remembered the first time she had seen him walk away from her just like that. She had looked at that spot beneath his curling hair, where his neck had shown above the collar of his coat, and thought it the most beautiful part of him. Something soft and vulnerable. Tender . . .

"Emma?"

She struggled to keep the knot of tears from overflowing as she turned and met Luke's gaze. He took her into his arms and held her tight.

The jury was gone, the judge was gone, everyone had left except their lawyer and a soldier who stood waiting at the door.

But she didn't care. She no longer cared who saw her with Luke. She let this man, this good man, hold her and comfort her.

One last time.

For whether they won or lost this trial, whether she loved Luke or not—though love him she did—she would never again risk giving her heart to any man.

John Sumner stood in the late afternoon sunshine, picking at the dinner pail Maggie had packed him this morning and thinking hard on all that had happened in these past few months. He thought of Maggie, how she had taken to Luke's mother and sisters. It broke John's heart that she was still so ashamed, so shy and quiet all of the time. Gone were the light and energy that used to fill her words and actions when she was young.

He thought of Luke's mother, Lenora Bowen. He smiled a little, taking a bite from his apple and blinking hard. She reminded him of his dear Martha. He'd lost his beloved so many years ago, when Maggie was just a little girl of four. Lenora not only looked enough like her that they could have been sisters; she also had that same strong, opinioned, take-care-of-everything way about her that Martha had possessed.

Lenora though, had something Martha didn't have: a strength from God. John could see that strength as Lenora struggled with her son's involvement with the Montclaires. He could sense this woman's determination to rest in her God.

In his own marriage he had been the one to trust God, to rely on God in all things. He knew his quiet meekness was a strength, and he was thankful to the bottom of his soul that God had placed that strength in him. But sometimes, times like today, he knew that strength looked like a weakness.

"God, I am going to need You." He swallowed the last of the apple. "I am holding on to You because you know these men. They look ready to believe Eric's side. He has many friends among them. And you know these men are looking out for their own interests where Montclaire is concerned. I don't think they care much about the truth, Lord. Correct me if I'm wrong."

The wind blew through the tree branches above him, shifting them enough to allow rays of the sunlight to spill across his face. John looked up and closed his eyes. He soaked in the warmth, feeling the strength he was being given.

A clanging of the steeple bell sounded from the building and told him that his reprieve was over. The jury was being called back in to deliberate.

He raised his face one last time and lifted his hands to feel the warm rays too. The wind blew stronger. He stood, straightened.

He was ready.

The courtroom was dark, and it took a moment of standing still and blinking for his eyes to adjust. After a few moments he saw that several members of the jury were seated in a semicircle near the judge's seat. He walked forward and sat down next to Dan Richardson, the town's baker, though the man's wife did the work while he spent most of his days in the saloon. John turned away the thought that the man might have been with his daughter. He had to resist that thought many times, and it was never easy.

"Sumner." Dan nodded to him.

"Hello, Dan." John nodded at the other men while they waited for the last two to join them. Once Gilbert Murphey, a farmer from outside of town, and Ron Crosby, one of the town's blacksmiths, had seated themselves, they began.

"Judge said we should choose a leader to run things," Ron Crosby noted. "Anybody want that job?"

"I think Mitchell Patterson should do it," David Brown said. "He always has an opinion about everything." The men chuckled.

"No, that won't do." Gilbert Murphey looked around. "We need someone who *doesn't* have an opinion about everything, someone who can keep order here but allow us each to have our say."

They all paused and then Gilbert spoke again. "What about John Sumner here. We all know his quiet nature. I'd listen to him."

John felt a shock go through him as the others agreed. God was answering his prayers already. "Well," he drawled out, "all right then. Would someone like to write this down as we go along?"

Louis Perry, the schoolteacher, volunteered. After coming up with a slate and chalk from the room's school cabinet, John got down to business. "Who believes that Luke Bowen murdered Mr. Frazer for the journal?"

Nine hands shot up. John motioned to Perry to write down their names.

"I see." Even though his voice was calm, his heart was pounding in his chest. Luke and Emma were in real trouble. "Who believes Luke Bowen and Emma Montclaire conspired to murder Judge Littleton?"

All hands went up.

All but his.

Luke and Emma walked side by side into the courtroom. Their shoulders didn't touch, their hands didn't clasp, but they were united, more so than ever.

"All stand for the honorable Judge Griffin!" A voice shouted out.

The assembly stood as Luke and Emma took their place behind the wooden table and chairs. They remained standing as the judge walked into the room, waited as he took his seat, and then they took theirs, the sound of the rustling of garments settling like the feathers of a flock of birds lighting on a branch.

The room grew silent and expectant. Everyone awaited the verdict.

Emma held herself within a small, still place. It was the secret place she had gone to so many times these past months. Times when Eric was breathing hard and fast in her ear. Times when her wrists ached from his grip and her body twisted beneath him. Times when time did a strange thing and ticked and ticked, slower than it should. She closed her eyes briefly, commanding her heartbeat to slow its pounding gallop.

"Will the jury please stand." The judge sounded more polite than he'd ever sounded during the trial.

Emma's eyes shot open, and her gaze swung toward the men that held her future—her life—in their hands. She clasped her trembling hands together in a tight grip against her lap and lifted her face toward them.

The judge looked at them for a long moment, and then, in a deep tone that spoke of the monumental moment, he asked them, "In the murder of Robert Frazer, how do you find Luke Bowen?"

John Sumner answered for the jury. "Not guilty, Your Honor."

Emma took a startled breath and looked up into Luke's eyes. She wasn't sure what to think, but she rejoiced. She rejoiced.

"In the death of Judge Littleton, how do you, the jury, find Luke Bowen?"

The room stilled, and Emma could feel the cords of muscle in Luke's hand stretched to the point of pain for both of them.

"We find Luke Bowen—"

John sounded so sad! Emma let out a little cry, suddenly knowing what was coming.

"—guilty, Your Honor."

The courtroom grew loud with celebratory shrieks from some, appalled gasps from others. Emma collapsed at the verdict. She fell forward as the breath whooshed out of her. Luke gripped her hands tighter in his. He leaned over, and his breath whispered into her ear.

"Be strong, Emma. Be strong until the end."

The judge's voice went on. "And Emma Montclaire? How do you find her in the death of Judge Littleton?"

John looked down at the hat clutched in his hand. He looked back up at Emma, his gaze shattered. "We, the jury, find Emma Montclaire, guilty of conspiring to murder Judge Littleton, Your Honor."

John Sumner's eyes held hers. She saw it then. How he had fought for her and Luke. How hard he had tried. And how he had been overruled by the majority.

Emma fell forward, a cry escaping her throat.

God! She wanted to scream, to wail. But even as those feelings swept her, something else, something more powerful flowed into her. *God . . . Father . . .* She lowered her head and let out a long, slow breath. *God, Your will be done.*

A sudden light shone from the back of the room, and the creaking of the door announced a new presence. A loud, gasping commotion sounded from the back of the courtroom.

Emma sat up straight. The judge's face had gone paper white.

She turned in her seat and looked, even as the others in the room were looking. A man shoved the door wide and took a few steps inside. Emma shielded her eyes against the light behind him, then heard the crowd's whispers turn into shouting.

One by one, people exclaimed as they saw . . . something, *someone—*

Emma gasped. It wasn't possible. But she heard the name before she saw his face.

"Judge Littleton! It's Judge Littleton!"

He walked into the room with that same, familiar gait. The steady step of a man who had wrestled with life and figured out a few things. He walked straight up to Emma, then stopped and put a hand under her chin, lifting her gaze to his. A big smile cracked across his broad face. "I promised you, beloved one. Emmanuel. God with us."

Chapter Thirty

*L*uke caught Emma as she fell back in a dead faint. The crowd went wild, babbling like a flock of squawking chickens. Luke reached for the cup of water on the table in front of him, dipped his fingers in it, and flicked some water onto Emma's face, to no avail.

"Here, son. Let me help you." Judge Littleton's deep voice resounded as the crowd grew quiet to hear.

Luke looked up and grinned at the man. "Good to see you again, judge. I can't *tell* you how good it is to see you."

The judge chuckled. "I reckon so. I would have been here sooner and saved you both all this trouble, but I had some folks I needed to look up before I made my reappearance. Hope you don't mind too much."

Luke grinned at the man. "Nothing that can't be forgiven and forgotten. Just glad you made it before the noose grew any tighter around our throats."

The judge patted Luke's shoulder and then looked at Emma. Luke realized everyone in the room had grown quiet to hear their exchange. A quick glance at Eric revealed that his face had paled. The cad looked ready to faint himself!

The judge's voice drew Luke's attention back to Emma.

"Let's see if we can't revive this lovely, young woman, shall we?" The judge leaned down and spoke in a low, steady voice to the unconscious woman. "Emma. Emma, wake up, darlin' . . . there isn't anything to fear. Wake up."

Emma roused, gave a small groan, as if she didn't want to awaken, but her eyelids fluttered and then opened.

She blinked several times and reached out to touch the judge's face. "Is it really you?"

"Yes, ma'am. Now you want to hear how I came to be here, don't you?"

She nodded, her lips pressed together in a happy, half-afraid smile.

The judge, with Luke's guiding hands, helped her sit up. Luke handed her the glass of water and watched while she took a sip, her eyes never leaving the judge's face.

Judge Littleton stood, hands on his hips, chest puffed out, and surveyed the room. He nodded to an acquaintance or two and then turned toward Judge Griffin. "May I approach the bench, Your Honor?"

Judge Griffin chuckled, then tried to look stern . . . and then chuckled again. "I think you had better."

The two judges talked in hushed tones. At one point Judge Griffin threw back his head and laughed so hard he was wiping tears from his eyes. After a few more minutes of whispered conversation, Judge Griffin faced the crowd. "Well, folks. The case of the murder of Judge Littleton has been dismissed, due to the fact that"—he paused and laughed again, wiping one eye with his hand—"Judge Littleton is standing in full health among us." He turned in his chair and glared at Eric. "But the murder of Robert

Frazer has new developments. Judge Littleton, would you like to call your first witness?"

Judge Littleton turned toward the crowd and then acknowledged the jury. "I know you are all curious as to how I am standing here, alive and well, and I will tell that tale for many years to come, I imagine. But right now we still have the death of a good man, a man that went with the Corp of Discovery, a man who kept a journal, not a very good journal he said, not something he thought to ever publish or sell. But a man who loved his life . . . and the adventure he'd had. This man was murdered. Strangled. And then his journal, his private thoughts and drawings, were stolen from him." Judge Littleton's sharp-eyed gaze scanned the room, then came to rest on Eric Montclaire.

Luke watched as a drop of sweat ran from Eric's temple down the side of his jaw—and it took all Luke's will not to break into a grin.

Judge Littleton reached inside his coat and pulled out a worn, brown leather book. He lifted it above his head and waved it at the crowd. "Ladies and gentlemen," he turned to the jury, "gentlemen of the jury, I give you Robert Frazer's journal."

He pulled the journal close and opened it. "'Tuesday, December 25. In honor of Christmas, Captain Clark issued a round of brandy to the accompaniment of a round of ammunition in the morning time. We'd given the Mandan Indians full warning that this day they should not come to visit as we were celebrating our Savior's birth. At one o'clock we raised the American flag for the first time above our newly constructed Fort Mandan and then had dinner. Later in the afternoon a shot rang out to announce the beginnings of a dance which continued until evening time. There were no women save our interpreters' squaws, who looked on and clapped in time with the music.'"

Judge Littleton lowered the book. He looked down at it in his hands for a moment and then back up at the jury. "Good people of St. Louis. I have spent the last several months looking into this matter. You might wonder why I would take time from my post as circuit judge to find the killer of the author of this journal, and I will tell you that I don't really know why. Something struck me as important about it. Something told me not to give up. In the last few months I have uncovered evidence that I believe will change your minds, gentleman, about one person. And that person is Eric Montclaire."

Luke felt Emma stiffen beside him. He reached for her hand again and held it tight beneath the table. She squeezed back.

The judge looked at Judge Griffin, his expression somber. "I would like to call Maggie Sumner to the witness stand."

John's daughter! Luke turned and watched as Maggie rose from the very back of the room. She walked toward the front, her head down, her black hair prim and neat beneath a straw bonnet, her dress modest and simple.

Maggie took the oath and then sat in the witness box.

Judge Littleton went to stand before her, smiled kindly, and showed her the journal. "Miss Sumner, do you recognize this book?"

"Yes, sir . . . judge . . . Your Honor."

Judge Littleton chuckled. "*Judge* will do fine for now, Miss Sumner. Now, please tell us, where and when did you last see this book?"

Maggie cast a glance at Eric, her face flushing pink as a new rose. "In my room at The Ace. Robert Frazer asked me to keep it for him."

"Miss Sumner, how can you be sure that this is the same book?"

Maggie took a deep breath. "I read it. Every last page. I remember the entry you just read. I can quote others. Robert Frazer wasn't a bad writer, and I wish I could have told him so. He . . . his story and all that went on during that journey . . . well, sir, it captivated me."

Judge Littleton looked down at the journal, pursed his lips, and then looked back up toward Maggie. "Miss Sumner, did Eric Montclaire say anything to you about this journal?"

Maggie's voice quivered a bit, but she went on. "He said he wanted to borrow it. When I told him I would have to ask Robert Frazer, as it wasn't mine to lend, he laughed and snatched it out of my hands. He waved it in front of me and said, 'I always get what I want, Maggie dear.'"

"Did you try to convince him to give you back the journal?"

"Yes, but he wouldn't listen, so I let the topic drop. I thought I would send a note to Robert when Eric left and let them work it out between themselves. I never questioned Eric about anything."

The judge cocked his head. "What do you mean by that, Miss Sumner?"

Maggie looked away for a moment, then faced the judge again to answer. "Eric didn't allow questions. I was afraid of him. I wanted to ask him why he came to me when he had a wife"— she glanced at Emma and then ducked her head—"who was so perfect. I couldn't understand it, but I was"—she flushed scarlet, her voice so low that Luke had to lean in to hear—"I'm sorry to say I was flattered. He never hit me, but he bragged about hitting and slapping and beating his wife. He would say it when . . ." She lowered her head, as though silently begging Judge Littleton not to make her continue.

"Yes, Miss Sumner? When did he tell you that he beat his wife?" The judge's voice was like still, calm waters.

"When he—when he was with me," she gasped out, then looked toward Emma as tears glistened in her eyes. "I'm sorry. I'm so sorry."

Luke felt Emma soften and then lean forward beside him. He watched as she tilted her head to one side and contemplated the woman. His heart swelled with pride as he saw her mouth the words, *I'm sorry, too.*

"And Miss Sumner, did you send a note to Robert Frazer telling him about the journal?"

Maggie shook her head. "I went to see him. I-I was the one to find him, his body. He was on the floor . . . dead." She put her gloved fist to her mouth and looked away.

"Thank you, Miss Sumner." Judge Littleton turned to Eric's lawyer. "Your witness, sir."

Mr. Reynolds opened his mouth, shut it, looked back and forth between Maggie and the judge, and then surged to his feet. Luke choked back a chuckle. Reynolds was a different man now that the cards were stacked against them.

"Miss Sumner . . ." Mr. Reynolds paused, then his eyes narrowed. "So you are a prostitute."

Maggie lifted her chin. "Not anymore."

"But at the time under discussion, you were a prostitute, is that correct?"

"Yes."

"And your testimony is that Eric Montclaire took the journal from you."

"Yes, he did."

"Mr. Montclaire testified that he never touched or saw the journal. Now, should we believe the word of a successful man of business or a prostitute?"

"Or a man who beat his wife, do you mean?" Maggie shot back.

"Again, your word against his."

"And the maid's word, and Luke Bowen's word, and Emma Montclaire's own word. Why would all of us lie?"

Mr. Reynolds turned away, waving a dismissive hand at Maggie. "That will be all, Miss Sumner."

Judge Griffin shared a long look with Judge Littleton and then directed his attention to the jury. It was the same jury that had deliberated in the case against Luke and Emma, except for John Sumner who had been replaced since his daughter was the judge's key witness. "Are you prepared to make a ruling on the guilt of Eric Montclaire in the murder of Robert Frazer?"

The whole jury, every one of them, nodded.

"Very well. I will give you fifteen minutes."

The gavel beat upon the desk for the last time.

While the jury of twelve men went outside to deliberate, the bystanders, the accused, and the two judges sat in silent contemplation. Emma leaned toward Mr. Barthom. "Might I speak for a moment privately with my husband?"

Mr. Barthom's eyebrows drew together. "I don't know why you would want to, ma'am—"

"Just for a moment. I have to tell him something before it's too late."

The lawyer contemplated her and then gave a slow nod. "I will speak with the judge."

Emma prayed as Mr. Barthom approached the bench. When he came back, he shrugged. "It is up to them. I have made the request."

There were only ten minutes left. Eric and his lawyer bent their heads together, speaking low. Eric looked over at her, then gave a demanding gesture with his hand.

He'd agreed.

Emma was escorted to a small, private room which was furnished with desks and benches, a map of the world on the wall, and a blackboard facing the chairs. She seated herself on a bench and bowed her head over her clasped hands.

At the sound of the door opening, she turned, then stood and started to smooth down her skirts—but stopped the automatic response to Eric's presence. She didn't have to do that any longer. Not ever again.

She clasped her hands tightly together. "I never used to do that, you know."

"Do what?" He sounded both angry and afraid.

She looked away from him and repeated the movement of smoothing down her skirt. "Worry so much, about . . . well, everything."

"What do you want, Emma?"

"When we married, I knew I wasn't perfect. I knew I was . . . clumsy sometimes and not as elegant as a woman should be, especially your wife." She took a long, slow breath and a step toward him. "But I thought I could make you happy. I never did, though, did I? And I've begun to understand that I couldn't. No one could. Eric . . . there is only one hope for you now."

A knock sounded at the door, and Emma rushed out the rest. "He loves you, Eric. God. He loves you now, in all your sin. Turn to Him. Pray God's forgiveness, Eric. That will save you."

Eric laughed—an ugly sound, full of condescension. "So you found religion, did you? Silly, silly woman. There is no God, Emma." Another knock sounded, and something flitted across his features. Could it be . . . ? Was it fear? He met her gaze again. "Will *you* forgive me, Emma?"

She couldn't tell if he was serious or mocking her, but it didn't matter. She wanted to answer him, to say she did forgive. But memories of all he'd done rushed over her—every taking touch, every time she'd suffered at his hands. Then she remembered Jesus, what He had taken for them all. Tears filled her throat and eyes, but she could not answer.

She turned and opened the door . . . and walked away without looking back.

Chapter Thirty-One

No one in the courtroom spoke. No one moved. Emma held her breath as Judge Griffin turned to the jury.

"Have you made your decision?"

The new leader of the jury nodded.

"In the matter of the murder of Robert Frazer, how do you find Eric Montclaire?"

"Guilty of being an accessory before the fact, Your Honor."

The judge turned toward the crowd. Quiet descended as he addressed Eric directly. "I hereby do sentence Eric Benjamin Montclaire to hanging by the neck until dead for the murder of Robert Frazer."

Emma's hand rose to her throat. Relief flooded her, but as she turned and looked at her husband, she felt a stab of fear for him—and profound grief that it had all come to this end.

Emma waited until the crowd had left the courtroom, then asked her parents and Luke to leave her alone for a few moments. She fell to her knees beside her chair and sent up a prayer of thanks to God. Tears, like freeing rain, washed down her cheeks as her shoulders shook with silent sobs. It was over. Luke was safe. She was safe. They would live!

Finally, she rose from the bench and, with unbound wrists, her steps light, she walked out into the open sunshine and looked up and up. She threw her arms out to each side as she twirled under the gray-blue sky, felt the sting of the cold air in her throat, and realized she would see the coming winter.

She smiled. There was only one place she wanted to go at this moment, and that was to an altar.

St. Louis had a small Catholic church. It wasn't the church her family attended as they always awaited the circuit preacher, but she didn't care. It was a church, and there she would find a wooden altar. She walked through the town, ignoring everyone—her parents, Luke, the few supporters who had believed in them. . . . All were waiting for her at the street's corner, but she didn't cast them a glance. She looked straight ahead and hoped the door was unlocked.

As she neared the church, she heard music. It was low and quiet, but there was singing too. She eased the door open and slipped inside. A woman was at the piano, playing a hymn and singing in a soft, sincere way.

Amazing Grace
How sweet the sound
That saved a wretch like me
I once was lost, but now I'm found
Was blind, but now I see
'Twas grace that taught my heart to fear
And grace my fears relieved
How precious did that grace appear
The hour I first believed

The sweet sound of the singer's voice shot straight into Emma's heart. She made her way to a back row of benches and sat down, closing her eyes as the music washed over her. The woman sang the chorus, and Emma lifted her head to watch as this beautiful creature sang the next verse.

When the song ended, the woman turned and saw Emma. She paused, and Emma wondered if she had angered her by listening uninvited. But after a moment the woman rose, turned from her instrument, and walked toward Emma.

As she grew closer, as her face came out of the shadows, Emma gasped. "Maggie Sumner?"

She had become a beautiful woman, Emma thought as Maggie sat down beside her and took hold of Emma's hands.

"I meant what I said at the trial, Emma. I am so sorry." Maggie leaned forward, her face pained and sad. "I have sinned against you."

"Sinned against me?" Emma shook her head. "You saved me today. What you said in that courtroom validated the truth, everything Eric has ever done to me. Every strike of his hand. Every bruise I've tried to cover. You made them believe me. And I thank you. I thank God for you. You were so very . . . brave."

Maggie gave her a small smile. "*You* were the brave one. I don't think I could have endured all that Eric did to you. I made my own bad choices, but you were swept along into an evil that you had no control over."

Emma looked down and bit her bottom lip. "Did he never hurt you?"

Maggie shook her head, her green eyes gazing into Emma's. "No. Not in that way."

Emma took a deep breath. "Maybe he loved you then."

"No." Maggie shook her head. "He only spoke of you." She gripped Emma's hands tighter. "I hated you for that. I wanted him to be mine."

Emma looked down at their clasped hands and pulled hers away. "I am sorry he wasn't. Maybe with you he would have been different."

"I'm thankful I didn't get what I wanted. I was so foolish, but Emma, I found God." Maggie rocked back and laughed a little. "It was strange. Love came in a jewelry box that my father made for you, but Luke Bowen . . . he brought it to me."

Emma looked up sharply. "You were with Luke, too?"

"No!" she gasped out. "Never! As everyone can see, Luke has only you in his heart."

Emma took a long moment to digest all Maggie had said. Then she looked up into Maggie's pleading gaze. "I didn't need a gift from Eric. He gave me gifts when he was sorry. I am so glad Luke gave it to you. I am so glad it led you to God."

Happiness and contentment brightened Maggie's features. "I remember you from school, you know. You were so shy then. So sweet and pretty but so different. I thought to talk to you once, but you seemed so . . . good. I didn't know what to say. You seemed so sure of yourself, quiet and happy just to be you even if you were all alone."

Emma gazed toward the altar of the church. "I was lonely. I never really had any close friends. I wish we could have been friends."

"It's not too late. I could use a friend right now too."

Emma motioned toward the piano. "Your singing was like angels singing. You should sing always."

Maggie laughed. "I will. I promise." She leaned back against the bench. "Thank you, Emma. You are truly all that they say you are."

Emma cocked her head to one side, felt one eyebrow raise. "What do they say I am?"

"A lady. A true lady."

Emma laughed. "I have been more a coward than anything of late, I fear."

"A person in the face of what you have endured is called a hero."

Emma looked down now, her throat clogged. "No."

"Yes. You have inspired every woman in that courtroom. I couldn't have endured what you did. I would have run away."

"I tried, remember?" Emma didn't try to restrain her rueful smile. "I tried many times and in many different ways."

"What will you do now?"

Emma looked up at the giant cross etched in the wood of the wall beyond the altar. "I don't know, except to follow Him."

They gazed at the cross together.

Emma knew, sitting there in silence, that she had found the friend she never had. She knew that somehow, some way, this woman would be forever in her life and that they would support and love each other.

"I think I would like to pray now." Emma rose from the bench. "I have much to be thankful for this day."

"Would you mind if I prayed with you?"

"No." Emma motioned her to follow. "I would love that."

They knelt down, bowed their heads, and prayed.

Side by side.

Separate but together.

Eric sat on the cot in his cell, the pillow pulled up close to his stomach, alone with his thoughts.

He would die tomorrow.

All his dreams of a life of wealth and power and meaning, taken away by a conversation with a hired man and a wife who told the truth.

Emma's face rose up in his mind. It was her face as it was on their wedding day when she stood before him and offered herself like a lamb to the slaughter. He had loved her that day, still loved her more than was comfortable. She was the one thing he had allowed into his life that he wasn't sure he could control. There was a quiet, steady grace about her that went core deep. He recognized it the moment he met her at the musicale soiree. Yes, she had a remarkable aptitude for clumsy accidents, but that was only on the outside. Inside, deep inside, he had sensed she possessed the kind of strength that could endure. Endure his pain.

That was why he'd married her.

He thought back on all the women—beautiful, wealthy, prestigious—he could have married. As he'd grown into adulthood, his beauty hadn't faded; it had only become more intense. . . . The more he wanted, the more it blazed from his eyes, the more they all wanted him. But Emma was the first one, the only one, that would allow him to spill out his pain on her like a sweet, overpowering nectar.

His mental gaze roved over her face. His hand lifted as if to touch the rounded curve of her cheek one last time. A crack creaked open in his heart as he remembered how he had treated her, all that he had done to her flesh, her soul. He blinked hard, and two tears raced down his cheeks—though whether for her or himself, he couldn't be certain.

A loud, short pounding sounded on the door. He bolted up and wiped his face with the backs of his hands.

A soldier walked in with a man following behind him. The man was in the shadows, but there was something so familiar about him. The way he walked, the slouch of his shoulders, the shortened gait, the head tilted up—

Eric jumped to his feet and strode over to the metal bars of his cage. The soldier stepped aside. "You have a visitor."

Everything in Eric stopped. His heart froze and then roared in his ears. His mind went blank. All emotion halted for a second, then two, then three . . . as he gazed at his father's face.

A sudden movement in his chest reminded him to breathe. He watched, dumbstruck, as the soldier turned and left them alone. His father shuffled a step closer, then hesitated, holding a flat book in his hands.

The silence stretched, wretched, interminable. Until finally . . .

"Son." His father hung his head.

"What are you doing here?" Eric's heart was now pounding so hard, roaring so loud in his ears, that he didn't know if he would be able to hear the man answer. "How did you find me?"

"I've always known where you were. Judge Littleton wrote to me right before he left to go after you." His father held out the book.

Eric stared at it. It was slim but almost as wide as it was long. He reached out his hand through the bars and grasped it.

Eric turned away from his father, took a step farther into his cell, and opened the book. His hand trembled against the page as he saw a newspaper clipping attached. It was an article about him, his first real success as a banker. He had struck a deal that had given that bank a lot of money, a lot of profit. He flipped the page and saw notes, torn off scraps of paper that had been glued down none too well.

Eric has moved to Philadelphia to work for the First Bank of the United States. And then Eric received praise from the bank president for his help to recharter the national bank. Another clipping came after the words, *My son goes to Paris as secretary to the United States minister to France.*

He turned the next page and saw his face sketched next to three more articles. *Eric has returned and is back at the bank. They say he worked on the Louisiana Purchase.* A few more pages and then, *The boy is moving west, to St. Louis. I don't know why.* And then an article from *The Missouri Gazette* announcing his engagement to Miss Emma Daring. The last page held an article about his position with the Ohio Company and his excursion to the Pacific.

Eric slammed the book shut and held it tight to his chest. He looked up at the far wall, unable to move. His life, his whole life and everything he had ever worked for, was in this book. He turned. "Where did you get this?"

His father shrugged, and Eric realized how old he had grown. He was still reed thin, still moved the same, though a little slower; but his hair was white now, and his tanned face had deep lines.

Rage boiled up from the depths of Eric's soul. *"Where* did you *get* this?" He walked over and thrust out his arm from between the bars. With a flick of his wrist, he threw the book at his father.

His father bent down to pick it up and then held it to his chest, just as Eric had done. The action, that reminder that he was like his father in any way, curled his lip.

"Son, I know you are angry with me, and you have every right to be."

"Don't say you're sorry. Don't you dare." Eric let the full force of his hatred infuse his words.

His father looked down at his dusty boots. He rocked forward a little, his grip still tight on the book. "I've been keeping track of you all these years. When you left . . . it broke your mother's heart. She wasn't ever the same." His father looked up into Eric's eyes with pain, remorse shining through. "She died about five years ago."

"That was your fault." Eric didn't feel pain or shock of his mother's death. There was no room. All within him was taken up with rage toward the man standing in front of him.

"Yes, yes it was. She didn't have the life she should have had and I'm sorry about that. I'm real sorry about that. So, like I said, I've been keeping track of you, son. I couldn't believe all you accomplished. I was so proud of you."

"I don't *want* your pride in me! I don't want anything from you! Now, get out!"

His father shook his head. "Not quite yet. I have to say what I came to say." He took a shallow sigh and then looked back up at Eric. "You might not ever forgive me, but this is your last chance, and I need to give you that. I read about this trial and what they are accusing you of and"—his throat worked up and down—"I know you did it. I know it because it's what I taught you. This"—his hand gestured toward the cell—"this is my fault too. You're right. Saying I'm sorry isn't enough. If I had something else. If I could take it back, do better by you, I would do it. I would do anything to have another chance at being your father." He took steps all the way to the cell bars. "Son, I am sorry. Please, forgive me."

Eric just stood there, felt his face go ashen, as if all the color had pooled out and run down his neck toward his thudding heart. Rage and searing pain throbbed throughout his entire body until he shook. He stared into his father's tired, worn eyes and then—

He reached through the bars and grasped his father's neck. He gripped it between his hands, held it tight, tighter, as tight as he could.

He didn't hear or see his father's struggle; there was only a red haze before his eyes. Then he let go, a sudden move, and stepped back. Coming out of the fog, he watched in horrified astonishment as his father's body slid to the floor.

Chapter Thirty-Two

*E*ric began to shake. The shaking turned into jerking motions and then convulsions as he backed away from the crumpled body. He fell to the floor, unable to look away from his father's still face and open eyes.

"Oh, God. God! What have I done?" He leaned over and emptied the contents of his stomach onto the floor beside him. Wretched, wretched life! A howling sounded in his mind, as though demons had gathered to gloat, to torment him, swirling around and through him. He brought his hands to his face and rocked back and forth, squeezing his eyes closed, unable to escape the nightmare before him.

A sudden shout brought his head up. A soldier stood there; Eric hadn't even heard him enter. Several more soldiers rushed in, then stopped short upon seeing the evidence of Eric's deed.

Running feet left the room and then another man entered, his decorated uniform proclaiming him the commander of the fort. Eric stared into the man's gaping stare. The commander walked over to the bars, his lip curling. "I should have you shot. Immediately."

Yes, shoot me. Please shoot me! Please take this horror away from me!

"This man claimed to be your father." The judgment and disbelief in the man's deep voice pierced what was left of Eric's shattered soul. "You were given leave to have a few private moments with him, last moments. I can hardly fathom what you have done."

Eric lowered his head as sobs tore from his chest, shaking his shoulders with their intensity.

"Have you nothing to say? Will you just sit there and bawl like a child?"

Eric buried his face in his hands, shuddering as bone-chilling shrieks filled the cell. They were horrible, desperate shrieks! Coming from a place of utter darkness. Shock turned his blood cold as he realized they emanated from his own throat . . .

"Take the body away." The commander's curt order struck Eric as though another physical blow. His father! His father's body. An empty, broken shell . . . all that was left of the man who raised him. The man who came to him in his darkest hour . . . who begged his forgiveness . . .

The man he'd killed with his own wretched hands.

Eric kept his eyes closed but heard them following the commander's order. Heard them all finally, mercifully, leave the room, slamming the door behind them.

It was dark. It was so dark. And he was utterly lost. He'd sold himself to that darkness long ago, and now . . .

Retribution howled his name.

Today she would become a widow.

Emma looked out at the quiet street from the parlor window. After leaving the church, she'd had dinner with her parents; and then, exhausted—emotionally, physically, and mentally—she told her parents she wanted to go home. She needed to go back to her own house, if only for one night.

Her mother looked at her askance. "But it will need to be aired out and cleaned. There won't be any fresh linens or even any food in the house."

Her father laid a hand on her mother's arm and spoke with quiet authority. "She will be all right, Anna. Let her go. She needs to do this."

Her mother huffed and then closed her mouth tight, but it was obvious to all that she wasn't happy about it. She sent Emma off with clean bedding and a basket of muffins and tea for her breakfast.

Upon entering the house, Emma had to shake off the dread and discomfort. She walked through the rooms, one by one, lighting all of the candles until the house was suffused with a soft, warm glow. Determination setting her chin, she walked into each room, pausing, letting the memories, the nightmare, play across her mind. As the images faded away, she squared her shoulders each time and proclaimed aloud: "Never again."

Feeling released, she walked to the parlor and took dust covers off the furniture, throwing them into a pile on the floor with sad abandon. Maybe she would become a waster for a while, just to see what that felt like. A choked laugh escaped her at the thought, and she collapsed to the floor beside the sofa, buried her face in the elegant cushion, and sobbed until her throat ached.

Too tired to climb the stairs and not wanting to see the bedchamber at night, she curled up on the small sofa, pulled a quilt over her, and drifted off into a fitful sleep.

Morning brought a great heaviness to her shoulders and upon her heart. She thought of Daniel from the Bible again and realized she had never wondered how he felt after his miraculous rescue. After Daniel was pulled from the lion's den, the men who had accused him, possibly over a hundred of them, and all their wives and children were thrown into the den. The Bible said that all their bones were crushed before they reached the floor. She shuddered. There must have been a terrifying number of ferocious lions to devour so many so fast.

Today Eric, her husband, would be devoured by another means. Had Daniel felt sad, sickened as he watched those women and innocent children being thrown to their deaths? Had he grieved the judgment of his enemies? She thought that perhaps he had. Perhaps he felt very much as she did this day.

"Give me strength, Lord. Give me the strength of Daniel again this day." Her eyes filled with tears as she reached for her bonnet. She turned and looked one last time at her home. No, not her home. Never her home. She would never live here.

The walk to the courthouse was long, but nothing could have prepared her for the sight that greeted her. It was as if the whole town and much of the countryside had turned up to witness the culmination of the shocking events over the last months. In the middle of the street stood a fresh-built platform with a rope dangling from a wooden arm above a wide hole in the floor. As people on the outskirts of the crowd saw her, mumbling and pointing sparked. Emma stood rooted to the ground, unable to move, unable to think what to do next. Where was she to go?

In a near panic her gaze swept over the crowd looking for a familiar face—her parents? Maggie? Luke? Where were they? The panic grew full-blown as her heart raced and her breath came in gasps. *Lord, I can't do this alone!*

Her name, shouted from the other side of the crowd, made her head jerk in that direction.

"Emma, I'm here!"

Blessed relief swept her as she rushed through the crowd toward the familiar, calming voice. The crowd parted as she ran toward the courthouse. She saw him then . . . Luke. His eyes shining with the love he said he had for her. His smile warm with concerned care. Then she saw her mother and father standing beside him. Maggie and her father were there too. And Judge Littleton, who came down the courthouse steps and walked to meet her.

She came to a stop in front of them, not knowing whom to go to first. It didn't seem right to stand beside Luke, and her parents looked as pale and stricken as she felt. Judge Littleton, compassion and understanding on his face, stepped forward and took her into his arms.

"It's going to be all right, girl." He patted her back in an affectionate gesture. "In time it will be all right."

Emma clung to him and her voice choked out. "It's hard to believe that."

"I know. I know." He pulled her tight arms from his neck and lectured in a soft voice filled with quiet authority. "Be strong now. We are all here for you. God is here for you."

Emma sniffed. The judge was right. She could feel His presence. "Thank you."

The judge turned toward Luke. "Mr. Bowen, why don't you take Emma inside, get her a cup of water, and sit with her until the soldiers arrive with Montclaire. She doesn't need to be out here being gawked at by all and sundry."

Luke nodded, deep concern etched on his face. He took Emma's arm and led her into the courtroom.

Emma sank down on a bench while Luke went to the water pitcher on a corner table. He held the cup out to her and watched as her trembling hand reached for it. She could hardly hold it without spilling it. "Here." Luke took the cup back. "Let me."

He tilted the cup to her lips and watched as she swallowed several gulps. "Are you all right?" He set the cup on the floor beside them and sat down next to her.

Emma started to nod, then shook her head. Truth. Always truth from now on. "I prayed God would save us, but I never imagined Eric's death. I don't know if I can witness it."

"You don't have to. You can stay right here if you need to. I will stay with you." He reached for her hand and squeezed it tight.

Emma looked up at him and then away, into the distance. "I don't know."

"You don't have to decide this minute. Wait and see. You will know what's right."

They sat in silence for a long moment, then Luke turned his head and half grinned at her. "I had dinner with Judge Littleton last night. He told me everything. Would you like to hear the story, or do you want to wait and hear it from him?"

As distressed as Emma felt, her answer was immediate. "Of course I want to know. What happened?"

Luke chuckled. "I guess he was in his tent, going over some papers before his dinner with you and Eric when he heard a voice.

God's voice, he said, telling him to go for a walk. He got right up, of course, not questioning it at all. You know the judge."

Warmth flooded Emma. She did, indeed. No man was more devoted to doing as God bid.

Luke's voice went on, soothing her soul in its quiet humor. "I can just see him standing right up, hiking up his trousers, and heading out the door."

Emma smiled a little. "Yes, I can see that."

"Well, as he strolled over toward the camp, he saw Eric talking with Billy and then saw Eric hand Billy a small packet. He said the memory of Eric inviting him to dinner flashed through his mind, and he knew, as clear as day, that Eric intended to poison him."

"That's incredible!" Emma breathed. "But he ate the food. I saw him eat it."

"I guess he just put a little in his mouth and then spit it out in a cloth. He said he did a lot of pushing his food around on the plate, like he did as a boy when he didn't want to eat something."

Emma pondered this. "Yes, I remember him talking most of the time, telling stories and asking Eric and me questions. It wasn't very long into the meal that he had his attack—" Emma caught her breath. "He faked the whole choking scene, didn't he?"

Luke nodded. "Said he spent some time on the stage when he was young. Even traveled around with a theater troop for awhile before he got serious and studied law."

Emma shook her head, her eyes wide. "He wasn't breathing when I ran over and sat beside him on the floor. And then I dragged his head into my lap. I am sure he wasn't breathing. How did he do that?"

"He said every time you looked over at Eric he would take a shallow breath. You were so distraught and yelling at Eric for help that it wasn't too hard to keep up the act."

"Amazing. Truly amazing. But what happened next? After I ran out? Didn't Eric go over to him?"

"Eric was in a lot of pain. The judge said Eric called for help and didn't move until some of the men came in. One of the men, I think it was Eisler, went over and looked at the judge, but no one touched his body until Eric had been seen to. He said it was one of the hardest things he ever had to do—lie motionless on that floor for a couple of hours."

"I can only imagine."

"I guess with all the men either busy with Eric or making plans to go after us, the judge was kind of forgotten. When they finally did give his body some attention, he said Lieutenant Arthur ordered he be taken out and buried before sundown. He was carried to a spot, praying the whole time because you took his gun and he had no way of defending himself if they tried to bury him alive."

Emma's hand went to her chest. "Oh, my. Can you imagine?"

Luke shook his head and chuckled again. "Turns out they were lazy sorts. They dumped his body on the ground and then sat down and shared a jug of rum that they had pilfered from the stores during all the excitement. The judge was laughing when he told me he was never so thankful for rum in all his life. It wasn't long before they didn't even notice if he breathed deep and moved now and then. When they left, the judge hid out in the woods for a few days."

Luke grinned at her, and in spite of herself, Emma's breath caught. She pushed the reaction aside and focused on Luke's words rather than his face.

"He said he lost so much weight he was looking good enough to go wife hunting."

Emma held a hand to her smiling mouth. "He *would* look for the silver lining of such an ordeal."

"Anyway, he hung out by the river, and when a canoe went by with two French traders, he chased them down and begged a ride."

"Just in time."

"Yes, just in time."

It all made sense. But there was still so much she didn't know. "What about Maggie? How did he know about Eric and Maggie?"

"He had been looking into Frazer's murder for weeks before chasing us down on the Missouri. It was common enough knowledge where Eric spent his afternoons, I guess, and the judge went to see her. She was still at the hotel, working. He said it wasn't too hard to get the whole story out of her. She already wanted to get her life right and return home. I think he helped her. I think he gave her the courage to leave that place and go back to her father."

"Luke, isn't he amazing? I mean"—she swallowed hard—"look what one man, one good, godly man has done for us all."

"He's our backwoods angel."

Emma started to agree, but there was a knock on the door, and then her father slipped inside the room.

"They are here, Emma. It is time."

Chapter Thirty-Three

*E*mma stood and braced her knees against the back of the bench. "Can I have one last word with Eric before—" She didn't say the rest, just pressed her lips tight together.

"Emma," Luke interjected. "I don't think that is a good idea."

Her father nodded, clearly agreeing with Luke. "Don't do this."

She closed her eyes. She didn't want to do it. Wanted more than anything to never see or speak to Eric again. But she had no choice. "I have to tell him something. Something important." Her gaze swung toward Luke. "I want to be like Judge Littleton. I want to tell Eric that I forgive him."

Luke took a long look at her, while her father stood mute. "All right then. I will go and speak to the lieutenant."

Gratitude warmed her chilled heart. Luke always listened, always heard her heart so clearly. "Thank you."

When Luke had left the room, her father came to her. "I don't want you to be alone with that . . . that monster."

She turned her face to her father's. She saw every care and worry written there. "It's okay, Father. I'm not a little girl anymore. I've grown up."

Her father came forward and took her in his arms. He felt small and frail and a sudden sad realization that he would die someday stabbed at her heart. He pulled back and blinked, his eyelashes white, his cheeks creased with lean folds.

Luke reentered the room, and when Emma met his gaze, she saw his features were drawn with revulsion. And something more. Something she recognized and cherished: a protective determination that she would not be hurt. "I'm sorry, Emma. You can't see him."

Her heart sank. "What did they say?"

Luke touched his fingers to his forehead, and it took him a few seconds to form the words. "Something has happened. Eric is bound. They will not leave him alone in a room with anyone, nor allow him to speak to anyone."

Emma stared hard at Luke seeing in his eyes that he was pleading her not to ask what he'd seen. "But I have to tell him. He has to know that I-I forgive him."

Luke studied her, his eyes scanning her features. "Maybe the forgiveness you feel is for you. Maybe it's not for him to know."

Emma gripped her hands together and raised them to her chin. "But if he doesn't know, it won't seem real."

"What if she wrote him a note?" Her father turned to Emma and pleaded. "That's the answer, my dear. Write it to him. Luke will make sure that he has read it before . . . before the end."

Emma looked away, seeking her heart. Would that do? Certainty flowed through her, and she nodded. "I will need a quill and ink."

Luke found the necessary writing tools and brought them to her. He and her father turned away while she bent to the task. Her mind filled with things to say, all the regrets and sadness of their life together pouring over her. She closed her eyes for a brief moment and then leaned over the paper. There was only one thing to say.

Eric—

I forgive you . . . everything.

Emma

She blew on the paper to set the ink, then she folded it in half and stood. She held it out to Luke. "Thank you."

And as her fingers let go of the paper, she felt it, deep within.

A releasing. Freedom.

Luke turned to go, Emma's note burning in his hand. He wanted to open it, to know what she had said to her husband, but he knew he could not. Instead he slapped his hat on his head as he traversed the crowd over to the scaffolding where Eric and the soldiers stood.

Luke thrust the note toward the commanding officer. "Mrs. Montclaire's last words to her husband, sir. Might he read them?"

The commander didn't hide his disgust toward Eric. "He doesn't deserve any privileges."

"No, sir." Luke was not going to argue that. How could he? After what Eric had done to his own father! "But Mrs. Montclaire does." He lifted his chin and stared at the commander. "It is her only request."

The soldier stared at the note, then at Luke, his lips pursed. Finally he took the note and read it. His brows creased, and Luke had the strong sense the man couldn't believe what he was reading. But with a slow inhale, the commander refolded the note and handed it back to Luke. When he spoke, there was a deep respect in his tone.

"Very well. Hold it in front of him so he may read it. I will not, even for Mrs. Montclaire, untie his hands."

Luke took the paper, not sure he could carry out such instructions. He could not look at Eric. If he did so . . . the image of what he might do made him pause, look to heaven for help, and then take a deep breath. Emma. The name and face resounded through his mind and heart, when she'd handed the note to him, so sad and resigned. . . . His back straightened. He had to do this for her.

He walked over to Eric, who had been listening to the interchange with voracious interest. Luke unfolded the note. Eric's chin rose, his back stiff as Luke held the paper out, trying to keep it from quivering in the wind.

Eric looked hard from Luke's stolid face to the paper and then back again. "What does she want? Tell me."

"I haven't read the note so I don't know."

Eric's once-handsome face twisted. "You didn't need to, did you? You already know who the winner is this day. You no good—"

The tirade of curses from Eric's lips made it even harder for Luke to stand still and hold out the paper. But he was determined. He kept Emma's face in his mind and blocked out the man in front of him, blocked his words and his snarling face. "I will hold it another few moments, sir. It is your choice whether to read it or not."

As he did exactly that, Luke realized the crowd behind them had grown still. People below them were straining, trying to hear the exchange.

Eric's gaze dropped from Luke's face to the paper. Luke knew it was taking a thrashing to his pride to do it, but the back and forth of his eyes told Luke that he was reading it. At the end, whatever it said, pure malevolence came into Eric's eyes. "Tell her I don't want it."

Luke took a step back. He didn't know what Eric meant, but that didn't matter. He would tell Emma nothing from this man.

The commander grasped the note, crumpled it, and then took strong hold of Eric's arm. "You, sir, are a fool." He turned to the other soldiers and inclined his head. "It is time."

Luke turned away from Eric just as Emma arrived at the front of the crowd . . . just as one of the lieutenants pulled a flour sack over Eric's head.

Emma shrank back, and Luke started toward her, then stilled when her mother came up from behind her and wrapped Emma in her arms. *Thank You, God.*

He made his way down the scaffold's steps and stood where he could see Emma and her parents, both of whom were now with her, supporting her from either side. He kept his eyes on Emma, not to intrude on this moment but to ensure he would be ready should she need him.

Sorrow weighted her beautiful features as they led Eric to the rope. She leaned back against her mother and father, her arms grasping theirs where they held her. Luke looked up at the scaffold just in time to see the noose placed over Eric's head.

It would not be long now.

The soldier tightened the knot around Eric's neck, and Luke turned back to see Emma close her eyes and lean her head to one side . . .

Luke heard, more than saw, the soldier push Eric off the edge, into the hole. His gaze was fixed on Emma . . .

Her face crumpled. A cry took wing, as though wrung from her very soul. Luke wanted to run to her, to take her in his arms, but he waited, always waiting for her to tell him when she needed him.

He turned from her agony to see Eric struggle against the rope's punishment, his legs, mere feet from the solid ground, kicked out. His head hung mere inches from the wooden hole. If his hands hadn't been tied, he could have easily pulled himself up and into freedom. But there was no escape. His body writhed and tossed like a drowning man until finally the struggle ceased. And Eric Montclaire, the most beautiful, vile man in the West, swayed, swayed, swayed with the wind.

Luke looked away, and his gaze flew to Emma. Her eyes were open, fixed on him, and in the next heartbeat he was racing toward her. When he grew close, she pulled free of her parents and threw herself into his arms. He enfolded her, capturing her against him, holding her tight. He leaned his face into the curve of her neck, drawing in the sweet lavender scent of her luxurious hair. He closed his eyes, loving the feel of her in his arms, wanting to keep her there forever.

But he knew what was coming next. What she would ask of him.

He would have to let her go.

Family rushed in on them from every side. There was Luke's mother, whom Emma had only just met but felt she had known for a long time. And she could see, in Lenora's eyes, she felt the same as she squeezed Emma tight against her.

"I can't imagine all you've been through," her tear-clogged voice whispered into Emma's ear, "but if you ever need me, need us, we are here for you."

Emma nodded as she let go, realizing someone had told Lenora everything.

Luke's sisters hugged her, one by one, more shy, less sure of why they were doing it. Except for Torrie, the eldest. Somehow Emma knew she understood more than her young years might suggest.

Luke came up to her as the others drifted away. The look in his eyes . . . the sadness . . . suddenly she knew. "You're leaving?" She hadn't thought it would come so soon, but of course, he would leave with his family.

"I don't have to . . ."

Emma shook her head. She could barely think what she would do now. Having Luke here, watching her every move—

She shook her head and grasped hold of his hands. "Of course. I'm sorry. It's just that everything is happening so quickly. You should go with your family."

Luke let go of her hands as a fleeting frustration flashed across his rugged face. He wanted her to ask him to stay. She knew it. But it was too soon.

Or too late.

Her heart felt ravished, her soul disconnected from the rest of her. She needed time. She needed to lick her wounds alone. And so she couldn't voice the words that would make him stay. That would make him . . . hers.

He waited in the silence and then eased his hat upon his head. Emma allowed a small smile as he turned his face toward the West, the setting sun. She pressed her lips together against the plea for him to stay, instead memorizing the dark slash of his eyebrow, the slope of his nose, his lean cheek, and the grim curve of his lips.

Everything in her wanted to say those three words, but she steeled herself against them. She'd told no lie on the witness stand. She loved the man standing here in front of her, but she knew she and God had some work to do. Alone. So she remained silent.

Luke turned toward her, his eyes piercing. "I'm going home, but I am not giving up." He held her gaze. "Not ever."

Emma's heart soared. As he turned and walked away, a tiny spark flamed into life within her, and she was able for a moment to smile through her tears.

Epilogue

Seven Years Later

*E*mma smiled into the darkness but didn't turn around as she heard the door open and then softly click shut behind her. Footsteps sounded, and then she felt a hand on her shoulder.

"They're finally asleep." Luke leaned down to kiss the spot just beneath her ear.

Emma turned her face into his and felt the shadow of his beard rub her cheek. She inhaled the fragrance of the field on him—nutty wheat and sharp corn mixed with their youngest child's scent. "He doesn't want to miss a thing, does he?"

Luke chuckled and came around to sit down next to her on the porch swing he'd asked John Sumner to build for their fifth anniversary. "He's like his mother that way." Luke put his arm around her shoulders and pulled her close.

Emma set the swing into motion with the tip of her toe and leaned into Luke's side. "Seven years. Can you believe it?" She took a sip of her hot tea and contemplated her husband's profile in the moonlight. His dark hair was still wet and shiny from the washing up he'd done before tucking in their children. He was tanned from the fields of growing crops that surrounded them on their Kentucky farm, his shirt partway buttoned, his sleeves rolled up to the elbows. Below the sleeve, she saw arms grown strong and hands that had become callused. He had crinkles around his eyes now when he smiled, but they only added to his undeniable appeal. Sometimes Emma made a joke about something just so she could see them.

She leaned against him, this good, good man. He'd waited so long for her to learn to trust again. Even after their marriage, especially the weeks right after, he'd been so very kind, so loving and patient until she'd slowly loosened in his light hold, letting him love her.

His breath was warm on her face as he spoke. "Yes, I can believe it. Do you remember the year and a half of he—"

"Luke!"

"Well, it was." His grip grew tighter on her shoulder. "Hell is a place where we are forever separated from God, right?"

She couldn't deny that.

"That year after Eric died, when I was separated from you. It felt like that."

It had been horrible and lonely for her too, but she'd needed that time to heal. After Eric's body had been buried, Emma took Maggie and John Sumner up on their offer to move in with them for a time. She couldn't go home to her parents; she had moved too far beyond being their child. Nor could she go back to the house where she and Eric had lived. She'd needed the fresh start that Maggie and John offered.

It had been a good decision. Eric's fortune had made her a wealthy woman, so she could have stayed in a hotel, or built her own mansion on a hill, or traveled the world. Whatever she wanted. But when she thought about it, all she truly wanted to do was to sit in the Sumners' parlor each evening after a day of working in his shop and hear the Bible read. It was the only salve that could heal her wounds.

"I'm sure glad I finally got tired of waiting and went after you."

Luke's lazy drawl sent prickles of delight along her nerves, and Emma laughed. "I couldn't believe it when you showed up on my doorstop with those drooping flowers in your hand, smelling like the road. . . . I realized right then and there how much I still loved you."

"Well, when I started out to win you back, I didn't realize my offering would wilt. I picked those flowers along the way, as you know. Every mile or so I stopped and picked you one, all the way from Kentucky."

Emma sniffed, the memory making her eyes sting. "They were the most beautiful flowers I have ever received."

Luke leaned his head back and gazed at the star-studded sky, a teasing tone in his voice. "You *did* seem to like them."

"And then I brought out your letters, all the drawings you sent me over that year. The drawings of me as your wife—Emma doing the washing, Emma cooking, Emma standing in the yard calling you in to dinner with my hand up to my forehead, shielding the sun, Emma playing with our children, Emma in your arms." As happened every time she thought of it, joy lifted her heart. She angled a coy look at her husband. "That last was my favorite. I saved everything you sent me."

Luke nodded. "As did I, though your letters were few. I thought you stopped loving me."

"Never. Not since the moment you picked me up off the street and held me in your arms."

"And then I got my first real kiss."

Luke's happy sigh sent a smile across her own lips. "Hmmm. Shortly after you gave me the flowers, if I recall." Emma leaned over and kissed him as she had that day, with her whole heart.

"And then"—Luke cupped her face in his strong hands— "you rushed me into a wedding."

Emma pushed against his side and huffed. "Only because you threatened to sling me over your shoulder and carry me all the way back to Kentucky. I had little choice. Didn't even have time to have a proper wedding dress made up. I looked like a farmer's wife for certain in that blue dress."

"You looked nothing like a farmer's wife that day, and don't ever think otherwise."

Emma blinked, leaning toward him. "How did I look?"

The look in his eyes stole her breath. "Like you were finally mine."

They kissed again, lingering over each other the way a musician remembers a beloved instrument. After a long while, they pulled away a little and gazed into each other's eyes. Luke's thumb caressed Emma's cheek. "I still can't quite believe you're mine."

"Forever and ever."

"And then my mother went and married John Sumner!" Luke pulled back, his grin broadening.

"I *told* you that was coming. It just took them longer than I thought. I think they were waiting for us to get married first." Emma shook her head against the back of the swing. "I didn't think she would ever give in to his slow, quiet calling on her."

"I'm glad she did. It's good to see her happy again, and the girls are so happy to have a father again. They've missed my dad terribly. He was a good father to them."

"As you are to your children."

"It's hard to believe Rebecca will be four next month. She's growing up too fast."

Emma took hold of his hand and squeezed it. "And Timothy just turned two. I don't have a baby anymore."

"I believe I know a remedy for that." Luke arched a brow, a devilish gleam in his eyes. They both laughed.

For a while the only sound as they rocked back and forth was the wind rustling through the night air. Emma snuggled up close as the summer breeze drifted, full and lazy, around them. "I love our life, Luke. Thank you for giving up so much for us."

Luke brought her hand up to his lips as they gazed out over their farm. "I gave up nothing. There is no place on this earth that I would rather be, day by day, every day."

She sat up then, plucking at his shirtfront, gaze teasing. "I have a present for you if you want it."

"I'm pretty sure I do." Luke smiled at her, the moonlight making his face look so handsome it nearly took her breath away.

Excitement tripped through her as she thought of what she'd bought him. He'd been so busy taking care of them that he had let too much of his other talents go by the wayside. She stood up, went inside their large, brick house, and then came back with a wrapped bundle in her hands. She held it out toward Luke, keeping her face normal and serious while a riot of glee rose within her.

Luke took the bundle and unfolded the paper wrapping. Inside was a new pen and ink set, graphite, paints in every color, pages of paper, rolled-up canvas, and journals. He looked up at her.

"Draw us again." Emma tilted her head toward one shoulder and finally let the tears flow down her cheeks. "Draw everything God has given you . . . draw our redemption story."

"Emma . . ." He stood and took her into his arms. He marveled at God and life and creation and, well, her. "Emma."

She snuggled against him. "Luke."

It was like Lewis and Clark. Two names, two people on this earth that belonged together. For together they could accomplish a heavenly kingdom's mission, a happily-ever-after fairy tale . . . and a legend.

Another beginning, another chapter, another gazing, embracing, two-becoming-one story that just might, if they believed in it as they always had . . .

. . . last into eternity.

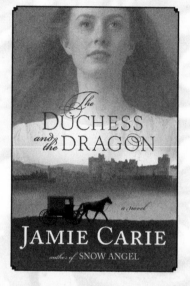
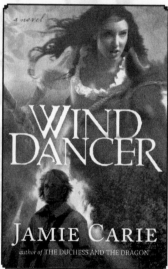
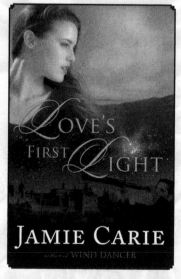